'SIMON RAVEN'S VIRTUES AS STYLIST AND ENTERTAINER SHINE ON UNVARNISHED.'
The Guardian

'Mr [illegible] theme is a vital one. For though he is writing of [illegible] much broader. His story is no[illegible]ty, but of the new ch[illegible]reatens our whole wa[illegible]

Also by Simon Raven in Panther Books

The Feathers of Death
Brother Cain
Doctors Wear Scarlet
Close of Play

Non fiction

The English Gentleman

In the sequence 'Alms for Oblivion'

The Rich Pay Late
Friends in Low Places
The Sabre Squadron
Fielding Grey
The Judas Boy

Simon Raven

Places Where They Sing

the sixth novel in the
Alms for Oblivion series

Panther

Granada Publishing Limited
Published in 1972 by Panther Books Limited
3 Upper James Street, London W1R 4BP

First published in Great Britain by Anthony Blond Limited 1970. Reprinted 1970

Made and printed in Great Britain by Richard Clay (The Chaucer Press), Ltd., Bungay, Suffolk
Set in Linotype Times

Contents

A LIST OF THE CHARACTERS WHO HAVE SO FAR APPEARED IN THE *ALMS FOR OBLIVION* SEQUENCE

In *The Rich Pay Late*, the action of which takes place in 1955 and '56:

Donald Salinger, a businessman.

Jude Holbrook, his friend & partner.

Miss Beatty, a secretary in the firm of Salinger & Holbrook.

Mrs Beatty, her mother.

Ashley Dexterside, friend and employee of Donald Salinger.

Vanessa Drew, Donald's fiancée and later his wife.

Penelope Holbrook, formerly a model; now married to Jude.

Donald (Donny) Holbrook, their four-year-old son.

Anthony Holbrook, Jude's father; a miser.

Mrs Anthony Holbrook, Jude's mother; a bluestocking.

Somerset Lloyd-James, editor of *Strix*, an economic journal.

Tom Llewyllyn, author, journalist and contributor to *Strix*.

Tessie Buttock, owner of Buttock's Private Hotel, where Tom hangs out.

Peter Morrison, a squire of substance in East Anglia and a Member of Parliament, where he leads the 'Young England' group.

Helen Morrison, Peter's wife.

Captain Detterling, formerly a regular officer of the 49th Earl Hamilton's Light Dragoons; now a Member of Parliament and a political supporter of Morrison's.

Carton Weir, Member of Parliament and another supporter of Morrison's; a friend of Ashley Dexterside.

Maisie, a whore.

'Young' John Groves, a dubious lawyer.
Jonathan Gamp, a not so young man about town.
Henry Dilkes, Secretary to the Institute of Political and Economic Studies and a member of the Board of *Strix*.
Robert Reculver Constable, formerly Fellow and Tutor of Lancaster College, Cambridge; now Vice-Chancellor of the University of Salop, in which he is also Professor of Economics and as such an *ex officio* member of the Board of *Strix*.
Lord Philby, son of the founder of *Strix* and now its proprietor.
Jimmy, a layabout and old associate of Vanessa Drew's.
Ivan Blessington, formerly of Earl Hamilton's Light Dragoons and now an attaché in Washington.
Lady Susan Grange, later Lady Philby.
Mrs (Angela) Tuck, an adventuress.
Tuck, sometime her husband.
Mark Lewson, a con-man.
Felicity Lewson ('the Contessa'), his wife and assistant.
Burke Lawrence, a publicity man and film director.
Jake Vincent, an East Anglian peasant.
Betty Vincent, his wife.
Max de Freville, a gambler and connoisseur of human affairs.
Doctor La Soeur, a confidential practitioner.
Alfie Schroeder, a journalist employed by the Billingsgate Press.
The Reverend Mr Purchase.
Gregory Stern, a publisher (of Tom Llewyllyn among others).

In *Friends in Low Places*, the events of which take place three years later, in 1959:
Mark Lewson, now a widower and temporarily living off . . .
Angela Tuck, who has inherited some money from her

dead husband and now lives quietly on it, and on drink, in the South of France.

Max de Freville, who has formed a Platonic liaison with Angela.

Stratis Lykiadopoulos, a Greek gambler and friend of Max.

Rupert Percival, a country lawyer of Bishop's Cross, Somersetshire.

Alastair Dixon, his friend, Member of Parliament for Bishop's Cross but now about to retire.

Peter Morrison, who has resigned his seat in Parliament in 1956 but now seeks re-election and wishes to be nominated as Conservative Candidate for Bishop's Cross.

Helen Morrison.

Nickie and Jeremy Morrison (aged eight and five), their sons.

Somerset Lloyd-James, Peter's competitor for the Conservative nomination at Bishop's Cross; still editor of *Strix*.

Maisie, still a whore.

Major Fielding Gray, formerly a regular officer of the 49th Earl Hamilton's Light Dragoons, but now retired because of wounds received in Cyprus in 1958 and ambitious to become a writer; an old friend of Somerset Lloyd-James's, to whom he applies for help.

Tom Llewyllyn, now much advanced in his profession.

Tessie Buttock.

Sir Edwin Turbot, a Minister of the Crown.

Patricia Turbot, his daughter, engaged to marry Tom Llewyllyn.

Isobel Turbot, Patricia's youngest sister.

Captain Detterling, MP, who has now purchased a directorship in the firm of ....

Gregory Stern, the publisher, who takes on Fielding Gray.

The Most Honourable the Marquis Canteloupe, a distant cousin of Detterling's; a successful operator in the

Stately Homes game and an amateur politician.
The Marchioness Canteloupe.
The Dowager Marchioness Canteloupe.
Carton Weir, MP, now aide to Canteloupe.
Burke Lawrence, now teamed up with . . .
Penelope Holbrook, who was divorced from Jude in 1956.
Henry Dilkes.
Robert Constable, now Provost-elect of Lancaster College, Cambridge.
Lord Philby.
Jonathan Gamp.
Jude Holbrook, now an 'agent'.
Alfie Schroeder.
Donald and Vanessa Salinger.
Lieutenant-Colonel Hookeby, 'Commandant' of Westward Ho, the first of Canteloupe's 'Country Culture Camps'.
Sergeant-Major Cruxtable, physical fitness expert.
Mrs Anthony Holbrook.

In *The Sabre Squadron*, which goes back in time to 1952:
Daniel Mond, a mathematician and research student of Lancaster College, Cambridge.
Robert Constable, at that time Tutor of Lancaster.
Jacquiz Helmut, a historian and research student of Lancaster.
Herr Doktor Aeneas von Bremke, a prominent mathematician in the University of Göttingen.
Earle Restarick, an American student at Göttingen.
Cornet Julian James, a national service officer of the 49th Earl Hamilton's Light Dragoons and an old college friend of Daniel Mond's.
Major Giles Glastonbury, officer commanding the 10th Sabre Squadron of Earl Hamilton's Light Dragoons.
Lieutenant Mick Motley, temporarily of the RAMC.
Captain Fielding Gray, second in command to Major Glastonbury.

Lieutenants Jack Lamprey and Piers Bungay, also of the 10th Sabre Squadron.

Trooper Michael Lamb, Captain Gray's driver.

Lieutenant Leonard Percival, of the Wessex Fusiliers, nephew to Robert Percival (*Friends in Low Places*).

The 'Ghost' of Conrad Stern (Gregory Stern's brother).

Herr Pappenheim, who is shortly to become an important staff officer in the new German Army.

The Graf von Augsburg, a duellist.

Tuck, at that time an official on the Control Commission.

Captain Detterling, MP, recently retired from Earl Hamilton's.

Squadron Sergeant-Major Bunce, of the 10th Sabre Squadron.

Corporal-Major Chead, of the 10th Sabre Squadron.

Mugger, a storeman.

Trooper Geddes, the Squadron barber.

Regimental Sergeant-Major Holeworthy, of the Wessex Fusiliers.

Ivan Blessington, an officer of Earl Hamilton's but currently employed as ADC to the Divisional Commander.

Alfie Schroeder.

Captain 'Bagger' Hennessy of the Coldstream Guards.

Colonel Haq, an obscene Turk.

In *Fielding Gray*, which goes still further back in time—to 1945:

Fielding Gray, at that time a boy of seventeen-and-a-half with another year before him at his public school.

Peter Morrison, Head Boy of Fielding's House and shortly to leave for the Army.

Somerset Lloyd-James, at the same school but in a different House.

Major Robert Constable, who has seen active service during the war and is released early from the Army to take up the post of Tutor at Lancaster College, Cambridge.

Ivan Blessington, a boy in Fielding's House.

Captain Detterling, at that time still serving as a regular officer in the 49th Earl Hamilton's Light Dragoons.

Angela Tuck, twenty-one years old and recently married to Tuck.

Tuck, at that time a tea-planter.

Christopher Roland, whom Fielding loves.

The Headmaster, a man of conscience.

The Senior Usher, a worldly and talented pedagogue.

Old Frank, cricket professional at the school.

John Aloysius (Jack) Gray, Fielding's father; a businessman of low tastes.

Mrs Gray, Fielding's mother.

Phyllis and Dixie, girls of the lower class.

'Glinter' Parkes, a small boy of resource.

'Squire' Morrison, Peter's father.

Johnny Pitts, tenant of the above; an amateur jockey.

Mr Japhet, a provincial lawyer.

A prostitute.

A private soldier.

Mr and Mrs Roland, Christopher's parents.

A garage proprietor.

A Colour Sergeant.

A Sergeant-Major.

In *The Judas Boy*, which brings us forward again in time to 1962:

Fielding Gray, now a novelist of some repute but little gain, living in Buttock's Private Hotel.

Tom Llewyllyn, now famous as a journalist and popular historian, presently under short-term contract to the BBC.

Tessie Buttock, still proprietor of Buttock's.

Maisie, still a whore.

Gregory Stern, Fielding's publisher and Tom's.

Isobel Turbot, now Mrs Gregory Stern.

Patricia Turbot, her sister, now Mrs Tom Llewyllyn.
Leonard Percival, a British agent.
Somerset Lloyd-James, still editor of *Strix* and now Member of Parliament for Bishop's Cross.
Captain Detterling, MP, Director of Gregory Stern Ltd.
The Marquis Canteloupe, recently made a junior minister to take charge of the newly formed Department of Public Relations and Popular Media.
Carton Weir, MP, still Canteloupe's aide.
Max de Freville, now living abroad.
Angela Tuck, his constant companion.
Earle Restarick, an American agent (Diomedes).
Robert Constable, Provost of Lancaster College, Cambridge.
The Director of Features (BBC).
Miss Enid Jackson (BBC).
'Baby' Llewyllyn, Tom and Patricia's infant daughter.
A Yugoslav head waiter.
An Austrian Customs Officer.
Spiros, an Hydriot tavern-keeper.
An Hydriot boatman.
A Greek sailor.
A Cypriot taxi-driver.
Savidis, Restarick/Diomedes' assistant.
A dead Jewish boy.
Nicos, a live Greek boy.
Dighenis.
Clito, a Cypriot tavern-keeper.
Assorted Cypriot males.
A long-nosed member of the American School of Greek Studies in Athens.
A bureaucrat.
Mrs (Harriet) Ongley, a well preserved widow.

Of the above, the following now re-appear in *Places Where They Sing*, the events of which take place five years later than those of 'The Judas Boy', in 1967:

Jacquiz Helmut (Doctor), now a history don at Lancaster

College, Cambridge.

Robert Reculver Constable, still Provost of Lancaster.

Tom Llewyllyn, now a Namier Fellow of Lancaster, holding his Fellowship for a second term of three years.

Daniel Mond, a don at Lancaster, teacher of pure mathematics.

Patricia Llewyllyn (*née* Turbot), Tom's wife.

'Baby' Llewyllyn, their daughter, now seven years old.

Isobel Stern (*née* Turbot), Patricia's sister, and married to ...

Gregory Stern, the publisher, who now loses Tom Llewyllyn to the Cambridge University Press but still publishes the novels of ...

Fielding Gray, now somewhat advanced in his profession as author and recently winner of the Joseph Conrad Prize for Fiction.

The Marquis Canteloupe, now Conservative Shadow Minister of Commerce.

Somerset Lloyd-James, MP.

Mrs Harriet Ongley, now Fielding Gray's constant companion.

Alfie Schroeder, still of the Billingsgate Press, but now promoted from reporter to columnist.

The following new characters also appear:

Ivor Winstanley, a classical don at Lancaster and a distinguished Latinist.

Hugh Balliston, an undergraduate in his second year at Lancaster.

Hetta Frith, his girl friend.

Mrs Robert Constable (Elvira), the Provost's wife.

Tony Beck, a young English don at Lancaster, well known as a critic.

Wilfred, a college porter.

The Honourable Grantchester FitzMargrave Pough (pronounced Pew), Senior Fellow of Lancaster, Professor Emeritus of Oriental Geography, at one time celebrated as a mountaineer.

Dinkie and Dudu, Choristers in the Choir of the Chapel of Lancaster College.

The Reverend Oliver Clewes, Chaplain to Lancaster College, a progressive cleric.

The Reverend Andrew Ogden, Dean of the Chapel of Lancaster College.

Balbo Blakeney, Fellow of Lancaster, a biochemist.

Lord Beyfus, Fellow of Lancaster, a social scientist.

Mona Corrington, his chum, a Fellow of Girton College and an Anthropologist.

Mayerston, a revolutionary.

Childer, Wine Butler to Lancaster College.

Mr Powell, a senior porter.

A Coachman.

The Head Porter of Lancaster College.

Job, Mayerston's lieutenant.

A Female Neighbour of the Llewyllyns'.

The Master of the Musick of Lancaster College.

Two Drum Majorettes.

A Naked Female ('Miss Liberty').

Assorted Students.

'That's it,' thought Ivor Winstanley: 'the *coup de grâce*.'

Away on his right a spiteful little bell tinkled in confirmation.

'Winning gallery,' squealed the professional's boy from the net-post: 'game, set and match to Doctor Helmut.'

Ivor waddled into the corridor which ran along the tennis court while Jacquiz Helmut stalked patronisingly behind him.

'Your game's holding up very well, Ivor,' he said, 'but you must remember to keep the ball away from your opponent's forehand when you're on the hazard side.'

Opponent's foreskin, thought Ivor crossly; how maddening these Jews could be, even the well-bred ones. Suppressing the temptation to remark that he had been playing tennis when Jacquiz was still in his kosher knickers (what a sight he must have looked, legs like the stalks of hock glasses), and remembering the universal tolerance which the modern age and his own calling required of him, he merely said, rather sadly:

'This will be our last game, I suppose, until the autumn.'

'I've never understood why they close the court for the summer term.'

'They don't close it,' Ivor said; 'it's just not done to play royal tennis during the summer.'

Jacquiz wound a scarf of many colours round his neck, then draped himself in a still more improbable blazer.

'Why not?' said Jacquiz, almost whining. 'The pro stays here, and so does that boy of his, both of them drawing good money.'

'Nevertheless,' said Ivor, slipping on his battered sports jacket, 'the custom is quite clear: no tennis from the first day of the full summer term till the last of the long vacation.'

'Why have a custom so wasteful and restrictive?'

'You're a historian,' Ivor said, 'and you understand this kind of thing as well as anybody. Now, the essential point is that the custom does not apply to the university strings who are to represent us against Oxford at Lord's during July. So plainly the original idea was to keep our only court clear so that the top strings could practice whenever they wanted to; but rather than have a rule, which people would have disliked, they started a custom, which everyone, this place being what it is, was delighted to accept.'

By now they had left the University Library behind them and were passing through the new court of Clare—two white-flannelled figures, one a foot taller than the other, grotesquely in step; for Ivor Winstanley had an accommodating nature, was, moreover, very sensitive about seemliness, and he would have found something scandalous in walking out of step with his companion.

'When?' snapped Jacquiz. 'When did they start this custom?'

'I don't know,' sighed Ivor. 'It was certainly observed when I came up in the late 'twenties.'

'And you did nothing to stop it?'

'I never was the interfering kind.'

'Well, it's high time somebody did,' said Jacquiz. 'I myself am not exactly radical, as you know, but I resent being deprived of my tennis.'

'All right, then: do something.'

'All right. I shall.'

Ivor and Jacquiz had had this same conversation, almost word for word, every April since they started playing real tennis together, which was now a long time ago. The truth was, however, that tennis was only one of Jacquiz' minor pleasures, and he had no intention of doing anything at all. Although they both knew this perfectly well, they would not have dreamt of omitting this discussion, which had become for them as significant a feature of the natural calender as the return of the cuckoo. Summer was icumen in, and this was their rite of welcome.

'I remember,' said Ivor happily, 'the first time you said that. It was in April 1953—a few days after you'd been elected to your fellowship and a few weeks before the coronation. You had some lunatic idea that the best way of beginning a new reign was to scrap a lot of old customs. But it is now 1967, and tomorrow is the first day of full summer term, and the tennis court will then be closed, as it always has been, to all but the university strings, and you would sooner fly off the roof of the chapel than do anything whatever about it.'

They both nodded with profound satisfaction, and turned to look at the gate of Clare New Court, which they had just left.

SUI MEMORES, the inscription read, ALIOS FECERE MERENDO.

'"Made other men remember them,"' translated Ivor, '"by their deserving." Worrying, you know. As a classical man, I am very unhappy about the use of *alios* in this context.'

'Why?'

'The plural of *alios* is normally used in pairs . . . some did this, others did that. *Alios* by itself is very dubious usage. However, the only alternative reading is *aliquos*, and if we adopt it the passage would mean, "Made *some* men—i.e. some *only*—remember them by their deserving."'

'I can't see much wrong with that.'

'Cynical.'

'Since when,' said Jacquiz as they crossed the Queen's Road and turned right under the trees, 'has cynicism bothered you?'

'It has no place on a memorial gate like that one.'

'But that's the whole point. The memorial gate says "*alios*", which isn't cynical.'

'But *is* doubtful Latin. Doubtful Latin has even less place on memorial gates than cynicism.'

'So what do you conclude?'

'That they should have chosen another quotation.'

'"*Dulce et decorum est pro patria mori?*"'

'No. Untruthful. Perhaps, "*Aspicit et moriens dulces reminiscitur Argos.*" "He looks up to heaven and dying he remembers his sweet Argoes."'

'Applicable?'

'Perhaps some of them remembered their college as they died. I think ... I think perhaps I might have done. But if you want my choice of a suitable quotation, it comes in plain English: "Dead is dead" ... A turn in the Fellows' Garden before tea?'

'With pleasure.'

They recrossed the road and went up to a tracery gate; Ivor felt in his pocket and produced a key; Jacquiz smiled and opened the gate without one.

'Since when,' Ivor asked, 'has that gate been kept unlocked?'

'Since the College Council met in March. You were away in Greece. The Council, after strong urging by Provost Constable and others, decided to grant the undergraduates' request that they be allowed free access to the Fellows' Garden at all times.'

'Oh,' said Ivor, as if suddenly winded. 'I hadn't heard.' He waddled slowly over the lawn, past the Judas Tree and towards the summer house. 'What others?' he asked at length: 'what others beside the Provost?'

'Tony Beck—very vociferous *he* was. If, he said, we clung to out-dated privileges, then something called "the new awareness" would ensure they were forcibly taken from us. Daniel Mond and Tom Llewyllyn said much the same.'

'Oh ... oh,' puffed Ivor painfully. 'So now ... the Fellows' Garden of *Lancaster* College ... is open to anyone who wants to walk in?'

Jacquiz shrugged.

'Does it matter?' he said. 'They ruined the garden anyway when they built the new hostel right on top of it.'

Both men turned their faces to a prominent red-brick building which stood where there had once been a grove of ladybirch and now glowered over the rest of the garden as if threatening to advance and occupy it all in the name of utility and progress.

'The garden was a lost cause already,' Jacquiz said as he glowered back at the hostel; 'but it is important we should not lose any more. So I hope you will make a point of being at the Council tomorrow? I'm whipping all our people in.'

'What's up tomorrow?'

'The College is up ... by a very large sum of money from the sale of those farms in Lincolnshire. The question is: how is it to be spent? There are people who would like to see more of *those*'—he gestured, almost obscenely, at the new hostel.

'Where? Here?'

'Worse. In Scholars' Meadow.'

'But they can't do that,' wailed Ivor. 'Scholars' Meadow is set aside by the statutes ... *qua currant et ludant pupillares* ... for the exercise and sports of the students.'

'They haven't exercised or sported there for over a century. Not since the new playing fields were purchased.'

'Even so, the statute still protects it. Anyhow,' Ivor went on sullenly, 'it looks very nice as it is, and to build on it would wreck the view of Sitwell's from the backs.'

'Reformers,' said Jacquiz, 'disdain aesthetic considerations. And radical reformers, which is what we're dealing with, hold even statutes in contempt.'

'That's not to say they can break them.'

'There are ways of getting round them, Ivor. Bequests, trusts, statutes—you can subvert the lot these days. All you need do is claim that it's in the best educational interest of the college to do so, and no one will dare breathe a word.'

'And why should it be in the best educational interest of the college to build over Scholars' Meadow?'

'Because it would mean we could take more students.'

'And who in his right mind wants to do that?'

‘For God’s sake, Ivor. You must know *something* of what’s been going on in the last ten years.’

‘Yes. I heard we were to have sensible changes. Sensible changes, gradually introduced here and there, to make things better and fairer. Fewer tied scholarships, that kind of thing—and quite all right by me. What I did not hear was that we were going to ruin one of the finest views in Europe simply to increase our numbers.’

‘But that’s just what it’s all about, Ivor. Increased numbers equals democracy in action equals absolute good. Fine views equals privilege equals absolute bad. We have a large area called Scholars’ Meadow, which looks nice but serves no purpose. Its beauty provokes as much resentment as its uselessness, and certain people will not rest until it is covered from the Queen’s Road to the river with square, grey blocks of cheap and nasty bed-sitting rooms——’

‘—Full of cheap and nasty students, all reading sociology. Don’t tell me. Well, it’s got to be stopped.’ Ivor Winstanley breathed heavily through his nose, while little flecks of foam appeared at the corners of his mouth. ‘A hostel in the Fellows’ Garden is one thing; a tactful concession to the times, you might say. But to build on Scholars’ Meadow—an act of vandalism on that scale means the end of everything.’

‘So you’ll be there tomorrow?’ said Jacquiz.

‘With sword and buckler. We’ve got a majority. Even now, we’ve got a majority on the Council, and if all good men and true turn out, we have nothing to fear.’

‘Except,’ said Jacquiz, ‘that it’s no longer up to the Council. Or not entirely.’

‘You mean the Government may make trouble?’

‘Perhaps. But we can deal with them, because they talk the same language as we do and acknowledge much the same rules. I’m afraid, though, that there are far more sinister opponents than Governments—even Socialist ones.’

‘I find you very puzzling, Jacquiz.’

Ivor wiped his mouth with the sleeve of his coat and led

the way, rather quickly for him, back towards the gate. Indignation had made him hungry for his tea.

'There is,' said Jacquiz, 'a new element in these affairs. An element undreamed of in your philosophy or in mine. Until now.'

Ivor produced his key, as of long habit, to unlock and relock the gate.

'No,' said Jacquiz, twitching his cardinal's nose, 'no key. The undergraduates wouldn't like it—remember?'

'Most of them aren't up yet,' said Ivor, huffy and illogical.

'But tomorrow is the first day of full term,' said Jacquiz: 'they'll all be up tomorrow.'

Among those who were up already was an undergraduate called Hugh Balliston, who inhabited a room in the hostel by the Fellows' Garden. Hugh's room looked over the Garden, so that he would certainly have seen Ivor Winstanley and Jacquiz Helmut, had he been anywhere near his window. But as it happened he was lying face downward on his bed with Hetta Frith underneath him.

'Castro,' cried Hetta, 'you can't half do it. Castro, Lenin, Engels. Mao ... *Christ.*'

'Christ?'

'Sorry—*Marx* ...'

'Soon?'

'*Soon.*'

She snorted like a Derby winner and took in a great suck of breath.

'Mao,' she whimpered; 'Mar*cuse*,' she moaned with a mighty shudder; 'Fidel, oh Fidel,' she yelped, and at last subsided quivering with, 'Che ... Che ... Cheeee ...'

Hugh, who had come to climax at the same time but had characteristically kept quiet about it, eased himself off Hetta and off the bed and marched to the wash basin. Hetta watched him with pleasure: the thin, sinewy legs; the pale, narrow back, with the three large pimples on the left shoulder blade; the upper arms of alabaster, the fore-arms sprinkled with short, black hairs, disappearing round his body to do their hygienic work. Castro, but Hugh could do it! And now perhaps he would come back to the bed, talk to her for a while of what he had done during the vacation and what he proposed for the coming term, and then, with a little luck (Marx, Castro, *Che*) start doing it all over again.

But Hugh had other plans.

'Get dressed, duckie,' he said. 'You've got to go.'

'Oh Hugh . . . What about tea?'

'What about it?'

'Wouldn't you like some?'

Hugh turned to face her. He had a thin line of hair which ran down the very centre of his chest, the last place, Hetta reflected, where most people had any. Below his navel the stomach was flat and silky, inviting Hetta's kisses. She leapt off the bed, fell on her knees, threw her arms round his hams, and nuzzled her cheek against the soft skin. Firmly but kindly Hugh disengaged her, then took a hand towel and started to dry himself with minute and particular care.

'I've got some work to do,' he said.

'But just a quick cup. After all, it is tea-time.'

'No, it isn't,' he said: 'tea-time's at half past six. You mustn't keep reverting, Hetta. I know it's hard for you with Daddy a parson in Godalming and all the rest of it, but once you come over there's no going back to the rectory style—not even for the odd cup of tea.'

His voice was low, unaggressive and confident, easy yet precise; a gentleman's voice, one might have said, had it not been for a very slight grating of the 'a's. This one did not exactly hear; one just realised, some moments later, that it was present. Hugh's voice was like certain kinds of white burgundy, which are agreeable to swallow but leave an undertaste of phlegm on the palate. Or, as Hetta had sometimes told herself, it was like the de-odorant spray which Mother used for the kitchen: from being fresh and light, it turned, within seconds, to a smell of warm metal.

Sniffing this smell now (so to speak) and being disappointed of her tea, Hetta was provoked to mild counter-revolution.

'The sort of people who have tea at half past six,' she said, 'would not approve of sex in the afternoon.'

'I know. We're going to change all that. We're going to educate them to understand that there's nothing wrong with sex in the afternoon.'

'Then they'll realise there's nothing wrong with tea at four o'clock either.'

Hugh laughed and nodded, conceding her point. Overwhelmed by this generosity, Hetta at once felt ashamed of having been 'mardy' and skipped into her knickers.

'I don't want to be in the way,' she said, really meaning it.

'There's a good girl. I wouldn't do this to you, but I've got to get ready for a tutorial this evening.'

'A tutorial? But it isn't proper term yet.'

'Tony Beck wants to go over something with me. Something special.'

'That's because you're his special pupil. What with your First last summer, and that University Prize in the autumn ... The Members' English Essay Prize,' she proclaimed proudly. 'Awarded to the undergraduate with the largest member,' she giggled, and tweaked it fondly.

'We've had that joke before,' Hugh said stuffily, considering his academic success to be somehow tainted by such ribaldry. 'Now for God's sake take your hands off before I get another horn on.'

He put on a striped flannel shirt (collarless) and a pair of denim trousers, and went to his desk by the window.

'What is it you're doing for Mr Beck?'

'Just a short essay. I've got to make a fair copy before I see him.'

'All right. I'm going. What about tonight?'

'No good,' he said without turning. 'I've got a meeting. The old men are up to something.'

'Oh?'

'They've got their hands on some money, and we aim to see they spend it properly. Although Lancaster's a filthy rich college, it's too much to hope they'll send it somewhere else where it's needed. And we can't make 'em—not yet. But at least we can try to see they do something decent for the college itself.'

'Like what?'

'Like we're going to discuss tonight.'

'How interesting. Can't I come to the meeting?'

'Sorry, love. Private. Get going, will you?'

'I'm at the door. Wave to me, Hugh.'

Briefly, Hugh turned his bright simian face, already crinkled with concentration, towards the door. He put his hand through his black hair (thick, curly hair, but tidily trimmed at the nape) and then waggled four long fingers at Hetta. Hetta waggled four rather stubby fingers back, hitched her jeans over her lovely round bottom and on to her ample hips, and flicked a long blonde wisp away from her mouth in order to smile at Hugh. It was half a smile of innocence, bold and sweet and trusting; and half a prostitute's leer (want a dirty time in a taxi?). Hugh quivered with tenderness, gurgled slightly and then turned back with a shrug to the papers on his desk.

'Go along, bottykins,' he said softly. 'Come tomorrow at twelve.'

Although Hugh had told Hetta she could always go through the Fellows' Garden if she wanted to, Hetta felt this to be wrong unless she was accompanied by a member of the college. On leaving the hostel, therefore, she walked a hundred yards down the tarmac drive to a side-road, turned left up this and walked a hundred yards to the Queen's Road, then turned left up that and walked yet another hundred yards to the back gate of Lancaster College, which was exactly opposite the gate of the Fellows' Garden. Thus Hetta's residual bourgeois scruples had already made her walk three times further than she need have done; and even now they continued to operate. For although anybody in the world was at liberty to walk through Lancaster College, Hetta felt that one who had a lover in the college should not do so unless escorted by that lover, in case she should seem to be assuming proprietary rights; and she was now seriously considering going all the way round through Trinity, which would have taken her another mile out of her way. In the end, however, common sense prevailed, and she started up Lancaster Walk, under the elm trees and towards the Willow Bridge.

On Hetta's left, as she went, was Scholars' Meadow. What sort of playground it had provided for the scholars, and what games they played there, were now questions beyond any conjecture; for Scholars' Meadow was no longer, to speak properly, a meadow at all. Its most prominent feature was two magnificent copper beeches which grew on the summit of a small, steep mound. The mound itself was at the centre of a rectangle, perhaps two hundred and fifty yards long by a hundred and fifty across, which was covered by thickets of shrub and small, wispy trees, these being diversified by patches of moss, daffodil and pheasant-eye, and interlaced by little paths which would hither and thither, stopped here, started again there, dashed across one another and whipped back to cut across themselves, with no pretensions either to purpose or convenience. The wonder was that they survived at all, as no one ever walked along them and no one, indeed, was ever seen to enter the 'meadow', which (the story went) was tended by an unknown gardener who arrived at dusk and was gone again by dawn.

It had often been suggested to the undergraduates of Lancaster that, since the Meadow was dedicated by statute to their pleasure, they should frequent it more often ... a suggestion which had been renewed when they started to agitate, the previous winter, for unrestricted use of the Fellows' Garden. But the student committee which was conducting the affair had replied that they were not to be fobbed off with what they didn't want; and when asked why they didn't want it, they had answered that as no one had walked in the Meadow within living memory (since 1856, in fact, when the 'new' playing fields had been procured), the place had acquired an air of remoteness and even of hostility which they found uninviting. This, of course, was a rationalisation: all the committee really wanted was to embarrass and annoy the Fellows by challenging their exclusive right to their own property. Nevertheless, there was something in the claim that Scholars' Meadow was unwelcoming; for, despite its gay flowers and pretty paths, it had an intimation of mortality about it, as though it had been the last retreat (if allowance were made for botanical differences) of a decaying Emperor who was waiting hopelessly until the barbarians should come to sack Byzantium.

Why it should have given this impression was difficult to say. Though it was sometimes described as a 'wilderness', the word was used only as a conventional term of landscape gardening, and the area was in no way gone to seed or overgrown; quite the contrary, whatever the truth about the mysterious gardener, it was as trim, in its informal way, as the Fellows' Garden itself. Perhaps this was the explanation: for there is, after all, something rather sinister about a well kept plot of ground which has no visible gardener. However this might be, the general feeling persisted that Scholars' Meadow was mildly numinous in an undefined but disagreeable way, and people just did not care to set foot in it.

And yet, perversely enough, they loved it. They gazed at it in deep silence, from all angles, at every hour of every day. As did Hetta now. How pretty, she said to herself as she looked down a little path which ran through a mass of daffodils, jumped a stream on a tiny bridge, curved round a young green beech, and disappeared between two bramble bushes. How ... how satisfying, she thought, pausing a moment opposite the central mound; and then, passing along the upper half of the Meadow, 'why is it so sad?' One thing that made it sad was the lonely and nameless old horse, who was always grazing in the only piece of real meadow that remained, a narrow strip which lay between the upper end of the 'wilderness' and the river bank. And what made it even sadder, she reflected, was the long line of willows (half of them weeping) along the bank itself. These ran all the way from the far top corner of the Meadow to just short of Willow Bridge, where the line ended in a group of four trees which leaned out over and into the water, whether in grief or supplication Hetta could not tell. Melancholy, she told herself, but knew the word was wrong. Hugh could tell me the right one, she thought, he's so clever at English. Doleful? No, Mournful? Not really. Dismal? Definitely not. The word for which Hetta was looking and could not find was perhaps 'elegiac'; but it is doubtful whether Hugh Balliston would have told it to her, as it was not a word of which he approved.

The bridge was crowded with people who were staring down at the Meadow, and with others who were jostling for good places against the balustrade. Most of the men turned to look at Hetta, but she kept straight on with what she thought to be a disdainful carriage, not knowing that this sort of carriage only emphasised the twin oscillations of her delicious buttocks. To her left there was now a huge and beautifully mown square of grass; and at the far end of this, facing its entire width, was an elegant eighteenth century building (Sitwell's), in which, she knew, most of the dons and a few rich undergraduates (a very sore point with Hugh) had large and lavish rooms. Straight ahead of her, the gravel path she was on passed through a gap between the south end of Sitwell's and the College Hall (an engaging piece of Gothick pastiche), then led on into the Great Court of Lancaster; while to her immediate right were the steps which mounted to the main entrance of the Provost's Lodge, a late nineteenth century erection with a commonplace yet somehow imposing frontage. Hetta gave this a glance of angry contempt, as it contained the principal and therefore the most villainous of all 'the old men', and then walked on quickly, through the gap between Sitwell's and the Hall, and into the Great Court.

It was now her paramount duty to get through the Great Court without taking any notice of the chapel. This was less than a furlong away to her left, forming the north side of the court, and was one of the finest pieces of perpendicular in the kingdom; but she had been warned against it by Hugh during one of the most solemn passages of her 're-education'. 'We can learn lessons from the past,' Hugh had said, 'but we must not be distracted or corrupted by it. The great thing you've got to realise about that chapel is that it stands for a system of thought which is false, outmoded and repressive. You must not succumb to its charm.' Mindful of this, Hetta marched straight ahead, arms swinging and bosoms bobbing, eyes and nose pointing resolutely to her front. But Hugh or no Hugh, the chapel could not be long ignored, for the good reason that Hetta had to turn left at the top end of the path round the court in order to come at the gate. This meant that she could not avoid seeing the south-east tower and at least two of the southern buttresses ... unless she looked down at the ground instead, which Mother had taught her was a furtive and slovenly habit. So Hetta turned left and lifted up her reluctant eyes to the chapel, and now as always the sight was too much for her.

'Castro, how fucking marvellous,' she said.

Re-education forgotten, she turned towards the statue of the Founder, King Henry VI, who stood over a fountain in the centre of the grass.

'Beate Henrice,' she whispered, 'ora pro nobis.'

Then, having enjoyed this self-indulgence but full of guilt at her betrayal of Hugh, she hacked on to the Market Place, where she caught a bus out to the Institute of Pediatric Training in the outskirts of Cherry Hinton.

Robert Reculver Constable, Provost of Lancaster College,

had seen the passing Hetta snarl at his front door. He had been sitting at the desk in his study, had looked up from his work and through the window to refresh his spirit with the sight of the back lawn, and had observed Hetta very clearly, on the gravel path below his casement, as she flicked the fair hair from her mouth and formed her lips into a priggish pout which (Robert Constable surmised) was intended for a scowl of moral disdain. It happened, however, that just as Hetta's disdainful walk was even more sexy than her ordinary one, so her disdainful look was even more fetching than her face in repose. So much so that the Provost was tempted to fling open the window and ask her in for tea. This (he reflected) would be more or less permissible as he had actually met her, in the company of one of his own young men, Hugh Balliston, who had been walking her round the Fellows' Garden a day or two before. Since the Provost knew and liked Hugh, he had stopped him to speak a friendly word and had been, rather grudgingly, introduced to Hetta. Even so, he now reminded himself, asking stray girls in to tea was something which Provosts of Lancaster did not normally do, and something which he, Robert Constable, most certainly did not do. Besides, Hetta's scowl, however fetching, was a scowl nevertheless, and so it was reasonable to assume that she would have refused the invitation.

But *why* had the girl scowled? He supposed that she must have been listening to Balliston, who had said something to make her hostile. But again, why should Balliston do that? Constable had always made a point of being pleasant to the boy, whom he recognised as a very able scholar and a potential credit to the college. True, Balliston was a left-winger and anti-authoritarian of the most insistent kind, as he had made plain by his work on student committees and by several talented articles in undergraduate journals; but then the Provost himself was a Socialist of long and impeccable standing and had bent over backwards, during his reign at Lancaster, to promote reform and relax discipline to the furthest degree consistent with passably good order and the peaceful pursuit of knowledge. Surely that must be enough, even for Hugh Balliston?

But somehow Robert Constable was not quite reassured. There had been signs lately that some people (exactly who he could not have said) wanted yet more change and wanted it very much quicker. And not just change, the need for which Constable understood, but a new kind of change, the precise nature of which no one had explained to him, beyond hinting that the demands about to be made were no longer matters for debate and negotiation in carefully defined terms but were somehow both unrefusable and limitless. Beyfus had said something of the sort a few weeks ago: 'It isn't a question of adapting the existing structure any more,' Beyfus had said; 'one must acknowledge the principle of total fluidity.' Whatever that might mean. (Trust Beyfus to be both contentious and obscure.) But if it meant what he thought it meant, Constable did not in the least like it, and he could only hope Hugh Balliston had not been taken in. After all, the great things that had been fought for and achieved since the war could not be allowed to go up in smoke (total fluidity?) just because of some new and extremist fad. Balliston, Balliston of all people, must be of calibre to understand that.

Whichever way you looked at it, however, Hetta's scowl meant trouble from Balliston and those like him. So once again, why? It was only a few weeks since the Council had yielded over the Fellows' Garden: surely there couldn't be another point of dispute already? 'Total fluidity,' rasped Beyfus' voice in his ear. All right, but even so, and however limitless and unrefusable the demands to be expected, such demands must come in concrete form; one at a time or a hundred at a time, they must be *distinguishable*. So what was it that Balliston and his cronies wanted now? What was it that had caused pretty Hetta to pout so appealingly but with such evidently savage intent? Constable shook his marmoreal head (that of a late Emperor, one might have said, risen from the ranks in Bithynia or some such place, but not without breeding—a small local chieftain's son perhaps?) and passed a large, hard hand through closely cut grey hair. There was, he thought, one concrete and distinguishable issue which, above all others conceivable, would appeal to the disaffected just now: the disposal of one quarter of a million in sterling money.

For the college had sold land to the North-West of the Wash, and sold it for just twice its value as this appeared on the books (which still carried land valuations as last made in 1947). Of the monies realised by the sale, the statutes decreed that one half, i.e. the capital sum which the land had theoretically represented, must be re-invested immediately; but the other half, all £250,000 of it (not subject to Capital Gains Tax), was surplus—it was money to be spent. The cash was presently to hand, and with it trouble for the Provost. For naturally enough, the intended sale had been widely known about. The actual processes had taken so long (well over three years) and had been so hideously boring, that popular interest had lapsed; but there remained certain acute and concerned observers, within the college itself, who had followed the business right through and were well aware that it had at last been finally settled. It was men such as these who were now mustering: determined men, all with plans of their own, plans fully forged and highly polished, which they would thrust at the Provost like so many bristling swords the first moment that the news was officially broken.

Which would be at the College Council the next morning, on the first day of the full summer term in this year of our Lord 1967.

Once more the Provost lifted his wary eyes to seek refreshment from the lawn and from Scholars' Meadow; once again he brought them back to the gravel path below and this time saw no Hetta to enhance the scene. He sniffed fiercely and bent his head to the blank sheet in front of him. Tomorrow he was going to be set about by clever men who would have diverse and cherished schemes for the spending of two hundred and fifty thousand pounds. He was going to be made to listen to appeal, threat, common sense, moral blackmail, political rancour, sweet persuasion and idle dreams. He must be ready for all of them; how, then, did the dispositions lie?

First, he thought, myself. I would merely wish that the money should be invested in equities (which should appreciate considerably between now and the end of 1968) and left to increase until everyone who wishes has had time to present detailed suggestions which can then be calmly considered on their practical as well as other merits. What I do *not* want is that some theoretically plausible plan should be hastily adopted on moral or political principle and that we should thenceforth be committed to this and this alone. But that is just what the activists, in their different ways, will try to force us to. Very well then: who will emerge as the leaders and under what banners will they lead their men?

'Right wing,' he now wrote: 'Balbo Blakeney and Jacquiz Helmut.

'Helmut is opposed to change for snobbish, aesthetic and, to do him justice, for intellectual reasons. Ideally, he would like nothing at all to be done with the money for as long as conceivably possible. He might therefore support me in advocating delay. On the other hand, since he knows the money must be spent sometime, he may well want it used straight away (i.e. before the sun can grow by investment and become an even greater menace) and used, of course, on something neutral and familiar.

'In any case, it is far more likely that any positive suggestions on the right will originate with *Balbo Blakeney.* He has the upper-class gift of leadership (in which his foul tongue helps rather than hinders him) and an undeniable streak of imagination despite his narrow scientific training. What does Blakeney want? (Apart from ever increasing quantities of food and drink.) He can hardly expect us to finance his researches into the chemistry of the blood, which are already generously underwritten by his Faculty. Or again, while Blakeney loves buildings, and not only traditional ones, like Helmut he loathes the notion of admitting larger numbers of undergraduates. He could, I suppose, urge the erection of a College Laboratory for the convenience of our science students—were it not that his contempt for all students whatever is so pronounced he'd as soon see them to the devil. He could propose more bathrooms and lavatories—were it not that those in his own set are quite adequate and he wouldn't dream of worrying about anyone else's. All in all, I'm afraid I must admit that I cannot begin to foretell what Balbo may put up: I must resign myself to its being a surprise, almost certainly a disagreeable one.'

And what following, thought Constable, laying down his pen and looking across the lawn to the rose-brick wall at its far side, would Blakeney command? He would certainly command Helmut; but the important question was whether he could also take with him those who represented more moderate right-wing opinion. The chief of these were three in number: Ivor Winstanley, the Latinst and celebrated Horatian; the Hon. Grantchester FitzMargrave Pough, Senior Fellow, Professor Emeritus of Oriental Geography, and a noted mountaineer in his day; and the Rev. Andrew Ogden, Dean of Chapel. Such was the prestige and amiability of this trio that where they went all men who were right of centre, by however small a margin, would follow. Indeed, if Winstanley, Pough and Ogden were in accord, it was even possible that some of the moderate left might join them. That they would be in accord was like enough, as they frequently were; but would they be behind Blakeney? This must obviously depend on the line Blakeney took, and about this, as the Provost had already told himself, there could be no knowing. The only reasonable surmise was that Blakeney, realising that he depended on the support of Winstanley and the other two to make up his numbers, would temper his propositions to their tastes.

These reflections he now committed to paper with the rest, fully and accurately and without grudging a second of the labour: for it was Provost Constable's one vanity that he wished to leave behind him a record and a justification of his entire career; and he was therefore assembling notes, day by day and blow by blow, for a autobiography of such huge dimensions and such minutely interlocking detail that it would surpass anything that had ever been produced in its kind, even by the most tortuous of Alexandrians or the most prolix of Victorians.

So much for the right, he now thought as he penned his last sentence on the subject: tactics unpredictable and strength as yet undetermined. What about the left.

'The leadership of the left,' he wrote after some thought, 'will certainly go to Lord Beyfus. A life peer of recent creation, veteran of countless Commissions and Committees, he enjoys such enormous prestige both as a public figure and a social theorist that the left has no other choice. The point to mark, however, is that Beyfus himself will be led, in this as in all else, by Mona Corrington; and the kind of thing Mona will put him up to can be readily guessed at.

'At a recent meeting of the Girton Anthropological Society, to which I was bidden as guest speaker, she deliberately turned the discussion from the formation of élites in primitive societies (the proper business of the evening) to the survival of privileged élites in our own. This unwarranted transition she effected (as usual) by sheer effrontery; she simply remarked that dissolution, being the opposite of formation, was a subject relevant to our brief, and then asked me what was my "personal thinking, as controller of a residual élitist institution, on available methods of eliminating discrimination and eradicating bourgeois/hierarchical systemisations in order to finalise the comprehensivisation of educational resources and exclude all elements of social or intellectual selectivity'. Uncertain whether it was her impertinence or her abuse of the language that more merited rebuke, I simply replied that entrance to my college was at present determined, as far as might be, by mental competence alone, and that once here men either did their work properly or were promptly dismissed.

'Mona immediately went into more jargon about "the fascist connotations of subjective standard-maintenance", and then switched, when I was least expecting it, to being brutally concrete. Lancaster College, she said, was rich and getting richer: what were we doing with all that cash? Before I could draw breath, she told me what we should be doing, which was to make the fullest use of our space and resources in order to house "a much enlarged student-body, drawn from all sections of the community and indeed the entire human race, with complete disregard of outmoded notions of academic attainment". Mercifully, she was interrupted by the arrival of cocoa and stale biscuits; but she had said enough to show me what kind of nightmare she will try to inflict on us through the agency of her double-ganger Beyfus.

'Although we shan't know the details of Mona's scheme until Beyfus parrots them out at the Council tomorrow, I am pretty certain that young Tony Beck will go along with him. Beck is a shrewd critic of English literature with a keen and muscular style of setting down his opinions; he, if any man living, must realise the importance of academic standards; and yet, although nothing on earth would make him drop his own, he seems to think that the "new culture" requires their general replacement by something which he calls "co-operative evaluations". These, as far as I understand it all, are arrived at in committee or even, ideally, in public assembly. They represent the highest common factors, as it were, in mass appreciation—i.e. the highest level to which all members of the populace, given their own sincere effort and every educational facility, can be expected to attain. Necessarily, this level is very low; but to insist on a higher one is apparently an offence against new social theory, which holds that to transcend the prescribed level of understanding is an aggressive exercise of mental privilege. Apparently it causes "undesirable tensions", both in those who cannot follow and therefore feel themselves "deprived", and in those who can and therefore feel themselves "apart"—which for some reason is considered a hideous fate these days. How Beck reconciles his own undeniable "apartness" with his advocacy of these modern methods (under which, presumably, everyone would be awarded an identical degree) God alone knows.

'To leave all that aside, however, it is clear to me that any plan of Beyfus's which would sacrifice standards to numbers, and destroy both distinctions and distinction, would have Beck's support, if only because Beck delights, above all, in the discomfiture of established men. But how many others would back Beyfus here? Once again, we come to the all-important moderates. There are, I think, two respected left-wing moderates whose attitudes will substantially influence all other left-wingers. There is also a joker in the pink pack who cannot be dismissed out of hand for reasons I will come to in a moment.

'But first, the two moderates. These, of course, are Daniel Mond and Tom Llewyllyn. Although Daniel is a quiet, introspective character and Tom very much the opposite, they have been great friends since Tom came here in '63 and have one thing very much in common: both of them have seen enough of the world in action to make them sceptical of untried theories for the improvement of any part of it.

'Their respective experiences have been very different in kind. Daniel's were all concentrated into a brief period of time and a small geographical area—i.e. into a summer spent in Göttingen where he went to do research in 1952. God knows exactly what happened to him (though I believe Jacquiz Helmut knows more than most of us), but whatever it was cost him both the power of speech and the power of will to do any further creative work. He remains a very sound man in his own fields of pure mathematics (Finite Series and the Tensor Calculus) but only as a teacher of conventional methods, no longer as the brilliant originator which he promised to be before he left for Göttingen. He went away, I remember, an eager, innocent boy; when he returned he was a little old man, unable to speak above a whisper, his physical health and his intellectual enterprise alike entirely shattered. And yet he is never bitter or morbid; although he has lost half and more of what life meant to him, he is tender in his manners and humorous in his whispered comments, a loyal servant of his college and his faculty, content to pass the rest of his life in the routine work of an obscure academic station. But the important point of my present purpose is that he was once subjected, and that most rigorously, to "a crash course" in the ways of the world.

'If Daniel has been pitched about by the world, Tom has bustled in it. Prestige journalist, popular historian, BBC producer, he has spent many years amid the smoke (and the vices) of Rome, learning to move at ease with the near-great and to survive among the violent and corrupt. Although he was very glad to come here, and will stay, I think, as long as we let him, he will always keep one foot, or at any rate a big toe, in his old arena. Part of Tom will always be a Grub Street man, however seriously the rest of him is working on the treatise which he is here to write; he has been and still is a frequentor of coffee houses, market places, drawing-rooms and great assemblies, one ear to the arras and one eye to the keyhole; and this is his great value to us here and now. Thank heaven we waived the rule which bars Namier Fellows from college administration and elected him to the Council. For Tom, a socialist by his birth, which was both low and Welsh, has none of that moral smugness and intellectual arrogance which attach to your middle-class socialists by conviction. Any smugness he might have had has long since rubbed off in taverns and posedas, while his training as a working journalist has taught him to despise anyone who claims a monopoly on intellectual truth. What Tom will bring to the Council tomorrow is the much needed reminder that all crops depend on dung and dung comes from the anus.

'So much for Tom and Daniel. There remains the question of the left-wing joker . . . the Rev. Oliver Clewes, the College Chaplain. He is one of these new progressive clerics who hardly seem to believe in God at all and apparently picture Christ as some kind of revolutionary guerrilla from South America. As a nominal Christian, Clewes is mistrusted by most of the left, while as a declared socialist he is mistrusted by all of the right. The few people remaining merely despise him as an equivocating opportunist. The one important thing to be said of him, therefore, is that he will discredit whatever cause he may adopt in the eyes of everybody at all, so that one can only hope he will not support a good one.'

Not without satisfaction, Robert Constable read through what he had written, gathered the sheets together, then held them up vertically and tapped them gently against his desk until they were absolutely flush. His thoughts were now in order against whatever the morrow might send, and he could ring with good conscience for tea . . . when, that was, he had done just one thing more. With great care, he fastened the sheets together with a stapler (exactly half an inch from the top edge and half an inch from the left-hand edge), then carried them over to some long shelves of files and secured them with an elaborately sprung device in a file marked, 'Lancaster College: Academic Year October '66 to June '67.'

Having replaced this file with a happy sigh, Constable pushed the bell by the door: one long and three shorts, these latter meaning that today he would have three chocolate biscuits instead of his usual two (surely he had deserved them). He then cleared a small table and placed it near his desk to hold the tray; for he would not extend his indulgence to taking his tea in idleness, and he proposed, during this brief collation, to revise the whole of his new paper for the Keynes Society, thus alloying his pleasure but increasing his self-esteem.

Thirty seconds since he rang the bell: where was that damned woman?

And indeed, just as he sat down at the desk, there was a knock on the door.

'On the table just here,' Constable said without turning.

'Yes, dear,' said Mrs Constable.

'You're sure it's strong enough?'

Constable liked a sergeant-major's brew which would have killed most sergeant-majors.

'Six spoonfuls, dear, and two for the pot.'

'Thank you. That's all.'

While Elvira Constable fled gratefully through the door, her husband reached for his paper (Moral Justice and the Taxation Structure). But before he read the first paragraph (which would give the tea nice time to settle), he allowed himself one more look over the back lawn. Strolling across this very slowly, on a diagonal from Willow Bridge to the north end of Sitwell's, were Tom Llewyllyn and Daniel Mond. Tom's head was turned to Daniel's ear and his hand rested lightly in the crook of Daniel's right arm. While Tom mouthed fluently, Daniel nodded gently, and then, as Tom paused for breath, brought his free arm across his body and touched Tom's hand where it lay inside his own elbow. Robert Constable felt rather than saw the smile with which Tom responded; and for a moment his head drooped over his desk, as he thought to himself how sweet a thing it must be to walk across a lawn in April arm in arm with a friend.

Tom Llewyllyn and Daniel Mond were talking about an old acquaintance they had in common, a novelist called Fielding Gray. The reason why Daniel had touched Tom's hand was that Tom had become vehement about Gray's irresponsible behaviour some four years before (when Tom, as a BBC producer, had commissioned him to write a programme for television) and Daniel, who deprecated vehemence, wished to calm his friend down. So he brought his hand over to Tom's, and Tom, as Provost Constable had sensed from his window, smiled in response.

'Not that it made any difference,' Tom now said. 'For a variety of other reasons that programme would never have got on the air in any case. But the fact remains that Fielding simply rode off into the blue with some bloody Greek boy while he was being paid a lot of money to prepare a script for me, and not a word did I hear until weeks later, after he'd been picked up near the palace at Mycenae, crying drunk and stinking like a corpse.'

Since there was a threat of further vehemence here, Daniel patted Tom's hand once more and whispered:

'Fielding always had good taste in his choice of settings. Where was the boy?'

'He'd pissed off by then. That's why Fielding was in such a state. Anyway, along came some interfering Yankee widow woman and scraped him off the ground—quite literally, from what I hear—and took him off to Nauplion to be dried out and deloused. After a bit she brought him back to London and got him writing again, and I'm bound to admit that he produced a bloody good novel. *Operation Apocalypse*. It won the Joseph Conrad Prize for 1964.'

Daniel screwed up his eyes in his pinched, sallow face.

'I didn't care for it,' he muttered.

'Why on earth not? It's the best thing he's done—except possibly for *Love's Jest Book*.'

'It's based on . . . some events . . . which happened to us both at the time I knew him. In Germany it was, in 1952. I was there researching, you see, and he was with his regiment. Somehow he's made it all false.'

Daniel broke off into a series of quick, painful little croaks. Although their pace was sedate, both halted, and Tom was silent until Daniel had had time to recover what was left of his voice. Then,

'How was he false?' Tom said.

'When it all happened,' said Daniel moving slowly forward again, 'I was in great fear. I had good reason to be afraid, and Fielding knew this—indeed he was very kind to me for as long as he could be. But in this novel he makes out that I was just being hysterical—that I was a pathetic paranoiac suffering from persecution fantasies. This hurt me very much.'

'Perhaps it isn't really you. Perhaps he used what he remembered of your situation but gave it a different slant.'

'I was in the most terrible distress. He should not have used such distress for his work unless he was prepared to treat it honourably ... with compassion.'

'Novelists,' said Tom, 'are cannibals. Worse: they eat you *alive* for their nourishment. It's not surprising if odd things happen while they digest you.'

'You take a lenient view, Tom.'

'I once wrote a novel myself, Danny. Have you never tackled Fielding with this?'

'I've never seen him since that summer in Germany.'

'Then he's changed a lot since you knew him.'

They rounded the north end of Sitwell's.

'A quick cup?' said Tom.

'That would be nice.'

They went up the staircase nearest the chapel and turned into the front chamber of a set on the first floor. Although the furnishings were mean—three sleasy armchairs, a scruffy desk, an oval table smeared with ink and dry sweat—it was a tall and lordly room.

'Mind you,' said Tom, kneeling to light the gas-ring, 'I didn't meet Fielding till after he left the Army in 1958. What was he like back in '52?'

'Beautiful. Rather drunk. Thoughtful. Bitter. Accustomed to being obeyed—that was the Army, of course.'

'He isn't beautiful any more,' Tom said, 'and the only person who obeys him is Tessie Buttock.'

'Tessie Buttock?'

'She owns a hotel in the Cromwell Road, where he stays when he's in London. But he spends a lot of his time in the country these days, and not very far from here. Broughton

Staithe, on the Norfolk coast. He does all his work there—two novels in the last three years, not up to *Apocalypse* but not bad at that.'

'Is that woman—the Yankee widow woman—still with him?'

'Yes,' said Tom: 'though he's finding her rather stifling. Or so I gather from chums. I haven't heard from him or seen him since the Greek fiasco, which is absurd when we live so close.'

'Write and ask him over here. One of you must break the silence. I'd like to see him . . . despite what he did to me in that novel . . . now that he's no longer beautiful. Perhaps,' added Daniel wistfully, 'that explains it all.'

'I'm not sure he'd come. This college was always one of the things he was most bitter about.'

'I know. He was kept out of here because of some trouble at his school. That was one of the first things he ever told me. It upset him, he said, because he'd always wanted to be a don.'

'I see his point. It's an attractive life.'

'You've only had a few years of it,' whispered Daniel, 'and you've got special work to keep you happy.'

For a moment he looked very withered.

'Even when that's finished,' Tom said, 'I want to stay. If the college will have me.'

'They might. Your Namier Research Fellowship was renewed after its three-year term, which is very unusual. They elected you to the Council—which for a Namier Fellow is quite unheard of. They must think highly of you. But why do you want to stay, Tom?'

Tom Llewyllyn looked into the palms of his grubby hands, then rubbed them up over smooth cheeks and on into his abundant and gritty hair.

'It's peaceful,' he said; 'and as far as it goes, it's genuine. On the whole, the men in this college try to discover the truth in their own line and then to act on it.'

'But suppose,' croaked Daniel, 'their own line is irrelevant to anyone or anything else? It sometimes happens, you know.'

'It is still valid in itself. Satisfying, therefore, to the scholar.'

'Such truth can be horrible, believe me. The more horrible because you are alone with it.'

'But always genuine.'

'And totally destructive of this peace you talk of. But as for that,' said Daniel, 'it's threatened anyway. Even those who are still lucky enough to enjoy this peace of yours will soon find it can't last.'

'Why not? Guilt?'

'Nothing as suble as that. The threat, the danger, is on an everyday level and of the crudest possible kind.'

He was interrupted by a series of sharp gasps in his throat.

'There's a lot of trouble coming to us, you know,' he said at length.

His manner was casual, as of one who predicts a spell of disagreeable weather during the month of February.

'What makes you think so?' said Tom, uneasy but trying to maintain the same tone.

'The undergraduates. They're getting difficult.'

'Undergraduates have always been difficult.'

'Not in the same way. They used to be wild or lazy or lecherous or cranky, but they always accepted the framework. Drinking men, hunting men, whoring men—to use the nineteenth century idiom—dissenting men or reforming men, they all knew that if they went too far they would be disciplined or even dismissed, and they accepted this, much as they accepted that the world was round, as a natural condition of existence.'

'They still believe the world to be round, I imagine.'

'They also believe that its shape can be altered to suit their convenience.' Daniel put his cup down on the oval table and fingered the grimy surface with distaste. 'There's a theory about it, far too loose and speculative to be strictly applied, but it will give you some idea of what I mean. According to this theory, the present generation of students was the first to be treated, when babies, after the precepts of Doctor Spock. Whenever they so much as whimpered, they were lifted out of their cots and petted and pampered until they stopped. The result is, the theory says, that over the years they have come to believe, to believe absolutely, that they can have anything they want simply by whimpering for it.'

Daniel paused to wheeze for twenty seconds.

'Now, so far,' he went on hoarsely, 'they haven't whimpered for anything very important, just for small concessions here and there, so that we have found it politic to yield. But very soon now they are going to start whining, if not for the moon, then certainly for something far too valuable to be given them. And when they are denied, for the first time since birth, mark you, they are going to scream their little heads off.'

'Well,' said Tom, who was becoming angry at this prospect and was only controlling himself with an effort, 'we mustn't be reactionary. We must find out ... now ... what they want and discuss it with them like civilised human beings.'

'Do children ever know what they want when you ask them? Even if they do, they want something else two seconds later.'

'You really can't go on equating our undergraduates with children and babies.'

'*Spock babies,*' I said. 'It's a metaphorical way of describing an attitude: I WANT THAT TOY *NOW*. And there's an obvious corollary: if a Spock baby is not to be refused, neither is it to be restrained. If a Spock baby wants to defecate,' Daniel said, 'it defecates there and then. And Spock babies, of course, are often turned loose without nappies.'

'So what it comes to in your view,' said Tom crossly, 'is that either we give the students some belated potty training or else we get ready to pick up the shit.'

'Have it thrown at us, more likely.' Daniel backed towards the door. 'See you in Hall?'

'I'm afraid not. Patricia's expecting me home.'

'Tomorrow at the Council then. There's going to be big money talk, I hear.'

The white silk scarf, which Daniel always wore round his throat like a bandage, had worked loose during his exegesis and now slipped down slightly to reveal a long, flaring lesion. It was not the first time this had happened; now as ever Tom opened his mouth to ask the question he longed to ask, and now as ever, seeing the hunted look on Daniel's face as he lifted and tightened the silk, he thought better of it.

'Money talk, Danny?' he said lamely.

'Yes,' rasped Daniel. ' "If there were dreams to sell, what would you buy?" There's plenty of money come in, they tell me, and so there'll be plenty of dreams floating round the Council. To say nothing of all the Spock babies' dreams when the students get to hear of it.'

'What are your dreams, Daniel?'

'Approximately those of William Morris,' said Daniel, opening the door; 'so as far as I am concerned, it is unlikely that the college can command the appropriate currency.'

Provost Constable, in accordance with his schedule, finished revising his paper for the Keynes Society at the same moment as he took his last sip of lava-like tea. Having wiped a thick crust of sugar from his lips, he placed his cup on the tray, then crossed the room and placed the tray on the carpet near the door, thus ensuring that Mrs Constable, when summoned, would either (*a*) hit the tray with the door, or (*b*) just miss the tray with the door but put one foot right in the middle of it, and (*c*) and in any case at all, have to bend down to pick it up. Having made this disposition with some care, the Provost rang the bell and returned to his desk, picking up *en route* the latest popular work by

Professor Parkinson, which he had been invited to review in the columns of *The New Statesmen.* Normally, he only reviewed academic treatises, but he was presently distressed, being an honest man, by the fact that Parkinson's plausible common-sense contentions had for the most part been simply ignored by the left-wing press instead of being properly refuted. This he considered a shabby evasion, and so, busy as he was, he had accepted the *New Statesman*'s invitation.

The main thesis of Professor Parkinson's book was that a high rate of taxation discouraged personal effort and was incentive only of quick spending on consumable goods, which could not, once consumed, be made subject to a later wealth tax. Since Constable's mind, after revising, 'Moral Justice and the Taxation Structure', was very much tuned to such questions, he went to work with a will.

'The late Sir Stafford Cripps,' he wrote, 'is known to have believed that the British people would tolerate taxation to any amount. Despite the objections of the cynical or merely frivolous . . .'

And so on, about our seemly puritan heritage, for the best part of 300 words. However, just as he was framing the sentence which was to clinch his first paragraph, Mrs Constable, who had heard the bell but had been delayed while adjusting her surgical stocking, knocked on the door.

'Come in,' called Constable, looking up from his review while he rehearsed, at lightning speed, the rebuke he would deliver when the door hit the tray.

The door opened cautiously. There was a sound of very heavy breathing but no more. The door closed.

With a sulky pout, Constable resumed his composition. It now occurred to him that two key phrases on the sheet before him had been unconsciously copied straight out of 'Moral Justice and the Taxation Structure'. Although the phrases were apt and the piracy, in the circumstances, venial, Constable scorned to fob off the literary editor of the NS with second-hand goods. He struck the two phrases from his text, with difficulty found two more that would serve, realised that a slight shift of emphasis which resulted would disrupt the rhythm of all he had written so far, and then, gritting his teeth, tore the page to honourable shreds and began all over again.

When Hugh Balliston had finished writing a fair copy of his work for Tony Beck, he made himself a cup of Bovril (having time in hand but feeling bound, after his remarks to Hetta, to eschew tea) and relaxed for ten minutes, during which time he amused his mind with the imagined sexual antics of Provost Constable. He even constructed a scene in which the Provost tried to seduce Hetta; but when the shadowy Hetta refused to be contained by her allotted role as proud daughter of the proletariat, and instead flopped on to Constable's lap with jolly whoops of lust, Hugh desisted from this entertainment and set out for Tony Beck's rooms in Sitwell's.

As he crossed Willow Bridge, he saw Daniel Mond, who was returning after his tea with Tom Llewyllyn to his own rooms in Willow Close. This was a three-sided court, which occupied the space between the Provost's Lodge and the river, being open to the latter and facing across it to the west. The southern wing of the court came right down to the river and separated Lancaster from its neighbour in that direction; the northern wing stopped about a cricket pitch short of Willow Bridge and some few yards to its right (as Hugh was facing), allowing one to fork right as one stepped off the bridge and cut across on to the little lawn which was central to the Close. Set into the river-edge of this lawn was a stone quay for the mooring of punts, and overlooking the quay was a large weeping willow, which Daniel had now paused to inspect.

Since Hugh had a minute or two to spare and was fond of Daniel, whom he met often at meetings of the Cabbala (the college essay club), he waved and went across to him.

'Another term tomorrow,' whispered Daniel; 'the last of

another year.'

'Oh, Daniel. You make it sound like the last there'll ever be.'

'It could be, from my point of view.'

'You're surely not leaving?'

'Not that I know of, Hugh.'

'Then why so gloomy?'

'Because this way I am prepared for anything at all to go wrong and shall be delighted out of all proportion if even one tiny thing goes right. It's a form of insurance. Like taking a mackintosh with you on a sunny day. A precaution which you seem to have neglected this afternoon.'

'So have you.'

'My gloom serves instead of one. But *you* have neither gloom nor a mackintosh. That is presumptuous. I shouldn't be at all surprised if you were struck by a thunderbolt.'

The words were uttered from so straight a face that Hugh could almost have thought they were meant seriously.

'I'm only going to Sitwell's,' he said, 'to see Tony Beck. I might just make it that far.'

'Let's hope so. And if you *do* arrive safely, give Tony my love and remind him that he has had my copy of the late Professor Hardy's little book for the last eighteen months.'

'*A Mathematician's Apology?*'

'Yes. I shall now go indoors to compose my own. It will never be published, but perhaps God will give it his attention.'

Daniel raised his hand to his forehead in a quasi-military salute. He moved off towards the south wing of Willow Close and disappeared through the entrance to staircase Omega, in which he had rooms that overlooked the river.

'I met Daniel Mond on the way,' said Hugh to Tony Beck in Sitwell's a few minutes later: 'he says you've had his copy of G. H. Hardy's *Apology* for the last eighteen months. He was behaving rather oddly, I thought.'

'Hardy was one old woman,' said Beck, 'and Daniel's another.'

Tony Beck was a short, stout man with a very thick neck and an agreeably lop-sided face. Whenever he was displeased, however, he inclined his head to the left side, on which it was smaller, thus causing the right cheek bone, which was normally no more than noticeable, to jut out laterally in a massively aggressive fashion. This was a pity, thought Hugh, observing the phenomenon now, because it destroyed Beck's usual appearance of coarse good humour and substituted one of truculent conceit.

'Well, do you want to read my essay?' said Hugh. 'Or shall I read it to you?'

'No. I want to give you my ideas on the subject. On several subjects.'

'It took me a lot of work,' said Hugh.

Beck leaned over, whipped Hugh's essay away from him, screwed it into a ball, and tossed it through an open door into his bedroom.

'Now,' said Tony Beck. He ceased to jut his cheek bone and smiled at Hugh with crude charm. 'You are an undergraduate just turned twenty and in your second year of residence. At the end of your first year you took a starred first in Part One of the English Literature Tripos. You are going to take two years reading for Part Two; you therefore have no examination this summer and plenty of time at your disposal. But what do you do with it? Exactly the same as you would have done if you had been taking Part Two in a single year. You read hard, wide and deep; you write your very clever and percipient essays. And that's all.'

'What's wrong with it?'

'Limited. Limited and limiting.'

'I went in for that prize last autumn. And got it.'

'And what did you do to get it? You simply wrote yet another clever and percipient essay.'

'I've done a lot of stuff for the Cabbala.'

'More essays.'

'And for undergraduate magazines.'

'*More* essays,' snarled Beck. 'My point is, you haven't involved yourself in anything active.'

There had been a time, and that not so many years before, when this would have meant that Hugh should play more games or take part in dramatic productions. At this time, however, and to these two, it could only mean one thing: politics.

'Oh yes, I have,' said Hugh. 'I've sat on student committees, drafted memoranda and resolutions, I've even drawn up declarations of right. Who do you suppose was behind the student demand to be allowed to use the Fellows' Garden?'

'That's just it. You were *behind* it. You *drafted* the resolution and you doubtless *composed* the letter of demand. All of it cerebral, Hugh. You've done the whole lot at a desk. It's time you took a turn at the barricades.'

'This is England,' said Hugh: 'we don't have barricades.'

For the moment Tony Beck let this pass.

'This essay I asked you to do'—he gestured through the door to the bedroom—' "The Politics of the Novelist". Kindly tell me your broad conclusion.'

'If you'd had the patience to read it, you'd have found a complete analysis.'

'I'm sure I should. I've read a lot of those in my time, Hugh.' From Beck's tone, one might have thought he was rising sixty instead of barely thirty. 'Here and now I'm interested in your conclusion. Which was . . .?'

'That a novelist's political beliefs should be implicit in his novels.'

'Why not explicit?'

'Because explicit statements in the novelist's own voice,' said Hugh firmly, 'irritate the reader and, more important, undermine the structure of the novel. Take the early George Eliot——'

'—I'd prefer to leave her just now. You're saying,' said Beck in a hectoring voice, 'that novelists must eschew open declarations of political allegiance because these vitiate their art?'

'As you know very well for yourself. And as you also know very well, this does not prevent them making whatever political declarations they please in the form of separate tracts or essays.'

'Which they produce, just like their novels, sitting on cushioned chairs in cosy studies. But when, Hugh, do they get off their bottoms and *act*?'

'In times of crisis or oppression. Otherwise they should do what they are best at, which is, presumably, writing. Provided society is stable and tolerably fair, a novelist must get on with his work just like anybody else.'

'But society is the whole world, Hugh. The world is not stable or tolerably fair. The world is riddled with crisis and oppression. We must *all* get off our bottoms and act.'

'Look, Tony,' said Hugh. 'For the last seven years you've been sitting in this college teaching English literature and doing distinguished work as a critic. Although you have made no secret of your politics, you have not allowed them to affect your judgments as to literary merit; and although you have engaged in polemics up to a point, you have certainly not got off your bottom, as you put it, to act. So why are you preaching at me now?'

'Timing, Hugh. Until just recently, whatever was the case with the world at large, there remained in privileged England enough *national* stability to make any kind of radical action unpopular and futile and therefore thoroughly impractical. So I just got on with my criticism and did it as well as I could in its own terms, in terms, that is, of objective literary judgment. One should always play a game according to its own rules, Hugh, otherwise there is no enjoyment to be had from it; and that's why I kept politics out of my criticism. But it *was* only a game, and the time for it is nearly over. The national, the purely local stability which made it possible for me to play it in peace has been rotted right through to the piles and will soon collapse completely.'

During this exordium, Beck had been strutting up and down the room, which was amusingly furnished with Victoriana. He now sat down in a grandfather chair, as on a throne, and threw off the rest of his speech like an edict.

'Even though I've been observing closely,' he pronounced, 'I'm not at all sure why or how this has happened. I suspect that British energies have been sapped by a mixture of guilt for an imperial past and resentment at imperial decline. But the important point is that it has happened, and nothing can halt the process now, certainly not a flabby Labour Government with half-baked right-wing policies and sentimental left-wing sympathies. From here on, the order of the day, in England as everywhere else, will be crisis and flux: disobedience and mutiny on the part of the so called lower classes; despair and desertion on the part of the upper. In short, Hugh, things are just going to fall apart.

'This being so, there is no longer place and leisure in this country for well-fed men in warm studies to write novels upon which other well-fed men in warm studies will comment. The only relevant occupation must be to go out and burn away the stumps of diseased wood which remain from the old edifice and still clutter the site, and then to build anew in concrete, glass and steel. Destruction and reconstruction. So what part, my good Hugh, do you propose to bear in all this? Reading pretty essays to the Cabbala Club will hardly be enough.'

'What part do *you* propose to bear, Tony? The scene is of your setting.'

Tony Beck gave Hugh his asymmetrical look of displeasure.

'I'm going to show solidarity,' he said, 'with the forces of the future.'

'Since this apparently necessitates the use of clichés,' said Hugh, 'let's have another one: you're going to climb on the band-wagon.'

'If you like.' Beck grinned like a small boy caught playing 'doctors' with his sister. 'At least I'll be allowed an instrument to blow a tune.'

'Not of your own choosing. And suppose you turn out to be wrong? You'll look awfully silly climbing off again.'

'Timing, Hugh. Although it's time to warn friends like you what will happen, it's still not quite time to commit oneself.'

'Then why expect me to? All that stuff about manning the barricades.'

'That was overstating it, I grant you. Just have a look round them, that's all I meant. Get the feel of them. Then pick up a few cobblestones and take some practice shots through middle-class windows. You might call it "protest".'

'Only hooligans break windows . . . for practice or protest.'

'I'll tell you what it is with you,' sneered Tony Beck; 'you're yellow. You'll use up gallons of ink writing manifestoes, you'll gas away all night about progress and social justice, but when it comes to the crunch, you're yellow.'

Hugh flushed.

'I don't care for violence,' he said. 'Of course I know that in certain countries it's been necessary as a last resort, and I honour those that have used it for that reason. But here . . . no. Here we can still settle things like civilised men.'

'That's all done for, Hugh. The rot's gone too far. What people want is speed and certainty. They want violence; for violence is the instant detergent which will scour away filth and wash the world bright again. That is what the masses feel, Hugh—the masses of deprived people all over the globe. To pretend otherwise is sheer cowardice; it's hiding your head in the——'

'—*Must* we go on having these clichés?'

'People like clichés,' scowled Beck. 'They have a warm, familiar ring. So if you take my advice, you'll start learning some yourself. Whose side are you on anyway? Don't tell me the old men have won you over with a starred First and the Members' English Essay Prize.'

'Why are you baiting me, Tony?'

'I'm just trying to wake you up.'

'Then tell me something particular which needs doing. Stop mouthing about decay and violence and show me some one thing which needs setting right. And then, if I really have to, I'll throw cobblestones with you. But not just for practice.'

'Very well,' said Beck, leaning his head to the left. 'As you know, the College Council has sold some land and made a sack of money.'

Hugh nodded.

'You told me yesterday,' he said, 'that there was to be a meeting about that this evening. A preliminary meeting to decide what the students of this college want the money spent on. The only thing which bothers me is that most of the students aren't up yet.'

'Precisely,' said Beck. 'They'll be consulted later. Tonight's meeting is not exactly what you might have expected. The fact is, I want to introduce you to a friend of mine called Mayerston. He's only a year or two older than you, so I thought I'd bring you both together and then leave you to work out what action those of your age-group might take to see that this money is properly used.'

'We must first decide on a proper use for it.'

'That, as you have suggested, is for the students at large. But there's no reason why you and Mayerston shouldn't . . . discuss general tactics.'

'Look,' said Hugh: 'who the hell is this Mayerston?'

'He's . . . not of this college,' said Beck evasively.

'Then what's it got to do with him?'

'This business is of more than parochial interest, Hugh. There's a lot of people who feel very strongly about this money.'

'If Mayerston's not from this college,' persisted Hugh, 'which one is he from?'

'He's from outside the University.'

'Then what's he doing here?'

'I suppose a human being has a right to be in Cambridge ... even if he doesn't belong to the University.'

'Of course. I'm sorry, Tony. But what's his line?'

'He'll explain that better than I can. You'll find he has a very unusual and compelling point of view.'

'At least you can give me some idea of it.'

'For our present purpose, it amounts to this. Whatever the Council decide to do with this money ... even if they vote to spend it in the most enlightened way possible ... their decision must be protested.'

'Why, for Christ's sake?'

'Simply because it *is* the Council's decision. As Mayerston sees it, the students must decide.'

'Then let the students ask for consultations with the Council before it takes its final vote.'

'No. This isn't an exercise in co-operation. The whole point is that the students should impose their own absolute will. They must make the Council back down from any position whatever which it adopts.'

'Suppose the students have nothing better to offer?'

'Then they will simply say "no" to the Council and go on saying it.'

'Not very constructive.'

'It's not intended to be. The important thing is to beat down the Council.'

'Of course you are a member. I think it stinks,' said Hugh.

'You may think differently after Mayerston has explained the philosophy behind it.'

'I doubt it. I suspect he's going to talk a whole lot more of your old bollocks—a diseased society and violence the only way to cleanse it. It's not even original, Tony: it's been used by a great many people—most notably by Adolf Hitler.'

'You'll find Mayerston more subtle than that.'

'I shan't, because I'm not even going to meet him. Good

evening, Tony. Let me know when you expect another essay.'

Hugh navigated a velour-hooded chaise longue and a bronze-clad family lectern, and walked towards the door.

'Hugh...'

'Yes, Tony?'

'You must listen to Mayerston, you know. If only in order to refute him.'

For five seconds Hugh stood dithering on the carpet (pistachio-green and eglantine). There was a knock on the door.

'Come in,' called Tony Beck. '... Good evening, Mayerston.'

'In conclusion,' wrote Robert Constable, 'it is important to face up to Professor Parkinson's charge that a high rate of tax on earned income draws off creative and inventive energy, too much of which, he claims, is now unproductively employed in devising new methods of tax avoidance. There is some evidence to support this assertion; but the assertion itself demonstrates and strengthens precisely those attitudes of mind which modern social philosophy is concerned to discredit and destroy. For personal ability or talent must no longer be regarded as a means to personal enrichment but as a commodity, held in trust by some fortunate individual, whereby he may serve and enrich mankind. Indifferent to monetary returns, such an individual should find his satisfaction in the exercise of his skill (grateful that it releases him from the drudgery by which most men must earn their livelihood) and in the knowledge that he is providing pleasure or amenity for his fellow human beings. Such grace, I fear, is still far to seek; and it will certainly not be found in any quantity as long as influential writers like Professor Parkinson continue to regard society, not as an area of tillage to be held and harvested in common, but as a barren and bloody arena in which men mangle one another in pursuit of acclaim and gold.'

That, thought Constable as he lifted his head, is putting it a bit strong. Although there are real gladiators, the iron men of industry and commerce, for the most part the circus is occupied by perfectly decent fellows who are hoping, in return for a conscientious display of talent, to achieve a quiet independence and retire to a Sabine farm. But then again, thought Constable, if society is to be truly co-operative there is no place even for such temperate self-interest as this. It's not the economics of the thing that matter so much as the moral attitude ... the idea that one will make a part of human society for only so long as it takes to raise enough money to opt out of that society and buy a pretty house on the hill way up above the noise and the suffering and the stink. If society were justly ordered, thought Constable for the millionth time, if wealth were fairly spread, then no ability would win enough money to escape the suffering and the stink, and all ability would therefore be used to mitigate them. This, then, must be the argument for heavy taxes on earned money—that independence, even when earned, is a crime against humanity.

Yet of all men, thought Constable, I am by nature the most independent and by situation the most aloof. True, I serve society in that I educate its young, but I do so in circumstances of such calm and privilege that for many years now I have been unreached by its cries of pain. Perhaps, he thought, that is why the young are now so restless: they hear the cries from the world outside and cannot bear them, and are determined that those like me should hear them too. But where is the good in that? If one listens to those cries, one becomes unmanned, unfit for the task of curing the ills that cause them. In order to help the world, one must get knowledge first, and while getting it one must stop one's eats and live behind thick walls. The walls of Lancaster, thought Constable, are strong and shall remain so, for I am their guardian: I, like the knights who were my ancestors, am Castellan.

About an hour and a half after Daniel Mond had left him, Tom Llewyllyn finished the chapter on which he was working (An Analysis of the Random Element in the Reform Act of 1867) and walked across the Great Court to the Lauderdale Gate. He left his rooms, as he always did, with regret; for it was here that his work was done, here that his life was now centred, and he returned each night to his house in Grantchester with a bleak certainty that the day could now hold little more either of value or of pleasure. He loved his wife and he loved his daughter; but they represented a domestic duty which was at odds with the independence proper to a scholar, and, what was worse, they called him away from the company of Daniel and the rest at the evening hour, just when that company would have been sweetest. To dine with like-minded friends was the crown of any man's day; but even when he found excuse to dine in college, the occasion was spoilt by the nagging sense that Patricia was waiting and that he must leave directly after the dessert.

'Good night, Wilfred,' he said to the porter on duty in the Lodge.

'Good night, sir,' said Wilfred, looking up and smiling with tactful sympathy, as though (Tom thought) he had divined the reluctance with which Tom now stepped through the gate.

For a moment, as he saw his old Lagonda on the College Stones outside, Tom's spirits lifted. It was a lovely evening for a spin. But a spin, he thought, of barely three miles; and after that . . .

. . . 'So you're home,' said Patricia, as he had known she would; 'not staying *there* for dinner?'

'You know I always warn you,' said Tom, sitting down very heavily, 'if I'm staying in college for dinner. What have you done today?'

'I took Baby into Cambridge . . . by bus . . . to have her plate adjusted.'

'Let's have a look, love.'

Tom put his arm round his seven-year-old daughter's waist and drew her in between his legs. Baby squirmed away from him.

'I hate my plate,' she yelped.

'That dentist's no good with children,' whimpered Patricia: 'now, if we were in London——'

'—I've told you. You can have it all done there if you want to.'

'Privately?' Patricia mocked. 'And you a socialist?'

'Don't be bloody-minded, heart. Do you want it, that's the thing?'

'It's such a strain going up and down.'

'Then go up for a whole week. Stay in a hotel. Go up, and get her teeth fixed as you want them, and enjoy yourself.'

'And you?'

'I'd be all right. I could sleep in my rooms in college.'

'You'd like that, wouldn't you?' she breathed.

'And so would you,' he said levelly: 'you could get yourself some clothes while you were about it.'

Patricia looked down at her worn tweed skirt and then at two holes by the left knee of her thick brown tights.

'Hotels, private dentists, new clothes ... We can't afford all that any more.'

'Rubbish. I know I don't get much from the college, but there's all those back royalties coming in, and there's that money your father left——'

'—*That's* to be kept for Baby, thank you very much——'

'—To say nothing of all we save by living down here in the country. There's plenty of money if you care to make the effort.'

'Just so's you could be free to live in that hateful college for a few days. That's all you want, isn't it? Sometimes I think you'd be glad if Baby and I were dead.'

Baby started snivelling to stress the point.

'Don't be silly, heart. You're tired and so's Baby. Put her to bed while I get the supper.'

'Wirr, wirr, wirr,' Baby went.

'Tired I may be,' Patricia said, 'but strong enough to say this. When we came here, *you* said it was for three years. I hated the idea, as you very well knew, but you were so keen, and you promised it would only be three years, so I said I'd come. But now what? We've been here nearly five, and God knows how long to go. Why couldn't you keep your promise?'

'I wasn't to know they'd renew my fellowship.'

'You could have refused.'

'Wirr . . . wirr . . . wirr.'

'I hadn't finished my book.'

'Your *book*. As if anyone will want to publish that. By the time we get back to London—if we ever do—they'll have forgotten you ever existed. How can you expect Gregory Stern to risk his money on a million-page sermon, about a subject which interests nobody, and written by a provincial has-been.'

'I should have thought,' said Tom, nettled, 'that Power was a subject to interest a lot of people.'

'Not the way you're writing about it. All split hairs and preach, preach, preach. Remember what happened to those specimen chapters you sent Gregory? They came back without comment.'

'I don't think this is quite Gregory's thing. I rather thought the University Press might be more suitable.'

'There are some things,' said Patricia with spiteful glee, 'which even the University Press can't swallow. Have you tried them yet?'

'I've sent them the odd hundred pages . . . as you know.'

'Six months ago—and not a word from them.'

'The University Press works very slowly.'

'Everything about the University works very slowly. They can't even bury their dead. So they just leave them lying there rotting—like that ghastly Daniel Mond—and pretend they're still alive. That's what'll happen to you, Tom. You'll start to rot, but they'll tell you you're still alive, and you're so besotted you'll believe them.'

'Wirr,' howled Baby, 'wirr, *wirr, WIRR*.'

'You need two things,' said Tom quietly. 'An intelligent interest and a vigorous lover. You've let your mind go to pieces and the rest of you's following.' He looked at the hole by her knee. 'Fast,' he said.

'*CHRIST*,' screamed Patricia, and struck him over the chops. 'It's you I want. Why won't you do it to me like you used to?'

'I can't.'

'Of course,' she snarled, 'I know I'm not what I was before I had that miscarriage . . . brought on by the move down *here*.'

'It isn't that,' said Tom. 'I just can't. I love you very much, but I can't do that for you any more. Not for you or for anyone, any more.'

'Wirrrrr.'

'You don't know what you're saying, Tom.'

'Oh yes, I do. It's stopped, Patricia. Nothing stirs it at all. I look at young girls in the street, and I think, surely, a juicy little thing like that, plump buttocks, smooth thighs spreading, the little dark triangle and the red lips moist and open . . . but it's no good. My cock doesn't even twitch. It's all over for me. Dead . . . Now take that grizzling child to bed while I get the supper.'

I wonder, thought the Honourable Grantchester FitzMargrave Pough (pronounced Pew) whether I should ask Dinkie and Dudu to Sunday luncheon again. Dinkie and Dudu were the two choristers at the east end of the front row south. At this moment they were banging through the Magnificat in great style though without assistance from the organ, as this was a day for unaccompanied evensong.

The uncharitable, thought Grantchester Pough, may remember that it was these two I invited last time I gave a Sunday luncheon. If, therefore, I invite them to the next, the uncharitable might draw scandalous inference. On the other hand, my last Sunday luncheon was over a month ago, just before the Choir School broke up for the holidays. There has been a goodish interval. The choristers started their new term yesterday, the college starts a new full term tomorrow, and that means a clean sheet. You start again from scratch, last term's lists having long since been torn up, and there is therefore no reason why Dinkie and Dudu should not be at the head of *this* term's list of guests for my Sunday luncheons.

But then again, will they want to come? Pough, as always when perplexed, seized a large handful of his beard and scrabbled in it, as though hoping to find truffles. He glared down at Dinkie and Dudu from the Senior Fellow's stall, defying them to refuse his invitation. Even if they did not care for the wholesome vegetarian fare which he offered, they should find compensation, as had generations of choristers, in his tales of the Eiger and the Matterhorn. And of the narrow failure on Everest (that need not have been a failure if only his colleagues had trained, like himself, on raw cabbage instead of steak). What more could any proper boy want? And yet, he thought sadly, there were signs these days that his stories were not as popular as they had been. For the last three years or so, the choristers had listened with a certain lack of respect; not indeed with disbelief (for even they knew that it was all in the record) but with mild contempt, as though wondering why any sane man should be at agonies to climb a mountain the summit of which could be comfortably viewed from the cockpit of a light aircraft. Modern boyhood seemed to have got its values botched up; he must have a word with the Headmaster of the Choir School about it—though he knew in advance exactly what the wretch would say. He would say what he said to every complaint, whether about the deterioration of the Choir School's cricket or the lack of gloss on the choristers' top hats: 'What you forget is that my boys are the first children of the space age.'

And now Dinkie and Dudu, those twin children of the space age, as alike as two little robots, were going gaily through the Gloria, what time the Chaplain, the Reverend Oliver Clewes, was cringing up the nave to the lectern.

Oliver Clewes, though humble in demeanour, was inwardly full of gleeful pride at the shock he had in store for the congregation. A small congregation, as on any week day, but with igneous elements in it. Pough, the Senior Fellow, would be just plain furious. Andrew Ogden, the Dean of Chapel, who was conducting the service, would be bitterly insulted. And even Balbo Blakeney might be roused from his contemplation of the Screen to mutter some indignant obscenity. With the spiteful relish of a man about to plunge in a detonator and blow a sleeping garrison to shreds, Clewes ascended the steps up to the lectern. Amen, carolled the space children, and flirtily arranged themselves to listen.

'The second lesson,' said Clewes, 'will be taken from the thirteenth chapter of St Luke's Gospel.' He paused, hands on the plunger. 'It will be read in the new translation.'

Oh, what a dreary fellow, thought the Reverend Andrew Ogden, wiping his palms down his rusty surplus. I knew he was up to something—he's been walking round all day like Titus Oates. And now this is the best he can do. He really thinks he'll get my bate by reading the Parable of the Prodigal Son in the new translation. On the contrary: I've always thought it was a silly story, and I'm delighted that this flat, boring English will make it sound even sillier.

How very convenient, thought Grantchester Pough. I've been meaning to look at the new translation for months. I should be able to judge from this specimen whether it will be worth the trouble ... No, he thought after three sentences, it certainly will not.

God, what a cur, thought Balbo Blakeney, as he sat in the Inductor's stall high up behind Dinkie's and Dudu's blond heads. (The Inductor was the College Officer who lead new Scholars forward to take the oath from the Provost; he received a special emolument of two and a half guineas a year, payable every Lady's Day.) What a dribbling, mangy cur. To disgrace this building with *that* rubbish. Not that anything said in here makes the slightest sense; but at least the old words made the right kind of noise. And that reminds me, he thought. The singing's getting patchy. Quality still good, on the whole, but those little eunuchs down there need to concentrate harder. They need more discipline, and if they're not getting it it's the fault of that poxy Headmaster. Morale in the Choir School has been low for some time, and it's his business to set it up again. I'll not have this building discredited by so much as half a botched verse in the whole bone-aching psaltery.

His eyes moved up the carved stalls opposite, then up the coloured windows (dull but still rich in the fading light), and then to the ringed roses sculptured on the ceiling. Gazing at these, he remained seated for the whole of the rest of the service (including the Creed), and had to be roused by the verger forty minutes later when it was time to close the Chapel for the night.

Short gowns flying, Eton collars gleaming in the dusk, toppers rakish on the leaders and straight as chimneys on the infants in the rear, the Choir rattled off in file, all along Sitwell's and then sharp right for Willow Bridge.

'I saw Gloozer Pough looking at us,' said Dinkie to Dudu.

'Everybody looks at us.'

'Not as hard as Gloozer Pough. Perhaps he'll ask us to lunch again.'

'It's not our turn.'

'He was looking at us so hard I don't think that matters.'

'If only he'd give you a proper lunch.'

'His stories aren't bad.'

'The first time you hear them.'

'Shall we go if we're asked?'

'Oh, I think so,' said Dudu. 'It would be very unkind not to, if he looked at us like you said . . . Look, there's Lord Beyfus.'

'He's not a proper Lord. It was only Mr Wilson made him one.'

'He doesn't look like it either. He's so small . . . and sort of black.'

'That's because he's a Jew and never comes to Chapel.'

'That lady with him . . . she looks nice.'

'Why is she wearing trousers?'

'I expect she's got horrid legs. But her *face* is nice.'

'I don't know. There's something . . . unfair . . . about it. As if she was hoping to find someone enjoying themselves just so's she could spoil it.'

'Lord Beyfus doesn't look as if he ever enjoys himself.'

'Not with her around, that's certain.'

But in fact Lord Beyfus was really quite happy; for Mona Corrington was back after being away nearly a week, and during that time some interesting things had come up which they were now about to discuss. As the choristers went twittering off into the twilight, he took Mona's arm to guide her down the narrow and bicycle-cluttered passage (between the Hall and the end of the Provost's Lodge) that led into Dawley's Court, a small gravel close bounded by the College Library and four staircases of comfortable but unfashionable rooms. Having released her as soon as they were out of the passage (for Mona severely rationed their physical contacts, however innocent), he hovered fussily about her as they approached his staircase (Theta), and then followed her up to the second floor. Not until they were inside his rooms with the door closed did she open her mouth (a life spent in a women's college had given her a horror of being overheard), and when she did it was to say:

'Sherry.'

Beyfus poured two glasses of Dry Fly and gave one to Mona. She tossed hers down with a single gulp and put the glass firmly away from her on the mantel-shelf. One drink before dinner was Mona's rule. Straddling in front of the gas-fire, she started to boom at Beyfus.

'I am a bearer of good tidings. The atmosphere is becoming more propitious every day. London, Paris, Rome, Berlin—everywhere it's the same story. I've seen more than twenty distinguished Anthropologists in the last six days, and most of them were implicitly agreed that from now on we must ditch the past and concentrate on the future.'

'But surely,' said Beyfus, carefully and deferentially, 'the whole object of Anthropology is to establish the human patterns of the past. Only when you've done that can you turn to the future.'

'They were *implicitly* agreed, I said. The feeling is that the past shouldn't be researched any more but *codified*. The helpful aspects, that is, will be marshalled to form a definite body of knowledge. Instead of seeking to qualify this, we shall take it as established, once and for all, and use it as an instrument to analyse the conditions of the present—and so to predict the future.'

'A dangerous game, Mona. The present is fluctuating too fast for precise analysis. And prophets look very silly when they make mistakes.'

'By predict we mean ordain. In the light of past experience, we shall say, if present behaviour patterns are so and so, then future behaviour patterns can only be such and such. Provided we say this often enough and authoritatively enough, governments will deliberately enforce the patterns we foretell. They will regard them as historical necessities.'

'In other words, you're going to adopt my function. You're turning yourselves into sociologists.'

'With this difference,' said Mona: 'we shall have introduced our historical instrument. Where *you* say the present is fluctuating too fast for analysis, we shall say that our anthropological knowledge can distinguish certain human constants which are being arranged and re-arranged by the operation of random variables—i.e. by day to day events. Where *you* say these variables are changing too fast for you to cope, we shall say that our ability to recognise salient human constants enables us to plot a basic pattern (whatever the variables at work), and that any one present pattern can only be succeeded by a limited number of others, all of them known to us and all similar in type. In other words, we shall claim to have a formula.'

'A formula based on selected anthropological data which, you say, will no longer be subject to addition or investigation but simply accepted as holy writ. What sort of scholarship is this, Mona?'

'Don't start up about the purity of learning, Beyfus. Academic learning is of no value except in so far as it can be used to determine social method.'

She gave him a brief but very intense look, and started to put on her cloak.

'You've booked our usual table at the Arts Restaurant?' she said.

'Yes.'

'Then dinner.'

'Yes ... But look, Mona. Your body of anthropological data. To put it bluntly, you're just going to select what suits your political purposes.'

'Yours too.'

'Arbitrarily selected data could make an unreliable instrument.'

'It'll make a good enough stick to beat them with,' she said: 'dinner.'

'I've heard a good deal about you,' said Mayerston; 'all of it interesting.'

Mayerston was clean-shaven and neatly dressed in a suit of dark clothes. He had appealing hair (straight, blond hair of moderate length) and a seductive smile. He also had plenty of money; for when Hugh had suggested that they went to eat at Haq's, an eating house of low cost and demotic cuisine, Mayerston had simply announced that they would go to the Arts Theatre Restaurant and that dinner was on him. What was more, the Head Waiter had treated him with respect on their arrival and though obviously hard up for space had found the two of them a corner table which could easily have accommodated four.

'Yes,' Mayerston was saying now: 'I've heard more than you might think.'

'From Tony Beck, I suppose,' said Hugh. 'You know, he made you sound so foul that I didn't want to meet you. If you'd reached his rooms two minutes later, I'd have been gone.'

'Tony Beck is a good critic,' said Mayerston, 'but he'd make a bad novelist. He has no eye for people. No ear for them either.' He sipped the two guinea claret which he'd ordered. 'What did he lead you to expect?'

'A wild-eyed ranter in a boiler suit.'

Mayerston laughed. He had a deep, easy laugh and a deep, easy voice, both of which made a slightly disconcerting contrast with his boyish appearance.

'That's for children,' he said, 'for frightened children who want a uniform in order to be safely one of the gang. Though surely there can't be anything very strange to you about all that? You must have plenty of friends in the boiler suit set?'

'Yes. But they belong here and you didn't, which was the first thing against you. And then Tony made you sound very extreme.'

'And are none of your friends extreme?'

'They are all constructive, whatever else.'

'And Beck told you I wasn't?'

'He said your plan was to go on saying "no". Not to suggest anything, not to . . . participate . . . just to say "no".'

'As far as that goes, Beck is perfectly correct.'

Hugh felt a disappointment which amounted almost to misery. From the first moment that Mayerston had walked into Tony's rooms, Hugh had felt that here was a man who had something to contribute. Of course, there was no rational ground for supposing this; it was just something about the way in which Mayerston had carried himself, had shaken hands, had looked Hugh up and down with a thoroughness which might have been insolent but in fact seemed only appreciative. Here was a man of candour and intelligence, Hugh had thought; an ally. He had been further impressed when Mayerston cut short a pompous speech which Tony had started about the international freemasonry of students, and then, ignoring Tony's protests, suggested to Hugh that they should leave together at once. He had been childishly flattered by Mayerston's invitation to dine at the Arts; he had been charmed by the courtesy which Mayerston had shewn as his host; he had been amused by Mayerston's comments, spare and well placed, on their fellow diners. But above all Hugh had been expectant; he had been waiting for a message, even perhaps for a vision; and now ... now it seemed that all he would hear was the same barren tale as he had already heard from Beck.

'Perfectly correct, Beck is,' said Mayerston, 'as far as he goes.'

'Mere negation ... obstruction. Is that all you can offer?'

'It's all I'm going to offer to Beck. One doesn't tell men like Beck more than one can help, Hugh. No more than one needs to get one's way with them. Because men like Beck are greedy. They steal.'

Hope stirred again in Hugh's stomach.

'Why have anything to do with them?' he said.

'They have influence. They know people. They know you, for example, and introduce you to me. They have many uses. But one doesn't share one's ideas with them, because they steal.'

Mayerston waved a casual hand. The wine-waiter rushed from the far end of the room, where he was in the middle of taking another order, and bowed with pleasure at Mayerston's request for cognac.

'Then who,' said Hugh, trembling with excitement, 'does one share one's ideas with?'

'Grammar, Hugh. With whom does one share one's

ideas? With those who are worthy.'

Hugh opened his mouth but Mayerston lifted a hand to silence him.

'Before you ask any further,' Mayerston said, 'understand this: not all men have the same needs. You, for instance, have certain mental needs, because you are a man of intellect. Others have other needs at other levels. They are not inferior to you, but their needs are different and must be catered for in a different manner.'

The wine-waiter brought them two brandy glasses and a bottle of vintage cognac, which he left on the table.

'He knows I like to pour for myself,' said Mayerston, doing so liberally and passing the bottle to Hugh; 'he knows I must be catered for in my own way.'

Out of sheer nervousness, Hugh poured himself about twice as much as Mayerston had taken.

'I'm sorry. I——'

'—It'll do you good. Drink it slowly.'

Mayerston produced a leather cigar-case and carefully chose a medium-sized cigar.

'Now then,' Mayerston said: 'people's needs. Although these are different, there is one basic need which almost everyone has in common: to feel that he has some say in his own destiny. The difference lies in the various ways in which this basic need is expressed; from the crude ways, like demanding more money, to the relatively subtle ways, like seeking justice or fulfilment or personal recognition—or, as in your case, trying to determine intellectual truth. But in the end satisfaction, for every man, lies in being able to assert himself—or to think he is asserting himself—on his chosen level. You agree?'

'Yes,' said Hugh, and took a gulp of cognac.

'Slowly, I said ... Now, the trouble with contemporary society is *not* that it prevents people from asserting themselves on their different levels but that its responses are both feeble and dishonest. It gives in almost at once and provides whatever is demanded—but provides it in a form that it knows to be worthless. The higher wages, for example, lose their extra value almost as soon as they are awarded; improved status means the same old dreary job under a higher-sounding name; and so on. Hence the general discontent; and hence our problem, which is to reward those who assert themselves with something genuine in response to their demands, on whatever level these may be made. Otherwise the whole affair is a mockery.'

'And so it is bound to be,' said Hugh, 'as long as their demands are self-centred. More money for *me*; higher rank for *me*. What people are demanding are *distinctions* ... which can mean nothing at all unless they are confined to small minorities.'

'And that, of course,' said Mayerston with just a hint of irony, 'we cannot possibly allow. So the answer must be to persuade people to demand the kind of thing which is in both genuine and plentiful supply. In this way, they will be asserting themselves to some purpose. They will have a good chance of actually achieving what they're aiming at.'

'And what is that to be?'

'Never mind what it is just yet,' Mayerston said. 'The thing you have to get straight first of all is that people have to be persuaded ... or even compelled ... to want it. They must be forced to give up their old aspirations and to desire what we wish them to desire, because we know that it is only this which is worth having. In short, Hugh, we are not going to give people what they want; we are going to make them want what we have to give.'

'I see. You are going to dictate.'

'To educate. To persuade.'

'You said "compel", "make" ... "force".'

'Careless of me ... though our arguments will certainly be forceful and compelling.'

'*Our* arguments, Mayerston? How can I join you before I know what these ... forceful and compelling arguments ... will advocate?'

'Are you worthy to know, Hugh?'

Mona Corrington and Lord Beyfus came in. They sat down at a table in the corner opposite Hugh and Mayerston. Lord Beyfus, who knew Hugh slightly, smiled across at him. Hugh smiled back, and Mona, unexpectedly, simpered.

'You know Beyfus?' said Mayerston.

'A little.'

'A dedicated man but unoriginal. He is not worthy to know. I think . . . I hope . . . you are.'

'Tell me then.'

Here, surely, must be the message. The rest had been cautious and preliminary. Now ... surely ... the good news.

'We are to persuade people to want,' said Mayerston, 'something genuine which we know is there to give.'

'So you have been saying.'

'Fellowship,' said Mayerston. He spoke quietly and deeply, clutching his brandy glass very tightly, one hand over the other. 'Fellowship. Brotherhood. Love. Here in Cambridge, a University which shall know nothing of privilege and ambition, of menial services rendered and paid for, nor anything of that learning which is bought and weighed and sold again. A University in which men will gather round other and equal men to listen and to receive the wisdom and knowledge, which these, their brothers, have to offer, freely and as a right. A University which will refuse none and smile on all. An Alma Mater, Hugh; a kindly mother of her sons.'

There was a long pause. At last:

'And where does the Arts Restaurant come into all this?' was all Hugh could think of to say.

'No one, in that University, will want the Arts Restaurant.'

'Not even you? You seem very fond of it.'

'I shall be gone by then. Doing the work of persuasion elsewhere.'

'Where they still have restaurants—until, of course, you've done your work and gone on to the next place.'

And yet Hugh was moved by what Mayerston had said. The message was there; the news was good ... or seemed so after all this cognac. He felt rather ashamed of himself for making pert remarks about Mayerston's taste in restaurants; but surely the point was valid?

'When in Rome,' said Mayerston pleasantly, 'one may as well enjoy her amenities. Until such time as they are swept away. And then ...'

Mayerston shrugged in resignation, but not quite, Hugh thought, in abrogation. Wherever Mayerston was, one felt, there would somehow continue to be exclusive restaurants. Yet did this inconsistency matter very much? Perhaps a man of Mayerston's ... authority ... could be trusted to make his own rules.

'What you propose,' said Hugh, 'co-operation and fellowship, have always been realisable. The difficulty is to persuade people to want them. You are obviously very sensitive to this difficulty. How shall you meet it?'

'Before one can build up Love the Beloved Republic,' Mayerston said, 'one must first pull down the Scarlet City to make room. There will be plenty of volunteers for *that* part of the work.'

'Yes. People enjoy smashing things. Even metaphorically.'

'How strait-laced you are, Hugh. Have some more cognac.'

Mayerston poured; Hugh did not demur.

'So demolition,' said Mayerston, 'is no problem. The problem is how to persuade people to start re-building once the Old City is down.'

'They'll be too busy looting and raping, you mean.'

'If you like. *That* is when persuasion will really be needed. But I think I have the answer. To use your own terms, we let them gorge themselves on loot and rape, and then, when disgust sets in, we seize on their repentance and tell them to purge themselves of their guilt by building temples.'

'And the impenitent?'

'To them we shall suggest that they contribute their loot and their energies to erecting comfortable brothels—for by this time they will be tired of fornicating in the rubble. We shall provide the ground plans—and when the buildings are up the impenitent will discover that they too have been making temples unawares. Temples of love.'

'That's trickery, not persuasion.'

'Justified—for Love the Beloved Republic.'

'The men who thought they were building brothels may not think so.'

'Ah, but they will,' said Mayerston, very earnestly. 'When they see the Beloved Republic, they needs must love it. No man can help himself. They will forget their brothels and fall down on their knees to give thanks ... and a very elevating scene it will be,' he said, his earnestness suddenly gone; 'but here and now it is time to discuss a few practical details.'

'Who,' said Mona to Beyfus, 'is that young man over there? The one you smiled at.'

'An undergraduate from Lancaster.'

'His face has character. And his friend?'

'Him I don't know.'

'At their age, they shouldn't be drinking so much brandy. They shouldn't even be here.'

'A special treat, perhaps.'

'This is no time,' said Mona, 'for special treats. Work—that's what's wanted. And from now on you and I are going to have a lot extra.'

'I can't possibly take on anything more just now.'

'You can take *this* on. We're forming an International Committee of Anthropologists. Me and some of these people I've met this last week. We want you as Vice-Chairman, to make the thing reputable.'

'I'm not an anthropologist, Mona, and I'm quite sure it will be reputable without me.'

'We need a solid name. Some of the others are rather flashy.'

Beyfus shuddered.

'Sometimes,' said Mona, 'I think you're just a fussy old bourgeois at heart.'

'So you have this committee,' said Beyfus, refusing to be baited. 'So you have me as Vice-Chairman. So what do you do then?'

'We issue a pamphlet. The International Committee of Anthropologists issues a pamphlet called Educational Patterns in Megalopolitan Cultures.'

'Megalopolitan Cultures,' said Beyfus, 'aren't your business. Your business is savages.'

'Our business is the study of man. In this pamphlet we shall prove that all city-centred cultures throughout history have been compelled to adopt a quantitative approach to education.'

'Meaning?'

'That more people—many more people—have to be educated, despite the obstructionism of a tradition-orientated élite.'

'Meaning?'

'Higher numbers and fuck standards.'

Beyfus tittered.

'You are a funny girl,' he said.

'No, I'm not. I'm a serious middle-aged woman, who's trying to publicise the most vital truth of our century—that in an urban/industrial society we must use the last ounce of our educational plant to one hundred per cent capacity. *And* build more all the time.'

'But everyone knows this already.'

'So they may, but they don't act on it. This whole town is full of lawns and parks and gardens and tennis courts and God knows what. Good building land, Beyfus; land on which they could erect *sky-scrapers* if they turned their minds to it. Like that new one by Tottenham Court Road Tube Station. Just think, Beyfus, how many students we could pack into *that.*'

At High Table in the Hall of Lancaster, conversation turned on how the Chaplain (who was absent, skulking in his room) had read the Second Lesson from the new translation.

'It sounded,' said Balbo Blakeney, 'just like the scabby jargon in one of Beyfus's sociological tracts.'

'Flabby, not scabby,' said Andrew Ogden, the Dean of Chapel. 'And not jargon. Just clear but utterly sapless English.'

'Perhaps,' said Provost Constable, 'it really will lead to a better popular understanding.'

'Which will be disastrous for the Church,' said Tony Beck, gleefully. 'The Church is as good as rumbled already, and if people really understand what it's saying, they'll die laughing.'

'I understand you were there, Senior Fellow,' said Constable to Pough: 'what do you think?'

'I think,' said Pough, 'that these carrots are out of a tin. Since I pay extra money for the services of an under-chef to prepare my vegetarian diet, I do think I might be given proper carrots.'

'The nutritive values,' said Balbo Blakeney, 'are identical.'

'I was thinking of the taste.'

'At your age,' said Balbo, taking a huge portion of steak and oyster pudding from the serving-man's dish, 'you should be thinking only of your arteries. Childer,' he called to the wine-butler, 'red burgundy.'

'You've already had a bottle of white,' said Ivor Winstanley in admiring tones.

'And now I'm going to have a bottle of red.'

'What,' enquired Jacquiz Helmut, 'will happen to your arteries?'

'They'll seize up, in laymen's terms, by the time I'm sixty. And don't think I shan't be glad. Do you suppose I want to go on living in a world run by pinkoes and pansies?'

'The trouble is,' croaked Daniel Mond, 'that they may not seize up quite finally. You may just have a very nasty stroke, and stay alive but paralysed and imbecile. That is the sort of joke which God enjoys.'

'Come, come, Daniel,' said Andrew Ogden mildly.

'As a Jew,' said Daniel, 'or rather a half-Jew, I know a lot about God and His jokes. We invented Him, remember.'

'And killed Him,' said Pough.

'So the joke was on God,' said Winstanley. 'Childer, I'll have half a bottle of what Mr Blakeney's having.'

Constable wished that the conversation was more edifying, but failed to remember a time when it ever had been.

'I hear,' he said, 'that Mona Corrington is back. My wife saw her with Beyfus earlier this evening.'

'Where has poor old Mona been?' asked Jacquiz languidly.

'On the continent,' said Tony Beck, 'getting up trouble.'

'She's a grand girl, Mona,' Balbo Blakeney said: 'she stirs up the shit wherever she goes. Her politics are sheer cow's piss, of course, but I do love a spunky girl like Mona who goes round stirring up the shit.'

'... All of which reminds me,' Mona was saying to Beyfus in the Arts: 'this new surplus Lancaster's got. Half a million.'

'Quarter of a million.'

'Quite enough to build with.'

'Yes. I'm going to propose a new building on Scholars' Meadow.'

That at least should please her, he thought. But it didn't.

'Cost?' she snapped.

'A hundred thousand plus.'

'Then why only one new building?'

'There are other things to be done, Mona dear.'

'No, there aren't. Not these days. Now, Beyfus, you listen to me . . .'

First with depression and then with mounting horror Beyfus listened.

'And that,' she said at last, 'is what you will propose.'

As Beyfus opened his mouth, Mona gave him a long, hard look which could only mean one thing: do this, or there'll be no more of *that*. So Beyfus took a big drink of Vichy Water, which he supposed to be good for his nervous stomach, and then nodded humbly.

'Just as you say,' he said.

'. . . So you see,' Mayerston was telling Hugh, 'these are not the methods of reform but the methods of revolution.'

'Peaceful revolution,' insisted Hugh. For of course, he kept telling himself, all this talk of demolition and so on *was* only metaphorical.

'Radical in any event. *Radix*,' said Mayerston, 'meaning root. The roots come up.'

'But painlessly,' said Hugh, 'because first we shall have been careful to dig the soil away.'

'All right. And who more suitable for the task than our chums in boiler suits?'

'They don't like hard work,' said Hugh disloyally.

'Then occasionally we give them a little treat. We let them move some of the soil by a quicker and more amusing method.'

Demolition again, Hugh thought. He did not like it, even as a metaphor. On the other hand, he believed in Mayerston and wanted to go with him. Why, he thought, do I believe in this man, whom I have only known for a few hours? It's not the cognac and it's not the straight fair hair; it's not the beautiful deep voice; it's not even the vision of the Beloved Republic. It's just . . . that I want to follow this man. It would be the same if he were starting a club or making a film or proposing a two-man crossing of the Pacific. Whatever he's up to, I want to be there, I want to bear a part. I want to laugh when he does, to cry when he does—and to mean it. Above all, I want him to turn to me and say, 'Well done.'

'Where do I come in?' Hugh said.

'So you will come in?'

'Yes.'

'Despite your obvious reservations?'

'Yes.'

'And you will do all I ask of you?'

'If you ask. Not if anyone else does.'

Mayerston smiled, revealing very white but rather unevenly placed teeth. The left-hand upper canine noticeably overlapped its two neighbours and protruded over the lower lip with gauche and innocent charm.

'Good,' said Mayerston, and Hugh was pleased.

'But what must I do?' he said.

'You have a name for academic brilliance. You are ... somebody of repute. I want you to set an example to all those who have no repute ... to all those sullen, dirty young men in beards and boiler suits. And more than set an example: inspire them.'

'You could do that better than me.'

'I can't be everywhere at once. I have a lot to attend to. You will do for them,' said Mayerston eyeing him closely, 'what I am doing for you.'

Hugh paused to consider this. He knows his power, Hugh thought: well, and why not? Then, shaking his head modestly,

'But what must I do in terms of action?' he asked.

'You must initiate and encourage certain movements,' Mayerston said, 'which will in time shake down the whole structure of this University as it now stands. Or, to use our other image, you must conjure the wind to blow away the soil that nourishes the roots.'

'A rather ... nebulous programme?'

'You,' said Mayerston, 'will make gestures. The denim-clad mass will stir and charge. And down comes all.'

'Another metaphor, Mayerston. What do I *do*?'

'You direct your attention,' said Mayerston, 'to the large sum of money which your college has just received from the sale of land. You find out what are the early proposals for using this money—Beck will tell you that, one of his many uses. And what you then do, in the first instance, is this...'

For something over an hour, with great precision and much practical detail, Mayerston proceeded to tell him.

After the Fellows of Lancaster had drunk port, claret, madeira and Château Yquem in the Senior Common Room, they dispersed for the night. Daniel Mond, making tracks for Willow Close, found Jacquiz Helmut at his elbow.

'A word or two in your ear,' Jacquiz breathed.

When they reached Daniel's rooms over the river, Jacquiz spread himself out full length on the window seat and called for Orangeade.

'... With ice,' he said; and then, when Daniel had stopped fussing about, 'Where do we stand *in re* tomorrow's Council?'

'We?'

'We Jews.'

'What's that got to do with it?'

'There are three of us. Beyfus will do what La Corrington tells him. I shall support the *status quo*. What shall you do, Daniel?'

'I shall listen to all the suggestions and support the most sensible.'

'Suppose none of them is sensible? Or suppose that no sensible suggestion has any chance of getting through? For anything to be passed, remember, there must be 75 per cent of the Council in its favour.'

'If there is a sensible suggestion,' wheezed Daniel, 'I shall support it, whether or not it has any chance of getting through. If there are no sensible suggestions, then I shall support none at all. But I still don't see what being a Jew has to do with it.'

'People are going to get very angry, Daniel. When they get angry, they look for faces to punch. Jewish faces, because they tend to be sensitive and clever, are the most satisfying kind.'

'Perhaps, too, because they tend to be sanctimonious.'

'Good point,' Jacquiz said. 'And the moral is, not to look sensitive or clever or sanctimonious when fists are flying. Now Beyfus, of course, is going to look all three; but Beyfus is the darling of the left, so there'll be no fist in the face for him.'

'There are still,' said Daniel, 'a few right-wing fists about.'

'I'm delighted to hear it, but I doubt whether they will be much help to *us*. Both of us, Daniel, if we allow for our political differences, will be standing for good sense and moderation. Neither quality is popular in times like these, and neither is ever popular in Jews. They make us look superior.'

'Then let us cultivate modesty and get on with our work. You with your life of Garibaldi, me with my Tensor Calculus.'

'We must still attend the Council and vote. This will expose us to attention. In all our Jewishness.'

'The Council is not noted for anti-semitism.'

'And the students outside it?'

'The students are committed absolutely to racial tolerance. It's the best thing about them. Why all this fuss, Jacquiz?'

'I felt it my duty to talk to you about the dangers. To ascertain your attitudes.'

'Thank you, Jacquiz. Dangers there certainly are, but not, I think, of the kind you mention.'

'I'm glad that is your view, so long as it gives you peace of mind. You see, Daniel, I was afraid that you might have been thinking along the same lines as myself and that you might have been getting ready to . . . er . . . to——'

'—Play the poltroon?'

'Let us say, to come to some accommodation with the extremists. I'm glad to be reassured.'

'Look,' said Daniel, 'you had that reassurance almost as soon as you got into this room. But you still had to carry on at length about these ... dangers ... you envisage. Why, Jacquiz? Were you trying to frighten me?'

'Only to test you, my dear. To make absolutely certain. I mean, after all you've been through ...'

'After all I've been through, Jacquiz, I don't believe in bogymen. I've seen the real thing. Fairy tales don't bother me.'

'And yet ... you *have* got fears, you say?'

'Not as a Jew, Jacquiz: as a scholar.'

'No one can discredit your scholarship.'

'They can say that it is irrelevant.'

'Why should they say that?'

'Because from their point of view it is true. I am not a scientist. I am not even a creative mathematician any more. I am just a guardian of a body of abstract truth which is expressed in certain symbols. This truth, beautiful as it is, has nothing to contribute to the new society as they see it. Nor, come to that, has the study of Garibaldi.'

'But Garibaldi himself was a revolutionary.'

'Was. They are not interested in the past, Jacquiz. They are not interested in truth for its own sake, whether it has to do with your Garibaldi or my mathematical series.'

'Then in what are they interested, for Christ's sake? Why are they here at all?'

'They are here to better themselves. To get more of what is going ... by which I do not mean knowledge, but social status and worldly goods. They have decided that they are not getting more enough quick enough, and so they are now turning nasty with us and all we stand for. You must know that.'

'I knew they resented our privileges,' Jacquiz said. 'But our scholarship ... why, we are offering to share it with them.'

'And they don't want it, because very few of them can understand it, let alone enjoy it.'

'Then why not just leave it to us?'

'Because if they don't want it, no one else is going to have it either. Anyone that did might get pleasure from it, you see—a pleasure which they can't share, *ergo* a privilege. For scholarship *is* a privilege, Jacquiz, and it's going to be destroyed with the rest.'

After the goodies in the Senior Common Room were finished, Balbo Blakeney had invited Ivor Winstanley and Tony Beck to drink brandy in his rooms in Sitwell's. Since these were on the staircase nearest to the college hall and therefore to the Senior Common Room which adjoined it, the journey was short and the three men managed it without disaster—though in Ivor's case only just.

'So,' said Balbo Blakeney, gathering up the Prunier Grande Champagne 1928 from his eighteenth century sideboard, 'the boys are back tomorrow. What trouble,' he said to Beck as he handed him a generous half-tumbler of cognac, 'are they hatching up this time?'

'The usual stuff, I expect. Protest against privilege and divisiveness. Justifiable resentment at the frivolous uses of superfluous affluence. And so on.'

'And where do you stand?' mumbled Ivor Winstanley into his brandy.

'Where I always did,' said Tony Beck. 'Waiting to join them when I'm certain they've won. And they will win, you know.'

'Then why not join them now?'

'Because I want to enjoy the old things in the old way for the very short time that's left.'

'If you leave it too long,' said Ivor, 'they might not let you join at all.'

'Don't you worry,' giggled Balbo, his gnome's face pursed in affectionate malice, 'our little Tony is taking care of all that. He may not have joined them yet, but he's dishing out hints on the sly. He's telling them that for the time being he can be more help to them where he is, listening to our counsels among the flesh-pots and then passing the word along.'

'I am showing,' agreed Beck good-naturedly, 'discreet sympathy with the student cause.'

'Which means,' said Balbo, 'that he can go on guzzling with the rest of us right up to the night of the long knives. When that comes, he slips away from high table, changes into his dungarees, and hey presto, there he is waving his sweaty nightcap in the middle of the mob. You are a bloody bastard,' he said, waving the bottle at Beck; 'have some more of this stuff.'

'The point is,' said Beck, having some, 'that I shan't be in the middle of the mob, I shall be the head of it. Grateful for my past advice and good offices, appreciative of my experience and maturity, the students will ask me to be their leader. Which is lucky for reactionary jackals like both of you, as I may be able to protect you.'

'Send us to labour camps,' muttered Ivor, 'instead of hanging us from lamp-posts.'

'You wouldn't protect your own mother,' said Balbo happily. 'You'll sentence us all to be drawn and quartered, in order to show revolutionary fervour, and then you'll set about finding yourself a pretty uniform and a big white horse.'

He went to the side-board for another bottle.

'Don't let's get over-excited,' said Tony Beck. 'All that is in question . . . at least for the time being . . . is a new kind of university. The young are discontented with what they've got and want something different.'

'Like what?' said Ivor, and slumped.

'Something which will make them feel more important,' sneered Balbo.

'That's about it,' said Beck. 'They have a legitimate aspiration, as they would say, to become a force in the present government and future planning of this university.

Now as ever—now more than ever—youth will be served. But no one is talking about labour camps or lamp-posts or big white horses. Simply about radical change, which has now become a necessity.'

'Ah,' said Balbo, 'necessity. I have an old acquaintance, a certain Captain Detterling, who is very fond of the expression. He uses it in the Greek sense, αναvχη, which as Ivor here will agree—wake up, you fat bag of guts—means essentially that which is unchangeable. Necessity, my dear Tony, is a conservative word: there is no such thing as necessary change.'

'Inevitable change then.'

'Change of some kind there will inevitably be, as things do not, unfortunately, stand still. But no particular kind is inevitable, Tony. Have some more booze to sharpen up your wits.'

'My wits,' said Ivor, staggering to his feet, 'are clean undone.'

He went quickly through the door and was heard being sick in the sink on the landing.

'Poor old thing can't hold his juice any more,' said Beck. 'Now then, Balbo. I agree with you that we can't determine exactly what change there will be; but the general direction is clear enough. There is an idealistic movement towards equality. The young will have it so.'

'Not all of them or even most of them. Most of them just don't care. In the good English tradition, they are moderate men.'

'Apathetic would be a better word. Apathetic but slightly uneasy, because they somehow feel that idealism is the new thing and that they would be safer as idealists. So when the movement gathers way, they will go with it.'

Outside the door, Ivor started down the stairs, keening loudly.

'It takes more momentum than you think,' said Balbo, 'to move a mass of the apathetic.'

'There will be very considerable momentum. You haven't

met my new friend, Mayerston. A prophet, Balbo, to bring the people out of Egypt.'

'The people always end by throwing prophets out, Tony. They nag too much.'

'Precisely. And that is when worldly men like myself step in. Mayerston the prophet does the donkey work and brings the people through the desert. When they're heartily sick of Mayerston and the short rations he imposes in Moab, I take over just in time to lead them into the land of milk and honey.'

'And the land of cognac, Tony? Of red burgundy and white?'

Balbo proffered the bottle.

'Yes,' said Tony Beck. 'We allow all those things again once Mayerston is dead and we're out of the desert. Or at least, since they're probably in short supply, we allow them to our leaders and those we value.'

'Privilege, Tony?'

'Of course, Balbo. Revolutionaries are only human, after all. I would wish to see you among the privileged in Canaan.'

'I don't want to go to Canaan. I like it here in Egypt and shall stay behind.'

'There is no staying behind. You know that. When God's children depart, Egypt is smitten and accursed. You come with us or you die of plague.'

'I am a scientist. My skills will keep me alive.'

'Because of those skills we shall insist on taking you with us. We shan't want poor puffy old Ivor, but we shall insist on taking you.'

Both drank deep.

'So whether you like it or not,' said Beck, 'you will come to Canaan. If you come quietly and work well, you will share my palace and my cognac, my burgundies red and white.'

'And if not?'

'You will be thrown into Golgotha.'

'I thought,' said Balbo, 'that we were only discussing

changes in this university.'

'The allegory holds at all levels.'

'All right. So Mayerston/Moses is dead and you've come to the promised land, where you start relaxing a bit. Or so you hope. Because you seem to have forgotten that the Ark of the Covenant is still right up with you, and who should be there carrying the bloody thing but Lord Beyfus and Mona Corrington? Who will speak in the voice of their egalitarian Jehovah to rain curses on your palace and your cognac.'

'Unless, Balbo, they have started relaxing too. Even Mona and Beyfus must relax sooner or later. They might even be relaxing now. Do you suppose he fucks her?'

'I've often wondered,' Balbo said. 'I saw his cock once, in the Fellows' loo. It was like a cooked snail.'

Both drank deep and then deeper.

'Of course,' said Beck, 'you can't really tell unless you've seen it erect. It wasn't erect in the Fellows' loo, I take it?'

'No.'

'Not a snail but a limpet?'

Both of them honked with laughter and drank deeper still.

'But none of this proves,' said Beck after long thought, 'that he doesn't fuck Mona.'

'Can you imagine Mona opening her legs? There'd be a sort of rending noise——'

'—Like the veil in the Ark of the Covenant when Jehovah rent it——'

'—Or like Ivor being sick——'

'—And Beyfus would come bouncing up like a balloon——'

'—And Mona would give one squeeze of those huge thighs——'

'—And Beyfus would burst with a plop——'

'—But Mona would mend him and blow him up again——'

'—So that whenever he spoke it would just be Mona's hot air coming out——'

'—Which is what happens anyway,' said Balbo; 'therefore Beyfus fucks Mona, q.e.d.'

Balbo poured more cognac and goodness, how they both laughed.

But in fact Beyfus wasn't fucking Mona at all. He was sitting bolt upright beside her on the leather-covered sofa in his room, while Mona explained, at some length, how they were going to serve the cause of humanity during the whole of the next quinquennium. Having told him just how she proposed to manipulate the new International Committee of Anthropologists, and having firmly outlined his own tasks in the reconstruction and 'detraditionalisation' of Lancaster College, Mona passed from the realms of speculation (for even she admitted that her plans depended on highly volatile contingencies) into those of fantasy.

'By about 1970,' Mona said, 'we should be ready for the coup in reverse.'

Oddly enough, Mona was a keen and courageous gambler, being especially fond of Chemin-de-Fer, and from time to time she flavoured her speech with expressions picked up in the gaming house.

'The coup in reverse?' said Beyfus, who was not familiar with the idiom.

'You run your bank as long as you dare,' Mona explained, 'and then, when you reckon it must be beaten on the next coup, you reverse the situation. You let the bank pass; somebody else takes it on—and you go "banco" against your own bank, and win.'

'It sounds very pleasing.'

'It is.'

'But I don't quite see——'

'—A simple analogy. The present government, which, for the want of anything more radical, you and I support, can stay in office, run its bank, until March '71. But if it stays that long it will almost certainly be beaten in the elections, so the better plan is to pass the bank voluntarily, i.e. resign, in 1970—and then instantly challenge the new bank with a call of "banco". Which means, Beyfus, that one's going for the whole damn kitty. In this case ... the Monarchy.'

'*Mona,*' said Beyfus, deeply shocked.

'The moment parliament reconvenes, the new Labour opposition will demand a plebiscite on whether or not the country wants to keep the Queen and the Royal Family. The plebiscite will be refused, whereupon the idea will gain great appeal in all quarters. The sheer novelty will guarantee that. From then on, the new Conservative government will appear as an oppressive tyranny which has refused the people's right to free expression. The Cabinet will lose its morale and any impetus it ever had, the people will go on hankering for the plebiscite—and in five years' time they will certainly return Labour on the strength of our promise to give it to them. In this way we achieve re-election in 1975. But if we hang on till 1971 before dissolving, and then adopt only the conventional processes of opposition, we may stay out until 1981 or even longer.'

'Which way would the plebiscite go?'

'That doesn't matter. The plebiscite is only a ruse.'

'But it does matter,' said Beyfus petulantly; 'because if the Monarchy goes, my peerage goes with it.'

'Why should you care? You only took it on as a duty, because Harold said he needed men like you to make themselves heard at Westminster.'

'I've got very fond of my peerage.' Beyfus hesitated guiltily. Then, 'You know,' he blurted out, 'I get an almost sexual thrill of excitement every time someone calls me "my lord".'

'I don't want to hear any more infantile nonsense of *that* kind ... Time I was going.'

'But first,' said Beyfus, his little dark eyes pleading, 'can you? Will you? Please, Mona.'

'Apart from this prattle of peerages,' said Mona, deliberately, 'you've really been quite a good Beyfus. Not very good, of course, but certainly not bad. So the answer is ... yes. Go and get ready.'

Full of happiness, Beyfus hurried into his bedroom and

changed into his pyjamas.

'Ready,' he called out.

'Have you washed your teeth?'

'Sorry. Forgot.'

He cleaned his teeth carefully at the hand basin.

'Ready *now*,' he called.

Mona came in and sat down on the bed. Beyfus clambered up beside her and nuzzled against her shoulder. Mona stroked his hair.

'Beyfus baby,' she said fondly.

Still nuzzling, Beyfus placed his hands together.

'Our Father,' he said, 'who art in heaven, hallowed be Thy name. Thy kingdom come ...'

Mona stroked his hair and heard him out. Then she helped him into bed and tucked him up.

'Why a Church of England prayer?' she asked. 'Jewish prayers are much stronger.'

'And was not Christ a Jew? This was Christ's prayer, Mona. It belongs to no church.'

Mona went to the bedroom door and put her hand up to the light switch.

'Lights out now,' she said. 'Good night.'

'Good night, Mona. Thank you for my nice evening. See you in the morning.'

Mona turned off the light and closed the door very gently. She paced across the sitting-room, gathering up her cloak as she went, turned off the lights by the outer door, and walked down the stairs. Outside the stars were shining, Bootes and the Bear, which men also call the Wain, which ever circles in its own place and watches Orion. But Mona, who did not much care for Homer, looked neither for the Bear nor Orion. She stuck her head forward, fixed her eyes on the ground five yards in front of her, placed her hands behind her back, and then strode away through the sleeping college, thinking of good battles past and the better ones to come.

'Benedic, domine, nobis,' intoned Robert Reculver Constable, Provost of Lancaster College, '*et his consiliis nostris.* Amen.'

'Amen,' repeated the nineteen other Members of the Council, each standing behind his chair at The Great Table of the King's Matter, which was a massive rectangle of oak, twenty-five yards in length, and used only for such assemblages.

'Why do you summon us this day?' boomed Grantchester Pough, as Senior Fellow, from his place at the bottom of the table.

'To lend ear and give counsel.'

'And shall we speak with truth and without fear?'

'With truth and without fear and in good fellowship, for our Sovereign Lady the Queen will have it so.'

'Then God save our Lady the Queen,' bawled Grantchester Pough, meaning every word of it, 'and God be merciful to the soul of our good Lord and Founder, the Blessed Henry of Lancaster. Amen.'

And from all, 'Amen.'

'Is it your will that I proceed?' the Provost resumed.

'It is our will.'

All sat except the Provost himself.

'What matter, Master Provost?' called Pough up the table.

'Listen and mark.'

Since this exchange made an end of the preliminary formalities, Balbo Blakeney and several others lit cigarettes. The Provost rootled among some papers, cleared his throat, then rootled again. From behind him the portrait of Provost Lauderdale, who had been butchered on the College Stones when denying entry to the Parliament men, scowled over his head and all along the table. Jacquiz

Helmut arranged his scarlet gown to his liking, while the Senior Fellow produced, from somewhere about him, a Rabelaisian throat spray and with a noise like a cataract squirted his yawning tonsils.

Then there was silence in the Long Chamber while they all waited for what they knew the Provost must say.

'Principal Bursar,' the Provost said.

The Provost sat. The Principal Bursar rose, it now being a quarter past ten of the clock, and occupied them, until lunch time, with a reading of the accounts as cast on All Fools' Day. None might leave while this went on, and none might join the Council for the first time after it was done. The rule was quite clear: either members attended from the very first word of the meeting, or they stayed away. A very good rule it was too: for since the condition of being allowed to speak or vote on any measure was that a man must first sit through at least three hours of the Principal Bursar's arithmetical recitation, the frivolous or impatient, should ever such be elected in error to the Council, were speedily discouraged from bearing any part at the Great Table of the King's Matter.

At half past one, the accounts being by now threequarters read, the Council adjourned for the traditional collation of spiced herring and small beer.

'Shall I like this Mayerston?' said Hetta to Hugh, over a sandwich lunch in a riverside pub.

Hugh had an uneasy feeling that she wouldn't.

'You'll find out when you meet him tonight,' he said.

'Why not until tonight?' asked Hetta. 'I mean, if it's all so urgent and exciting.'

'I expect he's busy until then,' said Hugh, who suddenly had another uneasy feeling that perhaps Mayerston, like Dracula, never emerged from his lair until sundown.

'And you say there's an important part for me?' persisted Hetta.

'Very.'

'Then why not tell me?'

'Mayerston will explain it far better.'

'No one explains things better than you.'

'It's not just a matter of explaining,' Hugh said. 'We want you to *believe* in what you're going to do.'

'So long as you want it,' said Hetta, 'I'll believe in it.'

Hetta was still feeling guilty about her little display of weakness in the Great Court of Lancaster the previous afternoon.

'Nevertheless,' said Hugh, passing her a sandwich, 'you'd best hear about it from Mayerston. So eat up your nice salami, and then we can go.'

'Back to your room?' said Hetta eagerly.

'Not this afternoon. It's so nice I thought we'd take a punt down to Grantchester.'

'That's not your sort of thing at all. Punts down to Grantchester . . . Like a lord in an Edwardian novel.'

'It's one of the things,' said Hugh, 'that I want us to do while we still can.'

'What can you mean? You really are being most frightfully peculiar today. It's something to do with this Mayerston. I can feel it.'

'Look,' said Hugh: 'either eat up that fucking sandwich and come with me on the river, or go home. But for Christ's sake stop ticking like a bloody clock.'

Hugh, though sometimes brisk with Hetta, had always been tender at bottom. But the speech which he had just made now was not tender, at bottom or anywhere else. There was a new and ugly tone in his voice which made Hetta both resentful and fearful. Nevertheless, she bit back her tears and her salami sandwich and then, not asking for time to go to the loo though she wanted to rather badly, accompanied Hugh to the boat house which adjoined the pub.

At a quarter past four in the Long Chamber, Lord Beyfus was well under way. The Principal Bursar had finished his reading at half past three; the accounts had been put to the vote and passed; and the Provost had ordered that they would now discuss possible uses for the quarter-million pound surplus to which full reference had been made in the statement they had just approved. Lord Beyfus had then risen (underneath the portrait of Provost Dawley, who, having lost his faith in Christianity one bright morning in 1873, had hanged himself from the top of the south-east tower of the chapel soon after breakfast the same day) and asked the Provost's leave '*orationem severiorem exigere*'—to push out a stiffish oration, i.e. one longer than the fifteen minutes which custom prescribed as the normal limit. Constable had bowed and consented; Jacquiz had reminded everyone within earshot that in any case Beyfus, as a peer of the realm, did not need special permission; and now, at a quarter past four, Beyfus was coming round on his last lap. Or so everybody hoped.

'. . . All of which considerations,' quacked Beyfus, 'moral, social, educational, spatial and financial, can be satisfied by a scheme which I will summarise as follows:

'One. The erection, on Scholars' Meadow, at the approximate cost of £100,000, of a students' hostel to hold one hundred extra students.

'Two. The erection, on the rear lawn of the college, again at the rough cost of £100,000, of a second hostel to hold a hundred more extra students.'

'On the rear lawn of the college?' said Ivor Winstanley, in tones which combined horror at this proposal with something like reverence for its sheer enormity.

'I have the ear of the Council,' snapped Beyfus.

'But the rear lawn——'

'—Lord Beyfus has our ear, Mr Winstanley,' said Constable sternly. 'Lord Beyfus . . .'

'Three,' said Beyfus. 'The £50,000 which will then remain from the surplus should be spent on providing the two hundred extra students in their new hostels with a variety of attached amenities of an experimental nature. It will be neither possible nor desirable to cater for these students on the basis of the present facilities and social routines of this college: not possible, because there is simply not the space —in Hall, for example, or in the Junior Common Room, or in the College Library; not desirable because such facilities and routines are in any case retrograde. We must therefore experiment with new oecological patterns of a kind appropriate to the new society for which we are striving.

'The two principles behind these experimental patterns must be (a) rationalised co-operation in environmental function, and (b) social integration within the norm. The first requires that all domestic management should be undertaken by the students themselves: meals must be provided, cleaning and repairs performed, *by* students *for* students on a system of rota which will ensure that all bear an equal part. I do not propose to go into detail here and now; but a good example of what I envisage is the Student Co-operative Cafeteria, which will replace, for those in the new hostels and ultimately for every member of the college, the outdated institution known as Hall. Servants will of course be unknown. All service will be self-service. All food will be purchased, prepared and cooked by teams of students. No resident in the hostels will be exempt from taking turns of duty: even graduates and Fellows will assist in the meanest chores—which, however, will be much mitigated by the use of the most modern machinery and techniques.'

Beyfus looked to left and to right, surveying the looks of incredulity or disgust which had now appeared on nearly every face except that of Constable, which was frozen in regal indifference, and that of Tony Beck, which wore a sly grin as if to say, 'Catch me doing the washing up.' In one quarter and one only was there evidence of friendship unalloyed: Oliver Clewes, the Chaplain, was staring at Beyfus with a fatuous look of devotion such as would have discredited a half-witted Spaniel. Beyfus hurriedly removed his eyes from Clewes and raised them to the portrait on the opposite wall; this was of Dean Peregrine Runcible-Walpole, who, in 1897, had published a volume of lyrical verse containing the famous stanza:

'The boys on Belmont beaches
Do as nature teaches,
If no one's there to frown:
When from high the kind sun reaches,
They toss away their breeches—
Show behinds like ripened peaches
With the same soft down.'

Finding Runcible-Walpole's gooey gaze almost as intolerable as Clewes's, Beyfus flicked his eyes one portrait to the right (the 14th Lord Seymour of Saxmundham, a rather moderate major-general of Division in World War I) and launched himself down the home straight.

'The second principle behind the experimental patterns to be embodied in the new hostels,' he said, 'I have designated as social integration within the norm. By this I mean the encouragement of behaviour that emphasises communal awareness rather than personal preference. Communal awareness will already, of course, have been fostered by the common performance of domestic tasks; but the concept must be taken a stage further, to include hours and methods of study and even leisure pastimes.

'For it is no longer acceptable that certain individuals, who have a liking for intellectual pursuits, should be allowed to enjoy these in privacy for as long as they choose and at the expense of their fellow students. I say, "At the expense of their fellow students", because by shutting themselves off from their contemporaries they are not only making a claim to be different from them but also making a bid to achieve better degrees, and so higher esteem and reward, than the average student can expect.

'Thus the average student, going about his normative pleasure-cycle while the few remain immersed in their books, is made to feel excluded, guilty, insecure and inferior. To prevent this, students will be accommodated by threes:

three students to a good-sized bed-sitting-room, which latter cannot possibly be regarded by any single student as a place of privacy or retreat. If a student wishes to work, he must go to the hostel work-room, which will be equipped with specially programmed audio-visual devices (thus reducing individualistic elements in study-processes), and which will be open from 9 a.m. to 1 p.m. and from 4.30 p.m. to 6. This will ensure that outside the approved working hours no student will be able either to advantage himself by extra effort or to withdraw himself from the community into a closed and selfish world of scholarship. All will be compelled to participate in the normative leisure patterns appropriate to their age-group.

'Such patterns, in the past, have had a regrettable tendency to be distorted by aggressive and individual pleasure-pursuits. So in order to ensure that patterns of a strictly modern typology are developed and conformed to, we shall spend a large part of the £50,000 balance on recreation rooms of a socio-creative play-potential.

'In this way,' Beyfus concluded, 'the numbers of the college will be doubled, a large amount of unproductive land will be utilised, and new ideals of social obligation and community-orientated function will be introduced among us. I should add that to make the experiment really worth while, the residents of the hostels should be of both sexes. There is nothing in the statutes to prevent this Council from declaring that the college shall henceforth be co-educational—a reform much to be desired according to current theories of moral hygiene and sexual equality.'

Phew, thought Beyfus as he sat down; what I go through for Mona. I only hope she'll be pleased by what I've said, because nobody else will be.

But in fact he was to be proved wrong in this before many hours were out; even there and then, he was not wholly without allies. True, when the Provost called for a preliminary vote to determine how many members of the Council favoured the general sense of Beyfus's proposals, the only people who signified support were Tony Beck and Oliver Clewes; but Tom Llewyllyn and (surprisingly) the Senior Fellow both announced that they wished to make further propositions on not wholly dissimilar lines. When, therefore, the council adjourned for tea at half past four, the Baron Beyfus felt his cause was not entirely dead.

During the tea interval, Tom Llewyllyn remembered the conversation which he had had with Daniel Mond, the previous afternoon, about Fielding Gray. Bored and fretful after the slow hours of words and figures, he felt a sudden compulsion to make contact with someone—with anyone—outside Lancaster College, whose tedious business was holding him a prisoner in the Long Chamber through this bright day of gaudy spring. So he sat down at the writing desk in the Fellows' Parlour and wrote a brief note in which he suggested that Fielding propose himself for an overnight stay any time after May the first.

'As you probably know,' he wrote, 'Daniel Mond is here. He thinks you owe him an explanation, and I agree with him. But however that may be, we shall both be very pleased to see you here. It's been far too long...'

He did not know Fielding's exact address in Broughton Staithe, so after some hesitation he addressed the envelope to Major Fielding Gray (he'll like the old title, Tom thought) c/o Gregory Stern the publisher—Fielding's as well as his own. He then dropped the letter in the box for franking and despatch, and felt very slightly better. A door which had long been closed was about to be re-opened.

'Tea on the lawn?' said Hetta at Grantchester when Hugh suggested this. 'You'll be reading Rupert Brooke next.'

'What's wrong with tea on the lawn?'

'You said yesterday that no one must have tea till half past six. To be like the workers, you said.'

'When in Rome,' said Hugh, 'one may as well enjoy her amenities. Until they are swept away.'

'That doesn't sound like you,' said Hetta suspiciously.

'Do you or do you not want some tea, for Christ's sake?'

So nasty was his tone that Hetta wanted to say, No, she didn't; but her need to piddle was now scarcely containable, and she supposed that the tea place would run to a ladies' lavvy.

After tea, the Senior Fellow addressed the Council in the Long Chamber. Like Lord Beyfus, he said gleefully, he too was going to suggest an experiment. Mindful that their Royal and pious Founder had ordained that his college should be a place of 'godliness and good learning', he would like to depose that neither of these virtues was encouraged by the daily and swinish consumption of butcher's meat, which fuddled the intellects and overheated the blood. It was time this abuse was checked. He, Pough, therefore put forward the following scheme: let them build a new hostel, on Scholars' Meadow if nowhere else could be found for it, for the accommodation of up to one hundred students; let all these students be fed from a vegetarian kitchen which would be attached to the hostel, and let them give their solemn undertaking that they would not indulge at any time either in the flesh of fish, fowl or quadruped, or in alcoholic beverages. At the end of two years after the erection of this hostel, let them compare the moral and academic records of the hundred vegetarians with those of the other undergraduates in the college. When they were satisfied that the former were incomparably superior, let them set about making plans for re-organising the kitchens of the entire college on a vegetarian basis, and for the total prohibition of alcohol within its walls.

It was typical of the old gentleman that he should have satirised his own fads in order to ridicule someone else's. When he finished, there was a low murmur of appreciation from all except Beyfus, Clewes and Beck. Sanity had now been firmly re-established, everyone felt, and high time too.

'Better now?' said Hugh when Hetta came back from having her pee.

'Yes. I mean no. There was never anything wrong with me.'

'I'm sorry if I've been stroppy, Het. The thing is ... I've been upset. By Mayerston.'

'I thought you admired him ... Goodie, what lovely scones.'

'I do admire him. But the more I think about him ... and I think about him all the time ... the more I feel there's something wrong.'

'Don't you trust him?'

'I trust him all right.'

'Then don't you *like* him? Try this yummy cream.'

'I *do* like him. I find him very attractive.'

'*Hugh*, you don't mean ...?'

'No, Het. It's not a physical attraction. I only wish it were, because then it could be easily explained. As it is ... I almost feel as if there'd been some sort of transference ... as if in some way he were beginning to possess me.'

'Like a witch?'

'You mean a warlock. No. Warlocks use demons to do their work. Whatever ... is affecting me, is coming from Mayerston himself.'

'If you ask me,' said Hetta, 'it was all that brandy you drank. Half a bottle each, you said. No wonder you still feel peculiar.'

'I dare say you're right. Dear, sweet, uncomplicated Hetta.'

He raised her hand from the table and kissed it.

'Oh my goodness me,' said Hetta, flustered with pleasure: 'can I have some more scones?'

'We ought to get back.'

'There's plenty of time.'

'No, there isn't. You've got to go out to Cherry Hinton and change.'

'*Change*, Hugh?'

'Me too. Before we meet Mayerston.'

After Pough's little triumph, Tom Llewyllyn told the table a few home truths.

'It is not acceptable,' said Tom, 'either by the Government, or by the informed public, or by the student population throughout the country, that a college should occupy as much space as this one does and yet should have such a comparatively small role of undergraduates. Leave politics aside, you must still face up to the general view that Lancaster is an educational luxury . . . that it is *uneconomic*. I say this with regret, because in my opinion it stands for something which is not reckonable in terms of utility; but that is how the world reckons, and these days we must reckon with the world. When it is generally known that on top of everything else we have just acquired a surplus of £250,000, the cry will be for a visible and practical investment in the future of the nation's youth.

'Rather than have importunate suggestions thrust on us from outside, we must be ready with a scheme of our own. It should be a scheme prominent enough to satisfy the Government, utilitarian enough to satisfy the philistine public at large, and radical enough to satisfy student aspirations. It should also be . . . malleable enough . . . to fit within the existing framework. In short, gentlemen, it must be a scheme which combines a maximum of ostensible bustle with a minimum of real change.'

Elegant, thought Constable, but flippant. Still the journalist.

'You may find such a dictum surprising in the mouth of a socialist,' Tom continued, 'but the truth is that the only valid motive for changing anything is to improve what is bad while preserving what is good. Schemes of the kind which the Government, the public, the students at present favour would do neither. Such schemes simply represent change for the sake of change—as futile a thing as speed for the sake of speed.

'But this is not to say there is no room for improvement here. The college *is* rather too ample for the student body it contains; and while over-crowding will always bring banality and deterioration, under-crowding can make for sterility and smugness. I think, then, that institutional health and social justice alike require that we effect an increase ... a very carefully calculated increase ... in our numbers.'

My word, thought Beyfus, Mona will have a fit when she hears about this. Particularly if he gets his way. And what's more she'll blame me. She won't tuck me up for a month. She's so unfair, Mona is, even when a fellow does his best.

'On my view,' Tom was saying, 'we could contain 25 per cent more students, i.e. about sixty, without seriously compromising our standards. On my view also, that represents the minimum scope of the change we must make in order to remain unmolested. A 25 per cent increase will combine duty with prudence. But since it is, after all, a bare minimum, it will be necessary to publicise it in somewhat inflated terms. That is what I meant by bustle.

'So there must be a fanfare of trumpets, gentlemen, followed by the immediate announcement that there is to be a new building on the Western half of Scholars' Meadow. The noisiness of the announcement will satisfy the Government. The mean-spirited intention to build over a pretty wilderness will satisfy the parsimonious public. The breach of statute and tradition will satisfy the disgruntled students, who will conceive that a stone laid on hitherto protected property is a stone worthy of the New Jerusalem. As for ourselves, we shall not be without comfort if we examine the scheme closely. We shall still have half our Meadow, for it is, let me repeat, only on the Western half that we shall build; and since we need only build for sixty people, and have a great deal of money with which to do it, we can make ourselves a building both small and beautiful which will enhance rather than hamper the view of Sitwell's and the Chapel.'

A preliminary vote of eleven members (i.e. more than 50 per cent) in favour of Tom's general sense guaranteed that his project would now be debated in detail. Should it receive, after debate, as many as twelve votes (60 per cent), it would then go on a short list of selected proposals, one of which would ultimately be adopted. For ultimate adoption, a proposal would need not only more votes than any other on the short list but also a minimum of fifteen (75 per cent), so that even after it was established which proposal on the short list had majority support, a bloody-minded caucus of six could keep it out indefinitely. However, all that was still a long way off; Tom's job here and now was to win the extra vote needed to get his scheme short-listed; and this meant that he must throw some enticing inducement to one of the members who had voted against it. Tom would not get the chance to do this himself until he exercised the proposer's privilege of winding up the debate; in the meantime, therefore, while Jacquiz Helmut was making a pithy speech of objection, Tom studied the list of his opponents, pondering whether he had in his pocket a carrot red enough for this or that donkey.

The opponents of Tom's scheme were: Jacquiz Helmut, who was clearly quite beyond redemption; Lord Beyfus, who doubtless considered that Mona would not approve anything so moderate; Oliver Clewes, who was infatuated with Beyfus; Tony Beck, who presumably (like Mona/Beyfus) wanted something more extreme; Ivor Winstanley, an old ally of Helmut's; Andrew Ogden, the Dean of Chapel, a respected and temperate conservative; the Senior Fellow, Grantchester Pough, another temperate right-winger, who had previously supported the idea of a new building but had obviously done so only in order to introduce his own little joke; the Lay Dean, a man of no account except in this, that he had never been known to change his mind; and Balbo Blakeney, who had done nothing all day except smoke cigarettes and look bilious.

Of these nine, then, it was clear to Tom that only two might conceivably be converted to his cause in time to swing the impending vote. One was Balbo Blakeney, for the good reason that Balbo was fascinated by architecture and might well respond to Tom's appeal for a really beautiful and expensive building which would set off and not disgrace Balbo's beloved Chapel. Against this was the fact that Balbo had as yet shown no sign of responding, having scarcely even deigned to listen; he had simply sat there scowling in a cloud of smoke and had cast his adverse vote without hesitation. This confirmed what Tom and others had already surmised—that Balbo was incubating some scheme of his own and was hoarding his entire will and energy for its later prosecution. And what, Tom wondered, would it turn out to be? As to that, time would show; meanwhile he must concentrate on his only other potential convert.

This was Andrew Ogden. True, Andrew usually voted with Winstanley and Pough, and he had done so firmly enough just now; but he differed from the other two in this, that he was very much more sensitive to the body of Christian precept and in particular to those parts of it which advocated, to use the rough lay equivalents, the qualities of 'fairness' and 'decency'. These, to Andrew, were more than mere gentlemanly attributes, they were a religious passion. It followed that one might probably get through to him, not by advancing politic reasons for letting sixty new students in, but by urging that it would be 'unfair' and 'indecent' to keep them out. This meant, thought Tom, that his method would have to change from the rational to the emotional—no bad thing, perhaps, in a speaker who was winding up. Having settled his tactical approach, he assumed a mild and ingenuous expression, and beamed charitably across the table at Jacquiz Helmut, who was now concluding his address.

'... Only necessary to say,' perorated Jacquiz, 'though

without any malice, that Mr Llewyllyn's suggestion has the audacity of total inexperience. For he is, after all, only a temporary Fellow, only recently co-opted as a colleague on our Council, and we need seek no further than this to explain the crudeness of his proposal and the simple-minded facility with which he has preferred it.'

Tom went on beaming at Jacquiz until he was seated, then turned his eyes up languishingly at Tony Beck, who had risen in the place next his own.

'The truly disgraceful thing,' said Beck, who wished to place himself on record, in case of future investigation, as having expressed the orthodox new-left attitude, 'is that Mr Llewyllyn should be so impervious to real human need. He has suggested that all of this huge sum be expended on a building which will hold only sixty students, and he is clearly far more anxious that it should be aesthetically pleasing than that it should fulfil any social function. In the face of such heartless irresponsibility, one can only respond with amazement and indignation. Let Mr Llewyllyn look out from his ivory tower at the mass of young faces which are turned towards us—bright, eager faces, hungry for truth and knowledge—and then let him tell them, if he dare, that he has room for only sixty of them because a larger building would block his cherished view.'

This speech cheered Balbo Blakeney up enormously. He positively rocked with pleasure all through it, and clapped his hands loudly when it was over.

'You beautiful, rotten bastard,' Balbo said; 'you keep it up like this, and you'll be king of the revolution.'

But after this little outburst he slumped back into his cloud of cigarette smoke and there remained while speaker succeeded speaker and Tom himself at last concluded the debate.

'... There is a lot,' said Tom, turning his eyes on Andrew Ogden and beginning to blink a little, 'in what Mr Beck has said about the heartlessness of denying entrance to those who are seeking for knowledge and truth.' A decided shift in emphasis from my first speech, he thought, but by this time of the day memories are short. 'With Mr Beck, I say to you that it would be ... shameful and indecent ... to turn such away from our gate.' Andrew Ogden was twitching: but was it in sympathy with his words or in contempt at his ploy? 'At the same time, since we cannot admit the whole world, let us ensure that those we do admit—and surely sixty is a substantial number—are received into surroundings and accommodation worthy of their noble and aspiring youth.'

Loathing himself for being capable of such a speech, Tom sat down to wait and see whether it had done the trick. When the Provost took the vote, it was revealed that Tom had lost one supporter, in Daniel Mond, but that he had gained two—Andrew Ogden, as he had hoped, and also Oliver Clewes. On the final count, then, Tom now had twelve votes for his proposal, which would therefore be entered on the Provost's Tabula Rerum Graviorum, or short list.

'All right,' said Mayerston to Tony Beck: 'what happened in there today?'

Beck told him. Then:

'When are you seeing Hugh Balliston again?' he asked.

'Very soon now. And his girl friend with him.'

'A word of warning,' said Beck. 'The girl is honest.'

'So is Hugh.'

'Hugh is also clever and proud of it. He prides himself on being able to follow people, to appreciate their deeper meanings. Since he wants his appreciation to be appreciated, he is liable to go further than he would really wish in making it evident. To prove that he has understood, he acts out his understanding.'

'In short,' said Mayerston, 'he is obliging because vain.'

'Whereas Hetta, you will find, is neither.'

'She obliges him, presumably.'

'She loves him.'

'Then she will do what he tells her.'

'Unless,' said Tony Beck, 'she should think it unworthy.'

'Unworthy of her?'

'Unworthy of him. At bottom she is rather old-fashioned, you see, despite her parade of contemporary opinions. If Hetta has a friend or a lover, she is eager for his honour.'

'Why, Danny,' asked Tom, 'did you vote against me?'

'What does it matter? You got your way.'

'And not a bad way. You were in favour of it at first. So why did you change?'

'Because I didn't care for your last speech.'

'I had to do something . . . to get extra votes.'

'But you did yourself a disservice,' said Daniel, 'by making yourself cheap.'

'Andrew Ogden didn't think so. I won him over.'

'You also,' said Daniel, 'won over Oliver Clewes. Not a recommendation.'

'Yes, that did surprise me.'

'It shouldn't have done. Clewes has an instinctive affinity with the spurious. That is why he supported Beyfus earlier on.'

'But my proposal was not spurious.'

'Your speech was.'

'Don't quarrel, Danny.'

'I shouldn't dream of it,' Daniel croaked. 'You've got your way for the time being, and not at all a bad way either, as you remark. For most people . . . even for Constable . . . that is enough. But I value you, Tom, more than I value your proposal, and I was sad that you could be so false.'

'Shall you go on voting against me?'

'No. Provided you argue honestly from now on, as you did in your first speech, I shall support you . . . unless a better proposal is made by someone else.'

'Fair enough, I suppose . . . I've written to Fielding Gray, Danny. Asked him to come over for a night.'

'Good.'

'But they say this Yankee woman of his doesn't like to let him out of her sight. I hope she doesn't tag along.'

'Fielding has a sense of the appropriate,' said Daniel. 'He knows that women can't stay in this college.'

'But does she? Anyway, Yankee women love pushing their way in where they're not wanted.'

'All women do.'

'And once they're in, it takes a steam-crane to get them out.'

'I shouldn't worry, Tom. Fielding has a knack of gliding away when it suits him. Or had when I knew him. He just used to . . . disappear . . . often when one wanted him most.'

'Like he disappeared with that Greek boy, damn him.'

'So if he decides to give his American lady the slip for a night,' said Daniel, 'no power on earth will stop him.'

When Hugh and Hetta met Mayerston in the Eagle Tavern as arranged, Mayerston was dressed in a roll-neck sweater and whip-cord trousers. Since Hugh was in his best (and only) suit and Hetta was got up to the nines (on Hugh's instructions) in a shimmering cocktail outfit, this was rather disconcerting.

'How nice you both look,' said Mayerston, 'but you shouldn't have bothered. I thought,' he said to Hugh, 'that we might try that place you mentioned last night. "Haq's", didn't you say?'

'Dinner's on me,' said Hugh stiffly.

'As you like. But let's make it Haq's, eh?'

Hetta began to hate Mayerston already, and they went to Haq's, where they sat at a square plastic table with legs of differing length. Hugh had a jet black mixed grill, Hetta dropped a noodle in her lap because the waiter jogged her elbow, and Mayerston ate a huge plate of fried meat balls in curry sauce with evident enjoyment. On Mayerston's suggestion they all drank something called Seven Up, though Hetta made it quite clear that she would have preferred Coca Cola. What made things even worse was that Mayerston said absolutely nothing during the entire meal, except to ask the waiter for three more bottles of Seven Up, which Hetta thought, he should have left to Hugh. Only when three cups of gritty and light brown coffee (Turkish) accompanied by some cubes of scurfy gelatine (Delight) were set before them did Mayerston at last open his mouth with any purpose other than to shove curried meat ball into it.

'That was very nice,' Mayerston said. 'How clever of Hugh to know about this place.' He sipped his coffee. 'Delicious,' he said to Hetta: 'don't you agree?'

Hetta was too miserable to do anything but shrug.

'Cheer up,' said Mayerston: 'there's a treat in store for you.'

'What?' said Hetta.

'Tomorrow night,' said Mayerston, 'you're going to sleep with Hugh in Lancaster.'

'*What?*' said Hetta.

'All night long,' Mayerston said.

'It's a protest,' said Hugh, and looked exceedingly silly.

This was too much. Suddenly and fiercely, Hetta started to blubber. She couldn't find her hanky, and her nose was blocked by snot which bubbled like a cauldron every time she tried to draw her breath.

'Never mind,' said Mayerston, passing her a large silk affair which smelt of Verbena, 'use this. And then, I think, we'll have a change of scene.'

The change of scene turned out to be a tiny pub near Little St Mary's. Mayerston led them into a back room, where there was a sideboard on which stood a pot of coffee and several kinds of liqueur. Comforted by a cup of the coffee, which was very sweet and very strong, and then further consoled by two large glasses of something white which tasted deliciously of greengages, Hetta began to feel happier than she had all day. Although she still didn't care much for Mayerston, she was quite ready to tolerate him, and when, a few minutes later, he started talking, she listened politely and calmly, while sipping a third glass of the greengage drink which someone had thoughtfully poured for her.

'Let me explain,' said Mayerston, 'what this is all about. At the meeting of Lancaster College Council today, Lord Beyfus made a remarkable and far-seeing proposal of what might be historic importance.' He gave a brief précis of Tony Beck's account of this. 'And what is more,' he went on, 'he also suggested that all this be implemented on a co-educational basis.'

'Don't be soft,' giggled Hetta; 'they'll never let women in there.'

'Why not?' said Hugh fiercely.

'They'd spoil it,' said Hetta. 'Women spoil anything like that, if you let them interfere. It's our nature. Like reading private letters which people leave about, or making people talk when they just want to sit quiet and read.'

'Nevertheless,' said Mayerston, 'and although you may disagree with certain details, Beyfus has put forward a scheme of revolutionary significance. You do see that?'

'By Castro, yes,' said Hetta, banging down her glass.

'And what has happened?' said Mayerston.

'Well, what?' said Hetta.

'The College Council declined even to discuss it. Instead, they discussed at length, and then placed on their short list for later consideration, a miserable apology of a plan, which was supposedly liberal in conception but was in fact just a clever piece of reactionary obstruction. The Fellows of Lancaster are trying to fob society off by building a kind of glorified summerhouse.'

'Now hold on,' said Hugh: 'a new building to house sixty undergraduates, I heard.'

'In relation to modern educational problems,' insisted Mayerston, 'they might as well build a potting shed. Here is this golden opportunity, and no one except Beyfus has the imagination, or even the inclination, to rise to it. Beyfus has been turned down like a piece of bad fish. So what do we do?'

'We pro-*test*,' said Hetta, throwing her glass over her shoulder.

'Right,' said Mayerston. 'And this is how we do it. We shall give out, all over Cambridge and all over England, that in protest against Beyfus's rejection you and Hugh are going to sleep a whole night together in Hugh's room in the Fellows' Garden Hostel of Lancaster College.'

'What's that got to do with Beyfus's rejection?'

'It's a magnificent gesture. You'll be breaking the oldest and strictest rule of them all. You'll be asserting your human right to freedom and to love.'

'Love,' said Hetta, 'is just as much fun in the afternoon.'

'But you have a *right* to love at night.'

'Beds that size are a bloody bore for a whole night,' said Hetta, 'and a girl needs her sleep. I'm quite happy with things as they are, thank you. A good fuck in the afternoon or soon after supper, and then home sweet home to cold cream and beddy-byes.'

'Your personal preference is not at issue,' said Hugh. 'The point is, we have a right to nights.'

'Do stop that ridiculous jingle,' Hetta said. 'A rightful Night full of Petting and Sweating,' she improvised. 'I just don't want it.'

'Well, you're bloody well going to have it.'

'Just think of the slogans we can get up,' said Mayerston. ' "They may muzzle Beyfus, but they can't Lock Out Love." You see the association? Love equals freedom equals Beyfus's proposals for co-educational hostels.'

'I can't imagine anything drearier.'

'You'd be the heroine of the campus.'

'They don't have a campus here,' said Hetta, 'and I don't want to be a heroine. I like being private.'

'If I can risk my career,' said Hugh, 'you can risk your privacy.'

'And that's another thing—it's all a wicked waste.

They'd just chuck you straight out of Cambridge the very next morning.'

'Just let them try,' said Mayerston with relish. 'We'd get up a mass demonstration. We'd threaten so much trouble they wouldn't dare.'

'Demonstrations,' said Hetta, 'threats. It's all people like you can think of. Why must there always be people like you,' she snarled at Mayerston, 'to come along and spoil things.'

Mayerston looked at Hugh, who came very close to Hetta.

'Hetta,' Hugh said, 'you do believe in all the things I've been teaching you? All the things we discussed last winter—you do believe in them, don't you, Het?'

'Yes. But what's that got to do with it?'

'A time comes, Het, when you have to show that you believe.'

'I'll tell anyone who wants to listen.'

'You have to *act*.'

'Is that what he says?'

She glared across at Mayerston.

'Not only him. And anyway, heart, it's true.'

He put his mouth to her ear and whispered. Hetta slumped.

'All right,' she said dully, 'I'll do it.'

'That's not enough. You must *want* to do it.'

Hetta made a great effort. She drew in her breath and shook her hair back and smiled up at Hugh.

'I believe you, Hugh, and I believe in you. I want to do it for your sake.'

'For its own sake.'

'For its own sake *and* yours.'

'All right, heart.'

Hugh looked up and nodded at Mayerston. Mayerston smiled back at him, and Hugh felt a rippling surge of satisfaction like that which comes to a man when he rises and stretches his muscles after a long day in a narrow seat.

'Tomorrow night, then,' Mayerston said.

'As soon as that?'

'Tomorrow night.'

'I've decided,' said Patricia to Tom out at Grantchester, 'that I'll do what you suggested last night. I'll take Baby to London to have her teeth done there.'

'Good. Take your time about the arrangements. I want you to have a really nice little holiday. You look tired.'

'So do you, Tom.'

'This Council meeting. I had to make two speeches.'

But Patricia wasn't interested in the Council.

'Tom,' she said, 'this afternoon, at that place down by the river, there was a boy and a girl having tea together on the lawn. I saw them when I was walking past with Baby. I'd seen the boy before—when I came to your college once.' She described the boy at some length. 'Can you tell me who it was?'

'Second year man called Balliston,' Hugh said. 'He reads rather good essays to the Cabbala.'

'The Cabbala?'

'College essay club. Why do you want to know about him?'

'He had a look of you. When we first met.'

'I hadn't noticed.'

'You wouldn't. It's not a resemblance, Tom, it's something in the eyes. He wanted something, just like you did then.'

'I wanted success.'

'You already had it.'

'And I wanted you.'

'Why?'

'Because I loved you.'

'There was something more . . . something different.'

'Very well. I also wanted somebody . . . before whom I

could bow down. Bow down and abase myself.'

'That's it,' Patricia said: 'that's what that boy wanted. But the girl who was with him was no good for that. *She* wanted to bow down to him.'

'He'll find someone suitable,' said Tom: 'there are plenty of father figures around the place for him.'

'*Father* figures?'

'The sex doesn't matter. It's just a question of finding someone convenient with a large pair of feet to grovel at. In Cambridge there are more male feet than female ones, so the odds are he'll end up venerating some don.'

'How unhealthy.'

'Why? Do you want him to venerate you?'

'Don't be so *silly*,' Patricia said, and went to heat up the tinned stew for supper.

'So they turned you down?' Mona said to Beyfus.

'Absolutely flat.'

'Then they must be *made* to understand.'

'So what do you want, Mona? That I should put a bomb under the table?'

'We must talk to people in London. There must be pressure.'

'But my dear, if this proposal of young Llewyllyn's goes through, people in London are going to be perfectly satisfied. A new building, they will tell each other, and sixty more undergraduates—what more can we ask for, they will say, than that?'

'It's not enough, Beyfus.'

'Everyone else thinks it is, Mona, except you.'

'And you, I should hope.'

'And me. And Tony Beck.'

'What will Tony Beck do about it?'

'I think he will try to make trouble through the students.'

'In that case, Beyfus, we must join in.'

'For God's sake, Mona. Do you want I should be carrying banners and throwing bricks? At my age?'

'If I can do it, so can you. And there's no need to throw bricks. We just lend our support by showing ourselves.'

'Exhibiting ourselves is what you mean. Like two creatures in the Zoo.'

'If you're going to talk like that, Beyfus, I shall leave.'

'No, Mona. Please stay.'

'Only if you promise to do what I say. After all, the students will be supporting you; why shouldn't you support them?'

'All right, Mona. I promise.' Beyfus heaved an enormous sigh. 'Provided you will always be there to.'

Mona grasped his hand for a moment.

'Silly old Beyfus,' Mona said.

'You were very quiet today,' said Tony Beck to Balbo Blakeney.

'I had nothing to say.'

'I should have thought that scheme of Llewyllyn's might have interested you. I can't support it, of course, but it sounded rather good.'

'I know a better,' Balbo said.

'Oh?'

'You're going to hate it.'

'Try me.'

'You wait till tomorrow.' Balbo giggled and postured like a garden dwarf. 'If I tell you tonight, you might have me murdered in my bed.'

'That Council again tomorrow?' said Mrs Constable in the Provost's Lodge.

'Tomorrow and tomorrow and tomorrow,' her husband replied.

'Oh dear . . . Shall I turn the television on?'

'Why?'

'There might be some news.'

'Do you remember,' said Constable, 'how in the old days the announcer on Radio sometimes simply said, 'There is no news tonight?'

'That can't happen these days. People feel entitled to news, so news there has to be.'

And news there was. When the television set had warmed up, a voice said:

'Late night news flash from Cambridge University.'

The grey screen flickered and heaved, then gave birth to a grinning and greasy young man with daintily permed hair.

'The students of Lancaster College, Cambridge,' said the young man in a superior brand of common voice, 'are preparing a protest against the rejection of a scheme proposed by Lord Beyfus, the well known expert on social problems, for the erection of new student hostels.'

The screen flicked, and a still picture of Lord Beyfus appeared.

'We understand that Mr Hugh Balliston, the well known Lancaster student, has invited his girl friend, Miss Hetta Frith, to spend tomorrow night with him on the college precincts, to claim the right of all students to self-determination and freedom of choice. No woman has spent the night in any part of Lancaster College, except the Provost's Lodge, since the college was founded over five hundred years ago.'

Lord Beyfus was replaced by a still of the Chapel.

'Our correspondent informs us that Mr Balliston's gesture is intended to draw the attention of the college authorities to the demands of youth and the future and to demonstrate student solidarity with Lord Beyfus and his radical proposals.'

Constable switched off the set and went back to his book (Spengler's *Decline of the West*).

'What are you going to do about *that*?' said Mrs Constable.

'I'll decide in the morning.'

'You could become a laughing stock.'

'If you don't mind, I'm trying to read.'

'You haven't much time, you know. Tomorrow night, the television said.'

'So I heard, and thank you. But as far as I am concerned, "There is no news tonight."'

When the Council was seated the next morning, Balbo Blakeney asked and obtained leave to make an 'orationem severiorem'.

Let him draw the Council's attention, Balbo said, to the chief glory of the college: its Chapel. It was for this, and for the music that was made inside it, that Lancaster was known all over the world. Now, at the moment the Chapel, as far as was known, was in excellent structural condition; but it would be no news to members of the Council that other and older buildings throughout the country were deteriorating so fast that they could hardly be held together even by the most expert and diligent repairs, which were, incidentally, costing astronomical sums of money. The reason for all this was very simple: the surveys conducted at the critical period, i.e. when the buildings had attained an age of about five hundred years, had been inexpert and negligent, with the result that small but important flaws, having been patched over or simply ignored, had spread and multiplied until they constituted a massive and often radical threat to the entire fabric. Had proper attention been paid when such flaws first appeared, had their basic causes been sought out and fully investigated when found, then an early and comparatively inexpensive programme of restoration would have secured the future safety of such buildings as, say, York and Canterbury for many centuries to come. As it was, York Minster was propped about by brackets and crutches like a paraplegic, and Canterbury Cathedral was permanently encased in scaffolding like an old whore in a corset.

'My point is,' said Balbo, 'that our own Chapel has now just reached the critical age when the first serious flaws and lesions must be expected to originate. I have already, I think, detected a crack in that section of the roof which is over the choir stalls. It is quite plain what we must do if we are to avoid the disasters which carelessness has occasioned elsewhere: we must start, now, on an exhaustive survey of the Chapel from the foundations to the pinnacles, find out what faults are developing, and have them aborted, so to speak, in the womb. I will not trouble you with technical details; but I must stress that this is *not* to be merely a perfunctory routine inspection: every angle must be measured and re-measured, every inch of fabric must be examined, and the setting of every last pane of glass must be checked and tested.

'Furthermore, it will be necessary to determine what effect the continual passage of motor traffic just outside the college is producing on the Chapel's structure. If motor cars are found to constitute the slightest threat,' said Balbo with relish, 'then they must be stopped. As a Royal Foundation, we have powers within the University and the Borough (or City, as I believe it now calls itself) which can easily encompass the compulsory diversion of traffic. It will also be necessary to compute whether or not a serious threat is posed to structure or fabric by other forms of modern beastliness, present or foreseeable, such as supersonic aircraft. In such cases, remedies may not be so easily found as with the cits and their motors, but we are not incapable of exerting pressure in the highest places.

'All in all, then, this survey and the work which will be done as a result of it will be both long and costly; but neither as long nor as costly as it would be in fifty or a hundred years' time, when labourers and artisans will doubtless be even more pampered and overpaid than they are now. Indeed, if we neglect this opportunity we might never be able to afford another. We are entrusted, gentlemen, with one of the finest buildings in Christendom. By taking a relatively easy course of action now, we can ensure its survival, in its present and excellent condition, for perhaps another thousand years. Postpone this course of action, and the small patch of rot which we might find and root out today will become the loathsome and pervasive disease which is past cure tomorrow . . . just as the spirochaete multiplies from the single primary sore until the whole body is a mass of festering ulcers—and down comes all.'

So far, Balbo's proposal had been sensible enough; after all, no one could seriously maintain that the preservation of one of the most famous buildings in the world was a frivolous or unworthy object. But all those who knew Balbo were aware that he would never rest content until he had contrived to hurt or annoy someone. Even his most sane and sound suggestions had to be used as weapons; in his hands, even the most peaceable instrument must somehow be converted into a bodkin that could puncture somebody's hide and be twisted in somebody's entrails. In the present case, it seemed almost impossible that so beneficient a scheme could be sharpened, as it were, to draw blood; yet everyone at the table knew that this would soon be contrived, the only question being how.

'In concrete terms,' said Balbo, 'I propose that £200,000 of the money which has come into our hands should be set aside to pay for an immediate Grand Survey of the Chapel and for the immediate action which that survey shows to be necessary. Any monies then remaining in this fund can be kept for the subsequent works which, however thorough we are now, time and chance are bound to impose on us. However, you will notice that of the quarter-million surplus there is still £50,000 for disposal; and I propose that it be used as follows:

'For the Choir School, gentlemen. The provision of sacred music of the proper standard is becoming annually more difficult and expensive. More difficult, because parents in this deplorable age think their children are better employed playing with technological gadgets than singing in choirs—even when they receive large bursaries to do so. More expensive, because private schools of the size of our own Choir School are now uneconomical to run. The Choir School contains twenty-four choristers and sixty others—a total of eighty-four. The economic figure for such a school is now estimated at a minimum of one hundred and fifty. The Choir School therefore runs at a substantial loss, reserves are being depleted, the headmaster is a worried man, petty saving, particularly on food and entertainments, is the order of the day, and morale is low.

'The result of all this is easy to see. The obtuseness of parents means that good choristers are harder, and in some years impossible, to come by; the standard of singing falls; and even that standard which is still maintained is compromised by the discontent and uneasiness which is induced in the choristers by the shoddiness and penury of their school. Children respond instinctively to such conditions—with cynicism, slackness and contempt.

'However, the standard of music is still tolerable. Our Chapel is not yet disgraced. All will be well if we spend money, first on increasing the choristers' bursaries and so winning over mean-minded parents, and secondly on subsidising the School itself, to the extent that it can become a place of which pupils—and, once more, parents—may be proud, instead of a third-rate lodging house. More money, much more money, for the Choir and the Choir School, gentlemen: a fund of fifty thousand pounds.'

So there was Balbo's twist. He was proposing that £50,000 of the college's money should be spent on a preparatory school, thus provoking to bitterness and rage all those who were hostile to the private system of education, but at the same time ensuring the support of all the conservatives, who could never resist baiting the left on this particular issue. It was therefore a brilliant exercise both in malice and tactics: there could be, for Balbo, no more certain way of mustering a dependable body of friends and of causing real pain to his enemies.

The attitudes expressed in the subsequent debate were predictable. Beyfus and Beck utterly condemned the notion that a great college should condone and enhance private privilege; Tom Llewyllyn regretted that a proposal in many ways so enlightened should be vitiated by such insolent disrespect of contemporary opinion in the field of education; and Clewes, the Chaplain, proclaimed that Christianity was concerned, not with monuments to its dead past, but with 'the sweet and humane spirit of its living future.' The conservatives, on the other hand, spoke blandly and smugly of their duty to preserve 'all that was precious in Architecture, Music and Religion' for the benefit of aspiring humanity and 'of the newly literate masses who now, for the first time, are educated to the higher enjoyments.' The more ill-tempered the left, the more smoothly public-spirited became the right; and at the end of it all Balbo's proposal was adopted for the short list by a vote of 13 to 7, the seven against it including Provost Constable. The Provost's vote, however, carried no more weight than any other man's; while the credit which the opposition might have had from his name and *auctoritas* was more than cancelled out by the shaming adherence of Clewes.

By the time the vote on Balbo's proposal had been taken, it was a quarter to one. So far, no reference had been made by any member of the Council to Hugh Balliston's threatened act of protest, although several of them, like Constable, had heard of it on television the night before and most of the rest had read short but prominent paragraphs about it in the morning newspapers. The reason for their reticence was one of protocol: Hugh's behaviour was an immediate matter for college discipline and might only be discussed, therefore, at the instance of one of the college officers, such as the Tutor or the Lay Dean, who were responsible in this field. Since the senior officer present who was directly concerned with discipline was the Provost himself, no one might raise the topic until he did; and since Constable's plan was to play the whole affair down, he had deliberately kept quiet about it when the Council assembled, in the hope that his omission would indicate to all that he did not regard Hugh or his protest as being of importance. Plainly, however, he must say something sooner or later, so he said it, briefly, now.

'This business of young Balliston and his woman,' he remarked; 'we shall simply ignore it. The college servants have been instructed to do likewise.'

'And the Press?' asked the Senior Fellow. 'The photographers?'

'If we ignore the whole thing and do nothing, there will be nothing for them to photograph. All that will happen is that at some time this evening Miss Frith and Mr Balliston will arrive at the Fellows' Garden Hostel and at some time tomorrow morning they will leave it again. A very dull picture that will make.'

'The other students may demonstrate in their defence,' said Andrew Ogden.

'If we do nothing, there will be nothing for the other students to defend them from.'

'They might stage a celebration.'

'What celebration?' said the Provost. 'If they wish to sing bawdy songs outside Mr Balliston's door, then as far as I'm concerned they are welcome.'

'They might form a sort of guard of honour ... with banners and things ... when the pair of them arrives at the hostel. That,' said Ivor Winstanley, 'would make quite a good photograph.'

'The public,' said Constable, 'is sick and tired of photographs of foolish young men with banners.'

'This one will have special interest ... in the circumstances ...'

'Just think of it,' said Balbo: 'banners saying FUCK FOR FREEDOM and things like that.'

'I have thought of it,' said Constable; 'and let me assure you all that provided you take no notice of this puerile protest, nothing more will be heard of it.'

He's got something up his sleeve, thought Tony Beck.

I hope Mona won't make me be in the guard of honour, thought Lord Beyfus.

I wonder whether I could bless the union as they go into the hostel, thought Oliver Clewes.

'So I rely on you, gentlemen,' said Constable with finality: 'if we behave as though nothing were happening, then in effect nothing will happen.'

We'll see about that, thought Tony Beck.

Although Patricia Llewyllyn hated Cambridge (with much the same sort of jealousy as other wives hate their husband's regiments or clubs), she loved the walk there from Grantchester along the river. Normally she had to go by bus, because the walk was too much for Baby, and this of course made her hate Cambridge all the more; but this morning, since she had managed to park Baby with a neighbour, she was free to go on foot, and her enjoyment of the journey mollified her feelings towards her place of destination.

In any case, it would have been unreasonable in her to resent Cambridge just now, as she was going there entirely of her own free will. Usually she went only if there was some necessary chore to attend to, like special shopping or a visit to Baby's dentist, but today she was going because she felt like it. She had no particular plan; there was nothing which she especially wanted to see; nobody was expecting her. She just felt like it. The walk will do me good, she thought: I need to get right away from Baby for a few hours. In which case, she thought, why am I not walking in the other direction, which would serve as well if not better for exercise? Why am I walking towards this town which fills me with loathing, as a rule, whenever I even think of it?

For the time being, it was easy enough to look down into the river reeds and evade the question. She imagined that she was in a punt, and that the punt was moored in among the reeds, secret from all the world, and that she was lying on her back looking up at the chasing clouds. The clouds were moving fast across the blue sky, but there was no wind where she lay in the punt; there was only the sun, warming her along all the length of her body, wooing her patiently and gently, yet gradually growing fiercer and more greedy as it rose from morning to noon. There was no one else there in the punt, only her, so she could take off her clothes if she wanted to and expose herself to the quickening rays . . .

She looked down at herself as she walked, imagining her large white limbs stripped and prone in the punt—and noticed, to her surprise, that she was wearing her best costume and a new pair of stockings. She had made no conscious decision, when dressing that morning, to put on any but her ordinary day clothes; yet here she was, dressed almost as if she were to meet someone for luncheon at Fortnum & Mason, her sister Isobel perhaps, except that she had no hat and was wearing sensible shoes. For a moment she panicked: had she indeed promised to meet Isobel in London that day, remembered when she got up but forgotten later? No, she told herself firmly. Lunch with Isobel at Fortnum's was in three days' time; she had arranged it on the telephone last night, so that they could discuss plans for when she brought Baby up to see the dentist. (She had hoped Isobel might ask them to stay in her house in Chelsea, but Isobel, though she seemed pleased they were coming, had made no mention of this on the telephone.) Confused and annoyed with herself, for she could not afford to wear out her best costume walking through meadows by the river, she found herself asking a second and more difficult question about the purpose of her walk. It was no longer, Why am I walking to this town I detest? It was, Why am I walking there all got up as I haven't been for years, except on special occasions?

Patricia shook her head and walked slowly on. Once more she looked down into the reeds by the margin of the river, and once more she willed herself into her secret punt, where she lay without moving, embraced by the kindly sun.

Hugh Balliston spent the morning reading Matthew Arnold's essays on Heine, Keats, Wordsworth and Shelley, and T. S. Eliot's essays on Arnold, Shelley, Wordsworth and Keats, in order to strike a balance. He analysed the limitations of Arnold as a critic and those of T. S. Eliot as a poet writing criticism. He considered the defects of Heine as deposed by Arnold and of Shelley as deposed by Eliot, and then calculated to what extent these really were defects, as opposed to being virtues from a proper understanding of which Arnold and Eliot were precluded by their limitations as earlier determined by himself. Having spent a very happy four hours doing all this, Hugh left the Fellows' Garden Hostel, walked through the Fellows' Garden, across the Queen's Road, and up the avenue past Scholars' Meadow, skirted the rear lawn and headed through the Great Court (without looking at the Chapel) towards the Lauderdale Gate, outside which he was to meet Hetta for lunch.

But before he was out of the Great Court, he was stopped by Tony Beck.

'I'm very glad to see you,' Hugh said. 'In your view, is Arnold sound on Heine?'

'Arnold's sound on most things, given his limitations. I've got a message for you to pass——'

'—Agreed. But what exactly were his limitations?'

'The same as yours,' said Tony Beck. 'At heart, he was an academic who wanted nothing to do with human life or emotions if he could possibly avoid it. When do you see Mayerston? To make final plans for tonight?'

'Early this evening,' said Hugh, his face falling at the thought.

'Well, pass this on. The old men have a plan to deal with this protest of yours. They're simply going to ignore it.'

'Good,' said Hugh.

'What's that?'

'I'm glad there's not going to be any trouble.'

'There'll be trouble,' said Beck, 'because trouble is what Mayerston wants. But it may be a bit harder to raise it if the old men deliberately don't react, so you'd best warn Mayerston what they're planning.'

'Anything else?'

'Yes. I think the Provost has some other plan in reserve in case the Press shows too much interest.'

'What plan?'

'He didn't tell the Council. Damned ill-mannered, I thought.'

'Could it be,' said Hugh, 'that he doesn't entirely trust some of the members?'

Hugh smirked and passed out through the gate. No Hetta—though he himself was five minutes late. But what there was was some kind of tourist woman, sitting on the low wall which marked off the College Stones, and eyeing him as if she wanted to eat him. I wonder, thought Hugh, very theoretically, if she'd pay me. And then: but isn't there something faintly familiar about her? That really rather fine and statuesque appearance, and that face, worn but commanding, like the Lady Volumnia's? However, there was no time for further reflection along these lines, as panting Hetta now arrived at the double.

'Bus late,' she spluttered.

'Never mind, heart. Lunch.'

He doesn't recognise me, thought Patricia Llewyllyn as Hugh and Hetta walked away. Well, why should he? We've never met properly. And after all, I ought to be content: I've *seen* him, which I suppose is why I came. But what shall I do now? I can't follow them. I can't go on sitting here. Would Tom give me lunch, if I went in and asked? But no, she thought, he'll be having a special lunch with that Council of his, all tucked away in private where no woman can get at them. I'd better just go home, she thought. Home to Baby. And not come here again. No one here wants me, not even Tom, and certainly not . . . *him.*

But if Patricia Llewyllyn didn't know where the Council was lunching, Mona Corrington did. She wasn't allowed in there, but she jolly soon had Lord Beyfus brought out.

'This protest,' she said; 'tonight in the Fellows' Garden Hostel.'

'What do you know about it?'

'More than you, I dare say. One of those young men telephoned from *The Observer*. He'd heard, he said, that there was to be a special demonstration when the young couple arrived at the hostel. Did I know who'd be there?'

'And did you?'

'I knew of two people, and so I told him: you, Beyfus, and me.'

'Hetta,' said Hugh: 'if you don't want to go through with this, you needn't.'

'Do you want to go through with it, Hugh?'

'I'm asking you, Hetta.'

Hetta gave him a stout look.

'Now you ask,' she said, 'I don't much care for the idea. But we've promised your friend, Mayerston, so there's no going back.'

After lunch, the Provost invited members of the Council to put up further proposals for spending their quarter of a million pounds. There were several such. Jacquiz Helmut suggested that the money should simply be invested and the considerable income used to award a series of lavish grants for travel and research; but the general view was that since a large investment had already been made with funds realised from the sale, the quarter million of profit should be spent *in toto* on some proportionable undertaking which would otherwise have been beyond their means. Grantchester Pough was in favour of a new boat-house which should include a modern gymnasium, an indoor swimming pool and all the facilities of a Kurhaus or health-centre—an idea which attracted so few others that it was not even debated. Finally, the Senior Tutor advocated the rebuilding of the College Library, which, as he pointed out, was badly overcrowded with books and was now almost impossible to work in. Enough members approved of this scheme for it to be put to debate; but despite a husky speech in its support by Daniel Mond, who reminded them that the library was the main point of the whole college, no more than 10 people voted for it at the finish.

So the upshot was that no further proposals were placed on the short list. This meant that there must now be a straight two-sided contest between, on the one hand, Tom Llewyllyn's motion for a single new building on Scholars' Meadow and, on the other hand, Balbo Blakeney's plan for surveying and restoring the Chapel and for subsidising the Choristers and their school. The comparative merits of both plans would be further debated the next day; and whichever of the two received the more votes, provided it also received a minimum of fifteen, would be finally adopted. After this, a committee would be formed to work out the details; but the general sense of the scheme adopted must be made public as soon as the Council rose, which should be, with any luck, by noon on the morrow. Although Constable would be very relieved, as he reflected, to prorogue this time-consuming assembly, he was not looking forward to the promulgation of its decision. For whichever way the vote went now, the plan he must announce would be a moderate one; and while he himself approved of this, he also knew that in an immoderate age nothing would be more suspect, more resented, more persecuted, than moderation.

'So you see,' said Mayerston to Hugh and Hetta in the Bath Hotel, 'however the old men may choose to react, we already have the publicity to make a very big splash. I tipped off the television people in time to get us a nice little puff last night. And the Press this morning was gratifying.'

'A bit too gratifying,' Hetta said. 'The Warden at Cherry

Hinton was on to me like a battleship.'

'How did you cope with that?'

'Cherry Hinton isn't a real college, only a kind of lodging house. The Warden's supposed to be a sort of sympathetic aunt—she's got no real power over what you do, provided you don't hold orgies in the place itself. But she did ring up my parents.'

'And how did you cope with *that*?'

'I rang them up myself a little later and told them not to worry, it was only a student rag. I'm fond of them, you see,' Hetta said, 'and I don't want them to be hurt.'

'A bourgeois attitude.'

'My attitude.'

'Well, you'll have a lot more to explain away to them tomorrow,' said Mayerston, 'if things go properly tonight. Because I've arranged a full-scale reception for you when you get to the Fellows' Garden Hostel, and the Press will be there in force.'

'You've *arranged* a reception?' Hugh said.

'The word's gone out all over Cambridge about what's happening, so a lot of people will turn up out of sheer curiosity. Among them will be certain special friends of mine who will ... liven things up.'

This made Hugh and Hetta very silent. Mayerston went over to the bar and bought them stiff whiskies.

'Drink this,' he said, 'and start smiling. Your carriage will be here in ten minutes.'

'Our *carriage*?'

'That's right. Horse-drawn. The Press likes a bit of a spectacle.'

'Spectacle is right,' Hugh said.

'The ground's damp,' said Beyfus; 'I knew I should have put on my galoshes.'

Beyfus and Mona were on their way to the demonstration.

'Never mind,' said Mona; 'I'll find you a nice dry place to

stand when we get there.'

'It's getting there that's the damp part.'

'For Christ's sake, Beyfus. Think of yourself as a soldier.'

'A soldier, she says. Next thing, she'll have bought me a cannon.'

Grantchester Pough, Jacquiz Helmut and Ivor Winstanley were approaching the hostel through the Fellows' Garden. It was very dark, and Ivor, who was slightly drunk, kept making spook noises to amuse himself.

'Wheee—aiiieee—eeecchh,' Ivor went. 'What time does the balloon go up?'

'We have plenty of time,' said Pough.

They went through a back door, which led into the hostel from the garden, and down a long white corridor. At the end of this was a college porter in a bowler hat, which he raised as they approached him.

'Everything in order, Powell?'

'Yes, sir. There's a lot of them out in the drive, but there hasn't been no trouble yet.'

'Good. Then we'll all just wait quietly in your office.'

Robert Constable was bringing his autobiographical matter up to date.

'A demonstration,' he wrote, 'is promised for this evening, but I am fairly confident that we have the situation in hand. What worries me, however, is that once this sort of thing starts, there is never an end of it. People get addicted to protest, just as actors get addicted to public performance or young guerrillas to drawing blood. And then again, it gives the idle and restless a specious excuse to neglect their work, on the grounds that they "are fighting for their beliefs" or "serving their ideals". Anything rather than mind their books.

'The problem of maintaining authority in such circumstances is almost insuperable. For if one quashes a protest, there is a further and probably more numerous demonstration to protest against the method of quashing; if one gives way and yields what is demanded, another demand follows the very next morning; and if one simply ignores the whole thing, the protestors are liable to walk right in and smash the furniture, for not to be noticed is more than they can endure. Nevertheless, I believe that the last policy is the best, always providing that one arranges certain safeguards, as I have done in this present case . . .'

When Beyfus and Mona turned into the asphalt drive which led up to the main entrance of the Fellows' Garden Hostel, what they saw was this.

On either side of the drive, which was lit by lamps similar in design to those in the yard of St James's Palace, were long lines of young people waiting amicably for something to happen. To the left of the hostel entrance was a small brass band in a travesty of Hussar uniform; in front of it was a group of mature young men, all of them unknown to Beyfus except for the fair-headed boy he had seen dining with Hugh Balliston in the Arts, and all of them dressed very much alike in elegant yet somehow proletarian garments of leather; and loitering about on the left were Tony Beck and Oliver Clewes, the former trying to pretend that the latter did not exist. Also scattered around the region of the entrance were some six photographers, two of whom were inspecting a pile of placards which lay directly in front of the leather-jackets.

As Mona and Beyfus started uncertainly up the drive, Tony Beck walked up to the fair-haired boy and drew his attention to them; whereupon the fair-haired boy gave a flick of his hand, the band played several bars of a fanfare, and a number of leather-jackets took placards from the pile and raised them aloft. These were of ingenious fabrication, their messages being spelt out in small electric light bulbs which the bearers could switch on and off. Most of the slogans seemed to be about Sexual or Academic Freedom, but at least three, Beyfus noticed, were about Beyfus, and they were extremely flattering in their purport. One proclaimed him the prophet of the new liberty, the second demanded that he be given a fresh hearing by the Council of Lancaster, and the third appeared to assert his virility—BEYFUS, it announced, FOR SEX. Confused but rather pleased, heartened by the polite applause of the boys and girls who were flanking the drive, Beyfus went trotting on towards the hostel, Mona striding at his side, and was about thirty yards short of it, when there suddenly came from behind him a loud PIM-POM PIM-POM PIM-POM, and he found that he had been snatched off the drive, by two solicitous young men, only just in time not to be run down by a large ambulance which careered on up to the entrance. (Mona, who had resisted a similar rescue party, very nearly bought her lot.)

What happened now was stately and impressive. The figure of the porter, Mr Powell, came out through the swing doors with the measured dignity of a Major-Domo and gestured coolly to a second porter, who emerged behind him. Mr Powell held back one swing door, his colleague the other; and in the frame thus provided there appeared the Honourable Grantchester FitzMargrave Pough, limping very badly and supported on either side, indeed virtually carried, by Jacquiz Helmut and Ivor Winstanley. An ambulance man ran to their assistance; the driver of the vehicle started to turn it round (not an easy matter in the small space available); and Mr Powell approached the photographers. Removing his bowler hat with regal courtesy, he started to address them. Beyfus, who by this time had worked his way nearer the entrance, caught the phrase, 'Gentlemen of the Press', followed by others such as 'celebrated attempt on Everest', 'bad fall on his evening walk in the garden', 'feared gravely injured'. Meanwhile, the leather-jackets had been compelled to make way for the crippled man and his attendants, the band had been dispersed by the sorties of the turning ambulance, and many of the placards had been trampled on by people anxious to get a closer look at what was doing.

Just as the Senior Fellow was being lifted into the ambulance, there was a hubbub at the far end of the drive. Some sort of horse-drawn conveyance, it seemed to Beyfus, had tried to gain admittance; but since the kindly and intelligent spectators had realised that the drive was too narrow to accommodate both this carriage and the ambulance *en passant,* the former was now being waved firmly on down the road. Immediately after this a different hubbub started up at the hostel end of the drive, this caused by the gentlemen of the Press, who, having avidly photographed the disabled Pough, were now clamouring to be allowed to accompany this still famous man in the ambulance and get his statement of what had occurred; for although Mr Powell had been very plain that Pough was hurt by a fall, the reporters, who belonged to a simple-minded class of person, insisted on somehow connecting the injury with the demonstration they had come to witness. Since they would not be put off, Pough graciously yielded; whereupon the ambulance hurtled off into the night, taking every reporter and every camera with it.

By this time, the crowd had already begun to disperse, feeling, as assembled Englishmen always do in the case of death or accident, that decent respect for suffering required no less of them.

'They're all going home,' said Hetta to Hugh.

They were sitting in an open landau some way down the road from the entrance to the hostel drive. Out of this the crowd was now streaming, turning away, for the most part, in the direction of the Queen's Road. The few people who came down towards the landau walked sedately past, ignoring it completely.

'That ambulance which came out,' said Hugh: 'someone must have been hurt.' And then to their coachman, 'What are your instructions?'

'I were to put you down at the Fellows' Garden Hostel of

Lancaster College,' the man said in a heavy fenland accent, 'and that were all.'

'Well, I think you'd better go home. Thank you very much.'

Hugh climbed out and helped Hetta down. The landau drove off along the road, away from the diminishing crowd.

'I wonder,' said Hetta, 'where on earth Mayerston found that thing.'

Mayerston came out of the drive, paused, spotted them, waved, and walked down towards them.

'Well?' said Hugh.

'Home,' said Mayerston. 'Never reinforce failure.'

'What happened?'

'I'm not quite sure, and I don't much care. The important thing is to do better next time.'

Hugh's heart sank within him. If only Mayerston had not been so cool and unconcerned, if only he had shown depression or ill temper, then Hugh would have warmed to him, would have soothed him with kind words and listened to excuse. But as it was, Mayerston's confidence about 'next time' and his bland assumption that everyone else shared it made Hugh so miserable and so hostile that suddenly, for want of any other relief, he stamped his foot hard on the pavement.

'How much more have I got to put up with?' he snapped.

'Come, come,' said Mayerston; 'beaten already?'

'It was such an anti-climax.'

'So that's it,' said Mayerston. 'The star of the evening was cheated of his role.'

'It isn't that at all. It's the waste of time.'

'I don't know,' said Hetta, wanting pleasantness. 'It was a lovely ride. Where did you get that landau?'

'I saw it in a farmyard near Waterbeach, when I was out there walking. I like long walks,' Mayerston said: 'you must both come with me one day.'

And all at once the idea of lazing through the countryside with Mayerston, in quest of landaus and God knew what other curiosities, seemed so attractive that Hugh forgot to be angry and petulant and was eager to start walking that very moment.

'When?' he said. 'When shall we go?'

'We'll arrange it when we all meet tomorrow,' said Mayerston, 'which will be at 6 p.m. in the lounge of the University Arms. Bye-bye till then.'

He saluted Hetta and strode off towards the Queen's Road.

'No point in hanging round out here,' said Hugh. 'Want to come in to the hostel?'

'You heard what Mayerston said. It's all off.'

'There's no reason why you shouldn't come in for half an hour. It's still quite early.'

'For once,' said Hetta, 'just for once, I simply don't feel like it. Anti-climax, I suppose, like you said. I think I'll walk up through Lancaster and get a bus.'

'Want me to come?'

'I know the way,' said Hetta, 'so it would be rather a waste of your time, now wouldn't it?'

In the summer the back gate of Lancaster was left open until ten o'clock. As it was now only just after nine-thirty, Hetta's notion of walking up to her bus through the college was entirely feasible. But things did not go quite as she had planned.

In the end, Hugh saw her over the Queen's Road and waved her off through the back gate. Since she was irritated with Hugh, who, she felt, had been both querulous and grovelling towards Mayerston, she hardly returned his wave but stuck her nose in the air and lit off at a smart light infantry pace. Half way up the Avenue, however, she began to feel that she had been petty and unkind. After all, Hugh had offered to take her to her bus, which was pretty good as manners in Cambridge went nowadays, and there was certainly no reason why she should not have said a proper goodnight. Never part in anger, her mother always said.

Thinking of all this, Hetta slowed to a dawdle and then to a complete halt, wondered whether she shouldn't go back, imagined how nice it would be in Hugh's bed with Hugh on top of her (Marx, Castro, Che, whatever could have made her say she didn't feel like it?), turned round, thought how cross Hugh would be to see her if he had started on some work, turned back again bus-wards—and found herself looking straight into a gnomish face.

'Balbo Blakeney,' said the face.

'I know,' said Hetta. As part of her course in Pediatrics she had once had to attend a special lecture by Balbo on abnormal blood-conditions in infant children.

'And I know a bit about you, Miss Hetta. I've got something to tell you. Come and have a drink.'

'I was just going to get my bus.'

'You didn't seem too sure about that. Anyway, Missy, you ought to hear what I've got to say. It's about your young man.'

'Hugh?'

'Young Balliston.'

So Hetta, who was of a trusting disposition, suffered herself to be led away to Balbo's room and given a huge glass of the vintage cognac.

'Now then,' said Balbo, 'I'm not the interfering type, but I've got you up here to warn you. To warn you to warn young Balliston. Because if he doesn't take care he's going to spoil a very good thing.'

'Why not tell him yourself?'

'He wouldn't listen to me. He thinks I'm a fascist hyena.'

'So do I.'

'But you're a woman, so you'll listen to what a man tells you. And what it all comes down to is this. Tony Beck—that's what it comes down to. Tony's got young Balliston into all this, but he won't lift a finger to get him out of trouble—not unless it suits his book, and that book's so complicated that there's no knowing what'll suit it for two minutes together.'

'How do you know?'

'I know Beck. And a very amusing fellow I find him. But he's no good for young Balliston. Young Balliston's got a great deal going for him, but he'll lose the lot if he listens to Tony Beck?'

'Why are you taking all this trouble? You're not on Hugh's side. If you had your way, Hugh and everyone like him would be kicked right out of this college. You'd never have let him come here in the first place.'

'Wrong, Missy. He's a scholar, and here we've always liked scholars. Anyhow, I thought that by telling you this I'd be doing *you* a good turn. I like the look of you, Miss Hetta; I like it a lot.'

And Hetta found herself liking the look of Balbo Blakeney. Well, not exactly his look, she told herself, but his fatherly approach. Being given advice by Balbo was a curiously warming experience. So in order to lengthen her stay she told Balbo about Mayerston.

'I've heard a bit about him,' said Balbo. 'Tell me, where does he come from?'

'No one seems to know. But what bothers me is this hold he's got over Hugh. It bothers Hugh too.'

'Then tell him to cut loose.'

'He can't. He starts to sometimes, but Mayerston always knows exactly what to say to him, and Hugh falls flat on his face worshipping.'

'Not good, Miss Hetta. You want to pump some sense into him.'

'But it's so difficult. Because in a way Hugh's quite right to admire Mayerston. Mayerston's trying to do something that really matters.'

'That's what makes him dangerous. Beck's bad enough, Missy, but people see through Beck, and that's an end of it. They don't see through Mayerston because he believes in what he's doing.'

'And so does Hugh. And so do I.'

'I can't say anything about that. But look at it this way.

What is young Balliston best at in all the world?'

'His English,' said Hetta without hesitation.

'Then tell him to stick to that. People should do what they're best at—if they're lucky enough to have the chance.'

'I suppose you're right,' said Hetta, who was liking Balbo more and more. 'But how can I convince Hugh?'

'Lysistrata.'

'Lysistrata?'

'A Greek play, Missy. All the girls in Athens told the men, "No more nice games of hot cockles until you stop this ridiculous war." '

'Oh,' said Hetta doubtfully; 'did it work?'

'Yes.'

'But that was a play.'

'Can you think of a better plan?'

'No.'

'Then try this one,' said Balbo; 'and if you want a shoulder to cry on, you know your way here.'

When the College Council assembled the next morning, the Provost made a brief statement:

'As most of you will have heard,' he said, 'nothing came of the student demonstration planned for last night. A crowd did indeed gather by the Fellows' Garden Hostel, among whom there was evidently a small body of organisers, these being equipped with placards and so forth. In so far as they had time and opportunity to display this apparatus, it would seem that they were protesting against our recent rejection of the proposal by our colleague, Lord Beyfus, that large experimental hostels should be built on Scholars' Meadow and the rear lawn.'

Lord Beyfus shifted his papers about and looked silly.

'However,' Constable went on, 'before the demonstration could reach any kind of climax, a regrettable accident, totally unconnected with the demonstration itself, occurred to the Senior Fellow in the garden nearby. The arrival of an ambulance effected what could not have been achieved by a whole brigade of policemen—i.e. the immediate and peaceful dispersal of the crowd. There is a moral here, on which those who advocate strong measures on such occasions might care to reflect.

'All reporters present transferred their attention to Mr Pough. The student Balliston entered the hostel unaccompanied and without incident at about 9.45 p.m. There is no report of the demonstration in the morning papers. Finally, you will be glad to know that the Senior Fellow, though unable to be with us here today, has returned to his rooms in college, where he is entirely comfortable in the care of the college nurse.'

Tony Beck pulled a sceptical face.

'This is all very well, Provost,' said Andrew Ogden; 'but we cannot suppose that this will be the last of these demonstrations, and the next time one occurs we cannot rely on the opportune arrival of an ambulance.'

'We can continue to rely,' said the Provost, 'on a show of dignified indifference ... and on the uses of our own good sense. And now, gentlemen, to the business of the day. I have before me on my short list two proposals, as to the relative merits of which I now invite you to discourse and arbitrate...'

'Castro,' squawked Hetta, 'it's never been so marvellous. Castroooo. Equaliteeeeee. Che ... Che ... Cheeee.'

A little later Hugh got off the bed and washed himself while Hetta looked lovingly on. But when he came back to her, she pulled herself together and prepared to tell Hugh what she was now convinced that she must say to him before it was too late.

'What time,' she began, 'are we due at the University Arms? To meet Mayerston?'

'Six o'clock, he said last night.'

'Well, don't let's go.'

'Hetta?'

'Don't let's go.'

Hugh stretched himself beside her on the narrow bed and began to fidget nervously with one of her thighs.

'Listen, Hugh,' said Hetta, taking this as a promising sign, 'you've done your bit. Ooowwwh,' she said, as he pinched a piece of thigh.

'Sorry, Het. Didn't mean to hurt.'

'You've done all that he can expect. You agreed to make this protest last night, and you did everything he asked——'

'—You too, Het——'

'And it's not our fault it went wrong. Now it's all over and we want nothing more to do with him.'

'We can't just walk out on him now. What he's doing is work that should be done. Anyway, I'm committed.'

'No, you're not,' said Hetta evenly.

It was clear to her that Hugh was ready to listen, because otherwise she would already have been silenced and sent home. The problem was, how to go on from here. She wondered whether to tell Hugh what Balbo Blakeney had said, but decided that any overt reference to Balbo would certainly weaken her case.

'You promised to help Mayerston with his work,' she now said carefully, 'but that work isn't what you thought it was. Can't you understand, Hugh? He's just trying to smash everything to pieces.'

'Only as a beginning. So that he can rebuild it all from scratch.'

'No, Hugh.' She pushed Hugh's hand away from her crutch, at which his fidgeting fingers had now arrived, and replaced it with her own. 'Smashing things is all that interests Mayerston, and he won't care the teeniest bit if he smashes you as well. And if that happens, don't think Tony Beck will help you either.'

'How can you know all this?'

Hugh's voice was cross but also uncertain. He was still ready to listen.

'. . . I just feel it. I love you, Hugh, and I feel . . . I *know* . . . that you're in danger. You've got so much, Hugh, so much that's worth doing. Why risk it all for Mayerston and Tony Beck?'

'To hell with Tony Beck. But Mayerston's another thing. I think, I *believe*, that his ideals are worth fighting for.'

Oh God, thought Hetta miserably, if only I could talk like he does, make things plain in the way he can. How shall I convince him? How?

'I've told you,' she said: 'all Mayerston wants is to pull everything down. Pull it down, and leave a pile of ruins, and move on.'

'So you say. And I say he wants to build something far finer instead. Why should I be wrong, Hetta?'

The question was not rhetorical. His voice was pleading with her to find a reason.

'Listen, lovely Hugh,' she said. 'Of all things in this world I love being here with you like this. But now I've got my hand over my cunt, and there it stays until you agree that you'll have nothing more to do with Mayerston. And if you don't agree, I shall get up off this bed, and put my clothes on, and go home, and I shan't make love with you ever again—until you break with Mayerston. It will half kill me to do it, but do it I shall, because I believe, believe, believe, darling Hugh, that you must free yourself, while you still can, from this man Mayerston.'

There, she thought. I've said all this because of you, Balbo Blakeney; because you wanted to help me and I trusted what you said. But what help can you be, kind as you are, Balbo Blakeney, if Hugh denies me? For if Hugh denies me, then I must keep my hand on my cunt and deny him (though at this very moment I long to open my legs to him as wide as the golden gates of heaven), and what help can you be then? You offered me your shoulder to cry on, but what use is a shoulder to a girl like me?

'And my promise to Mayerston?' Hugh said quietly.

'He got it under false pretences.'

Hugh put his hand on Hetta's and tried to move it, but it clung as tight as an oyster shell. Refusal roused him further; he seized Hetta's free hand and placed it on his groin; but the hand just fell limply away from him.

'You mean it, Het.'

'Yes.'

'You're crying, Het.'

'Yes.'

'Why, Het?'

'Because it breaks my heart, but I'm going to do it.'

With a burst of blubbering and a flurry of her splendid limbs Hetta heaved herself over Hugh and off the bed.

'Wait.'

She waited.

'If I . . . do what you want, I must tell him. I must go to the University Arms, where he'll be expecting us at six o'clock, and tell him straight out that I'm finished. I can't just leave him there. You do see that?'

Hetta stood pondering by the bed, then nodded.

'Well then?' he said.

He held out his hand to her. She shook her head.

'Not until you've gone and come back.'

'But if I promise you, Het?'

'Not until you've told him.'

'I swear that I will tell him as soon as I see him this evening. You can come yourself and hear me.'

'You swear, Hugh?'

'Yes, heart. Come to bed.'

'Go on, then: swear.'

'I've already sworn.'

'Swear again.'

So Hugh swore a second time; and then Hetta—trusting, randy Hetta—leapt blithely on to the bed and opened her legs as wide as the golden gates of heaven, that her lover might come in.

'So they're still talking,' said Mayerston to Tony Beck in the lounge of the University Arms.

'Yes . . . though I think we'd all hoped to get the Council

finished with today. But it seems a lot of people have a lot on their minds. Some reckon that Llewyllyn's idea is a sensible compromise which will keep the college out of trouble or controversy for a long time to come, and this appeals very much. They'd all like to feel safe.'

'Then why don't they settle for that?'

'Because Balbo Blakeney has struck a strong chord. They're proud of their chapel, and they see the sense in his suggestions for preserving it.'

'And his suggestion about the Choir School?'

'As most of 'em see it, that's pretty sound as well. If you're going to have a Choir and a Choir School, you may as well pay a bit extra and do the thing properly.'

'When will the debate be finished?'

'Some time tomorrow, I'd say. There's nothing more to be said, but there are still a few who'll want to repeat what's been said already.'

'Which way will it go?'

Beck shrugged.

'Does it matter?' he asked. 'You'll be against them whatever they decide.'

'It could make a difference to our tactics. For example,' said Mayerston, 'if they should decide to spend the money on the Chapel, well, the Chapel is actually standing there as a . . . possible centre of our activity.'

Beck raised an eyebrow and said nothing.

'But until we know the Council's decision,' Mayerston said, 'we can only be sure of our overall strategy. This must be to go on mounting protests and demonstrations until finally the authorities are compelled to take some action.'

'Such as?'

'Sooner or later they will have to discipline somebody. They'll probably panic and do it clumsily, but even if they behave calmly and sensibly, their act can be misrepresented so as to stir up the indignation of a great mass of moderate students, who will hitherto have had nothing to do with us.'

'You're sure they'll join you?'

'Yes. Suppose things had gone better last night, and suppose Hugh Balliston had been sent down——'

'—But that's just the point,' said Tony Beck. 'The Provost was quite determined that no one should be sent down. As he said, if we ignore what is happening, then in effect nothing will have happened.'

'He can't go on like that. Sooner or later, if we keep making a nuisance of ourselves, your Provost or somebody else in the University will have to put his foot down. If he loses his temper first, so much the better, but in any case at all down will come his foot——'

'—Preferably on Hugh Balliston——'

'—Or some equally respected individual, and then we shall have a martyr. Once we have a martyr, the big battalions will rally round him at our call, as has been their habit throughout history. From being a mere nuisance, we shall have become a serious threat.'

'And then?'

'As you know,' said Mayerston, 'I have a number of skilled assistants. These will immediately assume leadership of the battalions, in the way they have been trained to do and then we shall be ready to strike.'

'Strike at what?'

'As I've already indicated to you,' said Mayerston blandly, 'that question is best deferred until we know which way the Council has decided. Some time tomorrow, you think?'

'Yes,' said Beck sullenly, and put his head on one side.

'And meanwhile,' said Mayerston, 'we must revert to the phase which we are actually in. Our job at this moment is to provoke authority into making a martyr for us.'

'Well, here's your boy,' said Tony Beck, as Hugh Balliston entered the lounge.

'I wonder where the girl is.'

'Do you need her again?'

'No. But she was invited to come here. If properly

handled, she has a useful influence on Balliston.'

Although Mayerston could not know it, the reason why Hetta, the 'useful influence', had stayed away was to show Hugh that she trusted him to keep his oath without her supervision. Hugh himself was very touched by this delicacy of spirit; and now, as he looked round the lounge and signalled recognition to Mayerston, he was determined to be worthy of it. He advanced on Beck and Mayerston with poker face and measured tread.

'Drink?' said Mayerston.

'No thanks. I've only come to tell you that from now on you must do without me.'

'Now you look here——' began Tony Beck.

Mayerston gave him a quick look which killed the rising words.

'You look tired, Tony,' Mayerston said. 'You need a rest and a bath before your dinner. See you tomorrow.'

Beck opened his mouth, stopped another of Mayerston's looks, then heaved himself up and shambled out.

'Not a good man when things go wrong,' said Mayerston, raising one arm. 'Now sit down, Hugh, and have a drink.'

Hugh remained standing. A waiter appeared beside him. Mayerston looked from Hugh to the waiter and back again.

'What'll it be?' Mayerston said.

'... er ... a pint of bitter, please.'

'No pints in the lounge, sir.'

'A half of bitter.'

'No draught beer in the lounge, sir.'

'A lager.'

The waiter withdrew and Hugh sat down on the chair which had just been vacated by Tony Beck.

'We must arrange that walk,' said Mayerston. 'Some time next week, perhaps? I shall want to know how you're getting on.'

'You needn't worry about that,' said Hugh. 'I have a great deal of interesting work to do, and I shall get along very nicely.'

'I don't doubt it. But I shall want to know your opinion of what's happening. You see,' said Mayerston, 'there'll be quite a lot happening in the next few days, and naturally I'll be glad to hear what impression it's made on a ... spectator whose intelligence I respect.'

The waiter brought Hugh's lager.

'Who said anything about being a spectator?' Hugh said. 'We shall have plenty to say in Lancaster about all this, and we're quite capable of standing up to the Council. In our own way, Mayerston, which isn't yours.'

'You disapprove of my way?'

'It's too extreme.'

'We went into all this the other night, Hugh. You seemed quite satisfied then.'

Hugh took an unhappy gulp of lager.

'I liked you,' he said, 'very much. And I still do. But I've come to understand——'

'—*Liked me?*' said Mayerston. 'You said you *believed*.'

'I believe in your ideals but not your methods. They're so wasteful.'

There was an echo here ('It's all a wicked waste,' Hetta had said) and Mayerston was quick to catch it.

'Ah,' he said. 'So little Miss Hetta, the girl from the home counties, has been having second thoughts. Hetta, the play-time revolutionary, has discovered that the toys are sharp and dangerous after all, so she's taken her little Hughie by the hand to bring him indoors to bed.'

Hugh went scarlet.

'Hetta believes as I do,' he said. 'She wants equality and justice. Not blood.'

'Who said anything about blood? I'm disappointed in you, Hugh. An intelligent and independent man, as I thought, but what do I find? You've been got at by a woman.'

'That's not true.'

'Oh, but it is. You're like a suburban husband who's been nagged at by his wife because he wants to change his job. "What'll become of me and the kiddies?" ' he trilled, in a very fair imitation of Hetta. ' "What'll become of our dear little semi-detached?" So of course the poor sad sod knuckles under in two minutes flat. But at least he's got the excuse that he has his children to care for, whereas you, Balliston, all you're thinking of is yourself and your books and someone to tickle your knob. You're throwing me over because you want to go on writing your precious essays and being told how clever you are by a silly slut from Surrey who doesn't know Kafka from Cavafis but thinks you've got a cute prick. I'll tell you what it is with you, Balliston: you're just a mimsy little scholarship boy who's been swallowed whole by a cunt.'

Hugh was not certain which in all this he disliked the more—the venom or the obscenity. Never before had Mayerston shown a trace of either. But there was also something else which Hugh found more sickening than both together: the substantial truth of the accusation. For he had (he could not deny it) been won over by Hetta's tears, by her appeal to him not to throw himself away, and last but not least by her threat to refuse him his pleasure. He had, in truth, been got at by a woman.

'You're not to talk about Hetta like that,' he said feebly.

'I'm sorry,' said Mayerston, smiling penitence, 'but I hate to see a good man breaking up. People like Tony Beck, it doesn't matter what happens with them. But you, Hugh . . .'

'You shouldn't have said those things. It wasn't like you.'

'No. But I was upset. Wounded. Betrayed.'

First contempt, thought Hugh, now sorrow; and the sorrow because I gave cause for contempt.

'Perhaps I was too sudden,' he said.

'No. Better be sudden than equivocate. You were quite right, Hugh. You've got your life to live, when all's said.' Mayerston lifted his glass of Pimm's and took a long drink. 'Now then; about that walk. I thought we'd drive out to Cottenham and take the footpath over the fields to——'

'—I don't want to hear about anything else until we've

cleared this up first. I must know what to believe, Mayerston. You said you wanted to destroy in order to build. Hetta says you want to destroy in order to destroy. Which is true?'

'Although Hetta is an honest girl, Hugh, she is not a clever one. She hasn't understood.'

'Hasn't she, Mayerston? Can you prove she's wrong?'

Mayerston leaned forward, took both Hugh's hands in his, and looked straight into his eyes. Mayerston's irises were blue flecked with brown, by no means an unusual arrangement, except that the brown flecks seemed somehow to recede, as though some were more distant than others, as though they were minute clouds in a tiny sky, some riding higher than the rest and others higher still, so that as Hugh looked from one to the next he was drawn on and upwards into a blue empyrean that had no end, until he was hanging there in space, way up above the highest of the little brown clouds, supported only by the warm, dry, infinitely reassuring clasp of Mayerston's soft hands.

The hands released his; there was a terrible moment of panic as he started to fall, very fast, from what must surely be an immense height; then the hands clasped his again, and he was sitting in the lounge of the University Arms.

'You must believe me,' Mayerston said, gently kneading Hugh's wrists. 'Hetta means well, of course; but between you and me, Hugh, there is a different and much more powerful link. You felt what happened just now? When I let you go for a moment.'

Falling and falling, faster and faster, from a great height . . . Hugh nodded bleakly.

'You understand then?' said Mayerston. 'Next time I let you go, Hugh, it will be for good.'

Despite her resolution not to come near Lancaster again, Patricia had once more parked Baby and walked into Cambridge, where she had spent most of the afternoon hanging round the College Stones, hoping to see Hugh.

Since Hugh had been in bed with Hetta, Patricia had been out of luck; and after Wilfred the porter, who recognised her, had come out of the lodge for the third time and asked her whether he should fetch Mr Llewyllyn, she had given up and gone back to Grantchester.

By a quarter to six that evening (at which hour, had she still been on the Stones, she would have seen Hugh leave Lancaster *en route* for the University Arms) she had made up her mind what to do. First, she rang up her sister Isobel; then she started to pack for herself and Baby; and then, as soon as Tom arrived home, she said:

'I've decided to take Baby up tomorrow. Isobel's fixing rooms in a hotel.'

'Rather sudden?'

'I want to go at once.'

'As you like,' said Tom, who was too tired, after his day at the Council, to wonder why. 'Have you arranged with the dentist?'

'No. I'll do that when we get up there. Isobel knows a good man that Gregory goes to.'

'It may be some time before he can give Baby an appointment.'

'Gregory will arrange about that.'

'Gregory or no Gregory, it may take some time.'

'Then I'll have to stay longer,' snapped Patricia. 'Do you really care?'

'I want you to enjoy yourself. Not just to hang around up there waiting on the convenience of a dentist.'

'And what do I do down here—except wait on the convenience of Tom Llewyllyn?'

'One of the porters tells me,' said Tom in a puzzled voice, 'that you were waiting on the College Stones for two hours this afternoon. Was it me you were wanting?'

'No,' said Patricia, 'it was not.'

'Then what's all this about waiting on my convenience?'

'It's your fault,' she said, 'that I was waiting there. And it's your fault that I'm going to London a full week early and with nothing properly arranged. But I shouldn't let that bother you, because now you can do what you've wanted to for years—you can go and live in that precious college of yours until I get back.'

'And when will that be?'

As there was real anxiety in his voice, Patricia relented slightly.

'I'll let you know as soon as I can,' she said.

'Yes, please do,' Tom said seriously. 'The college is having great trouble getting servants these days, and the Domestic Bursar will want to know how long I'll need a bedmaker.'

Hetta was waiting for Hugh when he returned from the University Arms to the Fellows' Garden Hostel. Since Hugh had had a large dinner with Mayerston and Hetta had only had scrambled eggs, which she had cooked over the gas-ring in the gyp-room, Hugh was at a strong advantage.

'You're wrong about Mayerston,' Hugh said.

Hetta shrivelled slightly and said nothing.

'He's convinced me that he means what he says,' Hugh went on belligerently; 'so I must stick to him, Hetta. Can you understand that?'

Hetta still said nothing.

'Can you understand that?'

'You swore to me,' said Hetta. And then, in a very small, tired voice, 'How did he convince you?'

'He ... he just did,' blustered Hugh. 'You wouldn't understand. You haven't understood anything.'

'I suppose not,' said Hetta. 'Do you know, it just did not occur to me that you could break your oath?'

'I only swore because you said that Mayerston was a fraud. He only wanted to destroy, you said. Since I now know that's not true, I am absolved from my oath.'

'You swore,' said Hetta, 'because I wouldn't let you have me until you did.'

'That's not true. I meant to keep my word, and I did . . . at first. I went straight up to him and told him it was all over.'

'And then?' said Hetta. 'I suppose he talked you around.'

'Yes. But in a very special way.' Hugh shook his head angrily. 'You couldn't understand.'

'I'm tired of being told that. I think I shall go.'

'Het . . . I'm doing what I know to be right. You won't desert me now?'

'No, Hugh. I shall come to you and listen to you whenever you wish. But I meant what I said: I shan't make love with you again until you've broken with Mayerston.'

'But I've just told you. I can't.'

Hetta shrugged miserably and moved towards the door.

'Tell me one thing,' she said: 'what does he want you to do now?'

'It's a secret. It has to be. You'll find out when it happens—which will be soon enough.'

'Hugh . . . sweet Hugh . . . don't do anything to make them send you away from here.'

'How like a woman. All you can think of—degrees, careers, respectability.'

'I'm not thinking of that. I'm thinking of the work you love so much.'

This went home. At first Hugh's face just crumpled; then it reassembled itself, only to fall to pieces again in sheer fury.

'God damn you to hell, you blackmailing bitch,' he screamed. 'Stop interfering, will you? Just stop interfering and get out.'

Hetta got out, smiling and waggling her fingers to him, out of old habit, as she went.

'That's bad, Miss Hetta,' said Balbo. 'That's very bad.'

After leaving Hugh, Hetta had come to cry on Balbo's shoulder.

'Oh, Mr Blakeney,' she sobbed, 'what shall I do?'

'Put your head in my lap,' Balbo said. 'Sit there, on the floor, and put your head in my lap.'

This was taking fatherly behaviour a little too far. Hetta's face went rigid and she shook her head.

'Don't be scared, Missy. I know what's good for you.'

He put an arm round her waist, a surprisingly strong arm, and forced her slowly off the sofa and on to the floor. Then, holding her down with both his hands on both her shoulders, he shifted his own position in order that he might clasp her between his knees.

'Don't be scared,' he said.

Hetta wasn't scared, but she regarded all this as uncalled for. When she tried to get up, she found that Balbo's knees had her tight. When she tried to wriggle out frontways, all she managed to do was to turn slightly, so that now, when Balbo leaned forward, his stomach pressed against her cheek.

'What are you going to do?' she said.

'What your mother did when you were small.'

Balbo produced a comb from his breast pocket and started to comb her hair. Sometimes he scratched, very delicately, at the roots; sometimes he passed the comb firmly but strongly through the long outer tresses; sometimes he stretched a lock taut from the scalp and played the comb over it as a violinist might play his bow over the strings. Whatever he did was soothing and delicious; before very long Hetta relaxed completely, sticking her legs out over the floor and nestling her face against Balbo's friendly little pot.

'What shall I do, Mr Blakeney?' she murmured. 'What shall I do about Hugh?'

'From what you say,' said Balbo, steadily and sensitively combing, 'he's infatuated. Only one thing you can do, Missy. Let him go his ways and get ready to pick up the pieces.'

'Will you help me, Mr Blakeney?'

'I'll help you, Miss Hetta. And will you help me?'

'How can I do that?'

'By coming here, every so often, and letting me comb your beautiful hair.'

'But of course you may. You do it so gently, so marvellously.'

She turned her face up to smile at Balbo, and saw that two big tears were running down his face, one on either cheek.

'Oh, poor Mr Blakeney. Why are you so sad?'

'Brandy, Miss Hetta. It makes one remember things.'

'I thought it made you forget them.'

'So it does—the little things that don't matter. But the big things, Miss Hetta, it brings them up as clear as yesterday.'

Hetta had the sense to pursue this no further. If he wants to say anything more, she thought, he will. But Balbo simply went on combing her hair, now sweeping grandly through great skeins of it, now nibbling exquisitely at her scalp with the points of the teeth, while Hetta closed her eyes and wished that he need never stop.

The College Council concluded its discussion just before lunch time the next day. There had been a great many speeches, most of them repetitious, but what it all boiled down to was this: the extreme left, Beyfus, Beck and Clewes, were against either of the short-listed proposals, considering them to be merely impertinent, yet would support Tom Llewyllyn's for want of a better; the moderate left, headed by the Provost, also supported Llewyllyn; and the right, of all shades, was now solid for Balbo.

There were, however, certain subtleties in the situation. The continued absence of Pough reduced the Council to nineteen but did not reduce the number, fifteen, which would constitute the 75 per cent majority necessary to pass a motion for final adoption. Without Pough, moreover, Balbo's supporters were now reduced to nine; for though he had obtained a vote of thirteen to get his plan short-listed, three of those thirteen had been moderate left-wingers, who sincerely felt that the problem of preserving the Chapel should be fully aired before the Council but were nevertheless far more inclined, now it had come to the crunch, to support Tom's new building and the 25 per cent increase in student numbers. When the Provost took the vote, therefore, there was a count of ten for Tom's proposal and nine for Balbo's, which simply meant deadlock.

The procedure in such a case was clearly laid down. The Provost must now dismiss the Council with the warning that it would be reconvened to give another vote in seven days' time. By then, the theory was, private suasion and intrigue might have issue in a decisive majority one way or the other. But in practice, of course, such weekly reconventions could succeed each other for months without any perceptible realignment of the Council; and there were very few of its members, apart from the extreme left-wingers, who would not be entirely satisfied if something of the kind occurred. Tom was certainly in no hurry. Balbo knew that the Chapel and even the Choristers could wait another year and be little the worse for it. And Constable, as Provost, considered that a certain amount of mystery and delay (though more than six months might be dangerous) would invest the final decision with higher dignity. In any event, since nothing had been decided, nothing need yet be promulgated, which meant grateful respite from the world's comment. With a feeling of some relief, Constable rose to give his colleagues the formal word of dismissal:

'Nil est peractum, socii. Go hence and meditate, and return when seven nights have passed.'

Gregory Stern, the publisher, and Isobel Stern, his wife and Patricia's sister, lived in a jolly house in Chelsea which Isobel kept very bright and clean. Hither came Patricia and Baby, neither of whom looked bright and clean, as soon as they reached London; and Isobel served them a delicious soufflé of turbot, which she had cooked herself, for lunch.

The soufflé was wasted on everyone except Isobel.

Patricia, whose culinary method was limited to the incompetent manipulation of 'convenience foods', was jealous of the achievement and in any case regarded it as somewhat immoral. Baby, sensing her mother's displeasure and playing up to it, splashed her share round her plate and whined for fish fingers. The prospect for the long afternoon ahead would have been very grim indeed, had not Isobel, who wanted a tête-à-tête with her sister, taken one very sensible precaution. Shortly after the beginning of the meal she had given Baby a glass of orangeade in which she had dissolved a liberal quantity of aspirin; this Baby had swilled down, with bestial sucking noises and much discharge of nasal mucous, in twenty seconds flat; so that five minutes later, just as she was opening her mouth to grizzle about the soufflé or demand more orangeade (she had not yet made up her mind which), sleep fell on Baby like a hammer and stretched her prone in her chair. Isobel bore her off and deposited her, none too gently, on a couch in Gregory's dressing-room, then returned to catechise Patricia.

'You and that child,' she said, 'are in a bigger mess than ever. What's the matter with you, Patty? You used to think so much of yourself.'

'I still do,' said Patricia, miserably surveying her best costume. There was no doubt about it: the skirt was considerably the worse for her recent expeditions by the river. 'I may not look very elegant,' she said querulously, 'but let me tell you, it's not very easy for me, living down there in the country with hardly any money and——'

'—Knackers,' said Isobel. 'You lived in the country for years before you got married. You know how to manage in the country as well as any woman that breathes. And as for money, you're rolling in it. We both got exactly the same when Daddy died, and I know what it was to the last penny. You could carry on like the Queen.'

'That must all be saved for Baby,' said Patricia primly. 'It's Tom's business to provide for me, and now he's at that revolting college he earns practically nothing.'

'Balls.'

'I tell you, Tom earns practic——'

'—Balls to not spending Daddy's money. By the time Baby's grown up, the way things are going, it won't be worth the piddle in her plastic potty.'

Isobel splayed her long, thin legs on either side of her chair and leant over the table, her huge breasts bouncing on the edge of the soufflé dish.

'I know what's wrong with you,' Isobel. 'You look to me as if you haven't been fucked in months.'

'I . . . I don't care much about all that.'

'Yes, you do. We're a very sexy family. What's the matter with Tom? Can't he get his pecker up?'

'He . . . hasn't been very attentive.'

'Then you must find a little something on the side.'

'*Isobel.* Do you?'

'No, because Gregory *is* attentive. But I jolly soon would if he wasn't. Haven't you got someone you fancy?'

Patricia shook her head firmly. Then, because it had been her habit over many years to be honest with her sister, she started nodding it instead.

'Who?'

'An undergraduate. I don't know him. I haven't even spoken to him. But oh,' said Patricia greedily, 'how I could love that undergraduate.'

'Then love him.'

'He's got a girl friend.'

'They're hot at that age. He'll have plenty of energy for you too.'

'But look at me.'

'Spend some of Daddy's money and do yourself up. You've got lovely strong legs and a beautiful bloody great bottom. Your undergraduate will love that—if the rest of you's half way passable. I'll tell you what,' Isobel said. 'While you're here in London, we'll set you to rights. We'll buy you clothes and get your hair fixed, and have your face put together again. We'll send you back to Cambridge looking like a lioness, and you can *eat* your undergraduate.'

'But it's wrong, Isobel. Wrong, wrong. That's why I came up to London early—to get away before I did anything silly.'

'Let's get this straight. Are you afraid of sinning or just of being silly?'

Patricia thought a long time.

'I don't think Tom would mind,' she said. 'He's as good as told me. I should probably be much nicer to him . . . if I had something to look forward to every so often. But I don't want to look a fool, Isobel. How . . . how do I make the first approaches?'

'Will he respond to the mother act?'

'The what?'

'Will he accept your authority? You have quite a presence, you know.'

What was that, thought Patricia, which Tom had said the other night? Something about feet which were convenient to grovel at?

'Now you mention it,' she said, 'I think he might prove quite obedient.'

'Then drop something,' said Isobel. 'Tell him to pick it up for you and call a taxi, and to see you home in it because you're upset. Then, when you get home, tell him that *this* is how you're both going to spend the afternoon, because Mother knows best. He'll have to join in, if only out of politeness.'

'But suppose it's a failure?'

'I was coming to that. It's your job to see that it isn't. You're Mum and you've got to do the work. You've got to busy yourself round your little baby boy. You've got to feed him and clean him and change his nappies and kiss his little bottom and show him how to point his little prick. Do you understand?'

'Not quite.'

Isobel sighed.

'That girl of his,' she said; 'with her it'll have been very straightforward. Boom, boom, boom. With you it's got to be different. You're the older woman; the guide to secret places, the priestess of mysteries, the dispenser of curious pleasures.'

'Oh. I don't know much about those.'

'Hasn't Tom . . . ever . . .?'

'No. As you would say, he is—was—very straightforward.'

'You'd better come upstairs then,' Isobel said. 'Gregory has a very interesting collection of books.'

'It is a commonplace of all administration,' said the Leading Editorial in *The Times* the following morning, 'that important decisions must only be taken after much thought and discussion. On the face of it, therefore, it is by no means unsatisfactory to learn that the Council of Lancaster College, Cambridge, has not yet committed itself to a definite course of action as regards the disbursement of the £250,000 surplus which has recently become available to that venerable institution. One may conceive that the Provost and Fellows are conducting exhaustive and responsible deliberations about the best possible use of this substantial sum for the betterment of the services which the college has long tendered to the public weal.'

So far, thought Provost Constable, sipping his thin coffee and averting his eyes from Mrs Constable's flannel dressing gown, so good.

'However,' the leader continued, 'information has reached this journal which gives rise to disquieting reflections. According to a reliable source' (Master Beck, I suppose) 'the choice before the Council is now limited to two alternatives: a small new building for the accommodation of approximately sixty extra students; or the extensive survey and restoration of the College Chapel, together with increased subsidies for the upkeep of the Choir. Of the former proposal, it may be said that many will deem it inadequate, in view of the extensive funds in hand, to the needs of a rapidly expanding student population; of the latter, that, while the sacred architecture and music of Lancaster College must at all costs be preserved for posterity, there is nevertheless something of perverseness, at this difficult juncture of our social history, in applying to the premature refurbishing of a stone erection (however famous) what will rightfully be looked upon as the due of aspiring and at present underprivileged young people ...'

Great God, thought Constable, what unctuous drivel. Has the editor turned to jelly?

'There's a funny bit here,' said Mrs Constable, rattling an organ of the Billingsgate Press, 'by a man called Alfie Schroeder. Shall I read it out to you?'

'No.'

' "Dons delight to bark and bite," it says, "and those in Lancaster College, Cambridge, have certainly chosen some mouldy old bones to scrap over. Presented with a surplus of quarter a million pounds, the learned Fellows are squabbling like a load of Gorgons—about what? About whether to provide accommodation for a handful of extra students, or to pay more money to the Choir Boys, who've been letting their top notes get a bit grotty of late. But just in case anyone agrees with me that £500,000 is a little too much to lay out on improving the plainsong (dowdy old chants left over from the middle ages), perhaps they'd like to join me in reminding the dons of Lancaster that we live in an age in which science and technology"——'

Constable had been just about to tell his wife to hold her tongue (in so many words), when she was interrupted by a knock on the breakfast-room door. Bidden to enter, the Head Porter presented himself, wearing tails (since it was a saint's day) and carrying a silk hat.

'Mr Provost ... Madam,' the Head Porter said bowing. 'Someone has been a-writing rude things on the rear lawn. You, sir, I must ask to come and read them. You, madam, I must warn to avert your ladylike gaze.'

So Constable and the Head Porter went up to Constable's study, whence they could look out on the rear lawn. Constable saw two things. He saw a small, bent man, whom he knew to be one of the college gardeners, standing under the study window and crying; and he saw, burnt into the grass in letters ten feet high:

LOSE LLEWYLLYN;
BUGGER BLAKENEY;
FUCK THE CON;
BUILD WITH BEYFUS.

'Who,' said Constable after some thought, 'is the Con?'

'First three letters of your own name, Mr Provost. Making a Frenchie word, or so I understand.'

'I never knew they called me that,' said Constable. 'I must be getting out of touch.'

'All in all,' wrote Robert Constable, who was making up his record of the seven days which had passed since the writing had appeared on the lawn, 'this has been an uneasy and indecisive week. When I first saw what had been done to the back lawn, I was exceedingly angry, though I think I managed to conceal this from the Head Porter, who was with me at the time. What made it so much worse was the sight and sound of the third gardener, who was sobbing his heart out because his life's work had been destroyed. No one had thought of that, of course: it just had not occurred to the young men responsible that their fine and easy gesture had destroyed, in a few minutes, the achievement which had taken a fellow human being thirty years. Nor had they reflected that the human being in question was one of the "workers" they are always ranting about.

'However, I managed, as I say, to control myself, and having dismissed the Head Porter, I settled down to consider what should be done.

'Although I had been thinking of the culprits as "them", I now reflected that a single man could easily have done it on his own, and that whether or not this had been so, one agent in the affair must certainly have been Hugh Balliston. Why did I pick on him? Because Balliston, who is a great purist and a stickler for correct English usage, was the only man in the world who would have bothered to *punctuate* such a message and in such a medium. The careful semicolons at the end of each line and the full stop at the end of the whole were as good as a signature. True, the crudely alliterative slogans lacked Balliston's usual elegance, but they were terse and quotable, which was everything for their purpose. I was in no doubt about it: Balliston was my man.

'So what was I to do? My tactic so far had been simply

to ignore all protests and demonstrations; but whereas one can ignore the flouting of unimportant regulations and can even ignore personal insult (for in the end those that insult me merely insult themselves), one cannot ignore wanton destruction.

'In the end, I decided to back my hunch. I sent for Balliston (who came most promptly), told him that I knew he was guilty and whence I had inferred his guilt, and asked him to explain to me how he, of all people, could do such a horrible thing. Balliston, being a strictly truthful boy, admitted the crime; and then, being if anything even keener on self-justification than I myself, started to expound to me why I should not take his act to reflect adversely either on his intelligence, his morals or his aesthetic sense.

'The basic theory behind his actions, he told me, is that the University as it is must be destroyed so that a better one can be substituted. He had, on his own admission, destroyed beauty; but it would be urged by those who were behind him, first that such beauty was an irrelevance or even, much worse, an insult to the underprivileged, and secondly that in recording his "justifiable resentment" he had been performing "an act of conscience". Any punishment would thus be interpreted as "victimisation", and would lead to mass indignation, which he and his friends would be able to exploit for their initial purpose of destruction.

'Very well, I said: but did he really believe in the basic tenet behind his actions—that the University as it stood must be destroyed to make place for a better? Did he conceive that such an object was practicable? At this he became very shifty; he muttered something about the necessity for faith and his having encountered someone who had inspired him with faith, and then fell silent. Although he did not abandon his claim, although he even put a proud face on it, it obviously embarrassed him nevertheless, because with some part of himself he still knew that he had been cheated or charmed into betraying his critical intellect, that he was suffering from a temporary alienation from reason—to say nothing of plain common sense. So then I understood what was happening to Master Balliston. He was being piped by the Pied Piper (like many better men before him), and the question was, how to rescue him before he was piped away under the hill.

'With this problem in mind, I asked him whether he ought to have told me so much about his friends' strategy. Surely, I said, he had given away secrets? Oh no, he replied, he was perfectly certain that I had always understood what was doing, he just wanted me to know that he understood too, so that I shouldn't think him a fool. But I did think him a fool, I told him, for ever accepting the revolutionary programme in the first place—for accepting, that was, that an existing good should be destroyed for the sake of an improvement which was wholly putative. But my opinion shouldn't bother him, I went on, since potential martyrs must be prepared to put up with a reputation for folly and fanaticism as part of the burden of martyrdom. This, as I knew it would, made him both angry and unhappy. Master Balliston may be ready to assume a crown of thorns, but he wouldn't be seen dead in a dunce-cap.

'Even so, the piper's tune was still in his ears. Clearly, he was going to see the thing through. "I burnt those slogans into the lawn," he said, "and I can show you a jar still half full of the chemical they gave me to do it with. Although I'm sorry about the lawn, I'm not sorry about the implications of my act. Now go ahead and punish me." The punishment, I remarked, must fit, not only the crime, but the degree of responsibility for the crime. It was clear to me that he was not vicious, merely misled. I therefore proposed to hold him at the very considerable expense of having the lawn returfed where necessary ... which would be a suitable and durable reminder to him that he had allowed himself to be duped. The debit would be recorded in a suspended account against his name, and he could pay it off over the years ahead. And let his friends make what propaganda they could out of *that*.

'Since then, a week has passed and all, so far, has been quiet. But there is a very nasty smell in the air, and some of it, I think, is traceable to the sour frustration I have caused among the extremists by behaving so non-committally about Balliston. His friends wanted a martyrdom and have got instead a text-book example of liberal dealing; so they are (one may fear) turning nastier than ever. Yet what can they do without their martyr?

'The Council met again this morning, the Senior Fellow being back in his place again. He is voting, predictably, for Balbo Blakeney's proposal, which received ten votes, as did Tom Llewyllyn's. Deadlock. I don't imagine the vote will change for months to come; and I can't make up my mind whether this will help or hinder the promoters of future protests. Neither, I should say. The extremists' ostensible complaint is that Beyfus has been decisively rejected, and nothing can now alter that. Can they, one wonders, use Beyfus alone, without a martyr in his cause, to stage their holocaust? No. A martyr they must have, and it pleases me mightily to have withheld him.'

What the Provost did not understand, since he had been brought up to respect the truth, was the facility with which Mayerston and his associates were capable of tailoring the facts to fit their purpose. A formula had been readily devised to transform Constable's moderate treatment of Hugh Balliston into a deed of grinding tyranny, and the popular version which was now being put about went something like this:

'Hugh Balliston of Lancaster has committed an act of moral and social conscience in protesting against Lancaster's rejection of Lord Beyfus's progressive proposals. In order to make his protest significant, Hugh was compelled to deface college property. Since Provost Constable holds property more sacred than conscience, he is making Hugh pay for the damage.'

So far, the formula kept within hailing distance of the truth, but at this point there was an abrupt switch of the tiller.

'Hugh is a student of working class background' (the formula continued) 'who can not afford to pay the sum demanded even if his political creed permitted him to do so. But if he doesn't pay up by the end of the term, he is to be rusticated until he does. Since he will never be able to, he is in reality being sent down from the University and deprived of his degree—all because he has spoken up for equality and justice in defiance of age and privilege.'

'So you see,' said Mona Corrington, who was elaborating on this theme to Lord Beyfus, 'there has been a gross abuse of authority by your Provost. A week has passed since he penalised Mr Balliston in this intolerable fashion, and yet none of you in Lancaster has done anything about it. Why not?'

'Because,' said Beyfus wearily, 'what you have been saying is mistaken. Mr Balliston is not to be rusticated, nor is any other pressure to be put on him. As I understand it, he has his whole life-time in which to pay.'

'That's not as most people understand it.'

'Then most people have not understood it.'

'They've got the main idea,' Mona said; 'they know that Balliston is being punished for disrespect of college property, and they won't stand for it.'

'See here, Mona. Outside, on the College Stones, is parked a smart, green Jaguar. Yours. If you went out now and found someone scratching slogans on it with a chisel, you would do your best to detain him and make him pay for the damage. Right?'

'It would depend,' said Mona, 'on the slogans. Any right-wing rottenness, and I'd call the police at once. But if I approved the message, and if I felt it had come from some warm and youthful heart——'

'—Then you'd pat the culprit on his curly head,' said Beyfus, 'and you'd drive to your garage, where you'd shout and scream at the foreman until he promised to respray your car with absolute priority over all other cars whatever. And when the bill came in, you'd send it on to this college, claiming that your car was on college ground when it was damaged and that the porters should have been guarding it more carefully. I know you, Mona. You have everything both ways . . . you have everything a hundred ways.'

'If you're going to take such a stupid tone, Beyfus, I shan't be at all nice to you for a long time'—she paused for this to sink in—'and I shan't tell you the most important thing which I came here to say.'

'What's that?'

'Apologise first for being so offensive.'

'Mona, my darling,' said Beyfus contritely, 'I wouldn't hurt you for the world. It was only my little joke.'

'I've told you before, Beyfus: the times we live in are too serious for jokes. Now then. The big news is this. Although all of you in this college have been too flabby to do anything about Hugh Balliston, others are getting ready to march to his defence. The story has been put round, Beyfus, and anger is growing.'

'Everything seems quiet enough to me.'

'That's as it should be. Though indignation is already blazing, discipline is being used to contain it until the right moment. The authorities are being lulled, Beyfus. And meanwhile the troops are massing in the dark, ready to attack with the dawn, when the sleep of the authorities is always deepest.'

'And who told you all this, my dear?'

'I am in touch with the organisers.'

'That boy, Mayerston?'

'Those who help him.'

'Hmmm,' said Beyfus. 'He does know, I take it, that if he spends too long lulling the authorities he will also lull his own troops?'

'He knows that, Beyfus. He knows just how long he can keep the flame of anger burning, and he will strike when he has kindled it to its fiercest.'

'He certainly seems to have made an impression on you. All these fancy metaphors.'

'Don't be flippant, Beyfus. When the soldiers of liberation go over the top for the dawn attack, you and I must be with them.'

'Mona, sweet Mona. Let us have *either* the kindling flame of righteous anger *or* the massed troops of liberation. Let us please not have both. Let us for preference have neither. Exactly what is to happen, Mona dear, and when?'

Dropping her fancy metaphors and using the most precise and concrete of terms, Mona proceeded to tell him.

'Tell me, Miss Hetta,' said Balbo Blakeney, as he drew the comb slowly through her hair, 'have you seen young Balliston?'

'Yes,' said Hetta miserably.

'What does he say about this fine? Does he reckon it's fair?'

'He doesn't say anything much. He's got some secret, but he's not telling it to me. All I know is that he's sticking to Mayerston.'

'And you're still trying to prise him loose?'

'I've begged him,' Hetta said. 'I've told him how lightly he's been let off over this lawn thing, that next time they're bound to send him away, that he's ruining all he's worked for. But he won't listen to anything I say.'

'So you're still staying out of his bed?' said Balbo carefully.

'Yes, and I can't bear it. He looks at me and says, "I need you, Hetta." And I say, "All right. Just give up all this rubbish with Mayerston." "I can't do that," he says, "not now; but Hetta," he says, "if you'll only trust me and love me, I'll tell you what we're planning. I'll show it's not rubbish. I'll tell you everything, Hetta, if only you'll come into my arms." '

'But you won't?'

'No.'

'So all of this is getting you both nowhere.' Balbo grazed her scalp very gently with the sharp points of the comb. 'He gets no love and you've not the slightest idea what he's up to.'

'Not the slightest.'

'But he's up to something, Miss Hetta. Although it's been so quiet, they're all up to something—that I know. If we knew what, we might be able to help him before it's too late.'

'Then shall I make love to him after all, Mr Blakeney? Then he'll tell me what's going to happen, and I can tell you, and it can all be stopped.'

'You couldn't do it, Missy. If he told you, he'd be trusting you. You'd choke to death if you tried to breathe a word of it, to me or anyone else.'

'What can we do, Mr Blakeney?'

'There's one thing. I can try to find out what's going on from Tony Beck. I doubt they've told him, but he may know something.'

'Will he tell you if he does?'

'He might drop a hint without meaning to. I know him very well, Missy, and I'm good at picking up hints.'

'And then?'

'We'll see what we can make of it all and do whatever we can.'

'Kind Mr Blakeney. Oh, I do want to help him, to comfort him . . . to have him comfort me. I need him so.'

'And I need you, Miss Hetta.'

For a long time, while Balbo went on combing, Hetta was silent. Then:

'Like . . . like Hugh does, Mr Blakeney?' she said.

'Not quite like that. It'll be very easy for you, I promise.'

'Show me then.'

He took her hand and showed her.

'No,' she said after a while. 'Not like that. You're kind and good and patient. You deserve better than that.'

She shifted herself between his knees until she was kneeling up before him.

'Go on combing my hair,' she said, and lowered her head towards his lap so that he might do so.

'How much will it cost?' croaked Daniel Mond to Tom Llewyllyn.

They were standing together on the rear lawn, watching the last of the re-turfing. The damaged circle of grass which had represented Hugh's grammatical full stop had been cut clean out and a fresh and verdant disc, exactly measured, was now being eased into place.

'More than Balliston can pay.'

'He doesn't have to pay,' said Daniel: 'not until he's older. If then.'

'Even so,' said Tom, 'if anyone wants to twist it all to make trouble, it won't be difficult. A poor scholar is being put at charges to maintain a luxurious feature of the college decor. That's all the provocation they need.'

'You think they'll rise to it?'

'Of course. Not that it makes any difference. They'd have found or fabricated some "legitimate grievance" in any case. Once we turned down Beyfus, they were bound to.'

'Then why didn't you support Beyfus?'

'Why didn't you?'

'Because,' said Daniel, 'one cannot give in so easily. One cannot stand by and say nothing while everything is pulled to pieces.'

'Exactly. That's why I framed my scheme. It was workable, it conceded a measure of necessary change, and I hoped—I just hoped—that it would satisfy all parties for the time being and give us breathing space. But this plan of Balbo's for the Chapel—the mere fact that it's being entertained at all—will infuriate absolutely everyone. And with this affair of Balliston's thrown in . . .'

'Everything seems quiet.'

'It always does—until the next time. By the way, Fielding

Gray's written. He's coming to spend next Saturday night.'

'Oh good,' said Daniel. 'We'll all be able to listen to the Madrigals. He'll enjoy that.'

In London, Isobel Stern cooked a gala dinner in Patricia's honour, as Patricia was returning to Grantchester the next day. Although Isobel knew that her sister would not appreciate the attention, she was glad of the excuse, being very fond of food, for an extra special blow-out.

Luckily the chambermaid at Patricia's hotel had taken to Baby (God alone knew why) and had volunteered to baby-sit. So Patricia was able to come to Isobel's unencumbered, which was an unusual blessing, and arrived looking absolutely stunning. For Isobel had been as good as her word; during the last week she had had Patricia refurbished cap-à-pé. The result was somewhat in the Empire mode: a hair style of tight curls to frame the bold, seignorial face, and a loose and simple gown which disguised the slackness of Patricia's bosom while emphasising the strength and amplitude of her buttocks and her thighs.

'My word,' said Gregory Stern, 'Tom's in for a nice surprise.'

Neither Isobel nor Patricia bothered to explain that Tom was beside the point.

'You might tell him,' Gregory went on, as he tucked into his langouste flan, 'that I'm anxious to discuss this book he's writing.'

'Did you like the chapters he sent you?'

'Yes,' said Gregory, putting down his fork and rapidly fingering every button about his person one after the other, 'and no. You see, it's a very important subject, the nature of power, and Tom's apercus are undeniably very subtle, but it's all—what shall I say?—it's all rather donnish. Tom's public is used to something less demanding ... more friendly in tone.'

'So what are you going to do about it?' said Patricia. 'Whenever it's finished, that is.'

'I hoped Tom might make certain cuts and concessions. To please his loyal public and his loyal publisher.'

'Isn't it about time,' said Isobel, 'that you published a donnish book? Instead of grubbing after money all day long.'

'I dare say,' said Gregory, 'that Tom will be thinking about money too,'

'He certainly ought to be,' said Patricia. 'I'm sure I've got none to spare. Not after paying for Baby's dental treatment.'

'Mean bitch,' Isobel said. 'I hope young thingamabob comes off all over your new dress.'

'*What* did you say?' said Gregory.

'Nothing. Just an old nursery joke.'

Partly out of politeness and partly out of naivety, Gregory allowed this to pass without further comment. So, from different motives, did Patricia. For the truth was that Isobel's remark had conjured up so vivid a picture of Hugh Balliston in priapic flood that Patricia was half faint with lust and anxious to change the subject back again while a vestige of self-control was still left to her.

'What you must know about Tom,' she said firmly, 'is that these days he is not in a mood to make cuts or concessions to please anyone. That college has destroyed his sense of obligation.'

'Hark at her,' said Isobel, and set down a dish of truffled chicken's breasts cooked in cream and framboise.

'It's true,' Patricia insisted. 'All he wants for his book is the applause of the Provost and Fellows of Lancaster College. Nothing else matters to him.'

'Good for Tom,' said Isobel, 'and one in the schnozzle for poor old Fagin here.'

Gregory smirked. He always enjoyed it when Isobel insulted his Jewishness.

'That's all very well,' said Patricia, 'but he can't stay in that mutual admiration society for ever. At least, I hope not. It's time he started facing up to the world again.'

'When he sees you tomorrow,' said Gregory, 'back home and looking like an Empress, he will do whatever you say.' He raised his glass. 'To reunion,' he said.

Having no ready excuse for refusing, Patricia joined in the toast.

'Have some more hock, Miss Hetta.'

'Thank you, Mr Blakeney. It's delicious.'

Balbo was giving Hetta lunch in his rooms.

'Now then, Missy,' he said, having poured the wine, 'I did what I said I would. I've been to see Tony Beck, and I have to tell you that I got exactly nowhere.'

'He couldn't tell you anything?'

'Couldn't or wouldn't. Whatever they're up to this time, and whatever part they've fixed for young Balliston, they're keeping very close about it.'

'Oh.'

'So I'm afraid I've been no help to you at all. Which being so, if you don't want to see me any more, I'll quite understand.'

'But you have been a help, Mr Blakeney.' Hetta drunk a healthy draught of hock and lowered her glass. 'Don't you *know* how I enjoy coming here to see you?'

'Coming to see a wizened old thing like me?'

Hetta walked round the table and leant over Balbo from behind. She clasped her hands across his chest and kissed his neck.

'You're sweet and gentle and clever,' she said, 'and you've done all you can about Hugh. I still worry about him dreadfully, but he's a big boy now, and if he wants to behave so sillily, we'll just have to let him.'

Then she went back to her place and whacked into her lobster mayonnaise. After a little while, Balbo said:

'I've hired a car for the afternoon. A car with a chauffeur.'

'Goodness, how grand.'

'No, it's not. I've never learnt to drive, you see. I thought we'd go to Long Melford. It's a beautiful place, you'll find.'

'Isn't there a famous church?'

'Yes, Miss Hetta, there is. I particularly want to show it to you.'

'Do you know,' said Hetta, gaily cracking a claw, 'I think that's the best thing that anyone's ever said to me.'

A luncheon party of a very different kind was going on in Tony Beck's rooms: beer and cheese sandwiches, to give the occasion what Beck considered a suitably proletarian air, while at the same time saving him money. Present were Hugh Balliston, Mayerston, and Mayerston's principal lieutenant, a squat and snake-eyed youth who sported a fringe of beard and a light blue anorak.

'So you all understand,' said Mayerston, 'exactly how it's going to work?'

They all nodded, Hugh rather glumly.

'It's particularly important,' Mayerston said to him gently, 'that you should have the right sort of look on your face while it's all going on. You're the centre-piece of the whole show. Try not to look as if you were just about to be hung.'

'I'm the martyr. Isn't that how martyrs look?'

'No,' said Mayerston. 'They look long-suffering but radiant.'

'Not easy.'

'Agreed. We may have to give you a shot of something before we put you on. You can arrange that, Job?'

'Yup,' said the light blue lieutenant.

'One thing you haven't told us,' said Tony Beck edgily: 'when is it to happen?'

'From what the lads tell me,' said Job in a voice like tyres scrunching over broken glass, 'the student boys and girls have bought this martyr bit about Balliston here. Indignation is running higher all the time—in Cambridge and in other places too. But unless something new happens, they'll start to cool early next week, and once they do that we'll have to blow very hard to get the fire up again.'

'Thank you, Job. I think that makes our best time pretty clear, gentlemen. This week-end. Sunday, Sunday at ... half past twelve o'clock.'

'But the Madrigals won't be over,' said Hugh stupidly.

'The Madrigals?'

'This Sunday,' explained Beck, 'is Madrigal Sunday. They are sung between noon and 1 p.m.'

'What are madrigals?' scrunched Job.

'Madrigals,' said Mayerston, 'are songs of love set for unaccompanied voices. They are beautiful but somewhat repetitious, and I'm quite sure that by half past twelve on Sunday everyone will have heard enough.'

While he was working in his room that afternoon, Tom Llewyllyn received two telephone calls.

The first was from the Cambridge University Press. It appeared that the Syndics had considered, with great interest, the specimen chapters which Tom had submitted to them, and that they now wished to express their provisional readiness to publish his book on its completion.

The second call, which came only a few minutes later, was from Patricia.

'Patricia, oh Patricia, the University Press wants to publish my book.'

'Well, if that's what you want ... I'm very happy for you, Tom.'

'Thank you, darling. How's everything in London?'

'I'm not in London, Tom. Baby and I came down this morning.'

'Oh. Why didn't you warn me?'

'I didn't know. The dentist was much quicker than I thought.' She started to gabble. 'He saw Baby at once, and he gave us appointments every day—you know how clever Gregory is at arranging all that—and before I knew where I was it was finished. But Tom ...'

'Yes, Patricia?'

'There's no need for you to come back to Grantchester just yet if you don't want to.'

'But of course I must come back now you and Baby are home.'

'Listen, Tom. How long did you arrange to stay in the college?'

'Till the middle of next week. But now that you and——'

'—Tom. You said that the college would have a lot of trouble arranging bedmakers and things. If you told them next week, you must stay till next week. It's not fair to mess them about.'

Which was true enough, Tom thought. And not only that: since Fielding Gray was coming to spend Saturday night, the week-end arrangements would be very much easier and more enjoyable if he himself were still living in college. But it was most unlike Patricia to take such a liberal line; really most unlike her.

'Are you quite sure,' he now said, 'that you and Baby will be all right?'

'Quite sure, darling. I've had a simply marvellous time, and I feel absolutely wonderful, and the last thing I want to do is upset your plans. Now today is Thursday, so I'll expect you back today week.'

Well, thought Tom as he rang off, I was certainly right to make her go to London; it's done her a power of good. Thoroughly contented, he turned back to the quarto page before him. Now that he knew the University Press was backing him, the labour already seemed lighter. But it would never do to become over-confident. Careful with your words now, he told himself, you can't be too careful with words.

'True authority,' he began to write, 'must depend on reciprocal good will. There must be competence and justice on the one side, respect and trust on the other. But even where such conditions obtain, there is room for endless misunderstanding and mischance. Let just one clever dissident plausibly misrepresent the motives of one faltering minister, and the trust that has been won by a century of stable government can be shattered overnight...'

The following morning Patricia parked Baby with her obliging neighbour, got herself up to kill, and went slamming into Cambridge as fast as her rather large feet would carry her. There were just two things she wanted: one of them was to meet Hugh Balliston and the other was not to meet Tom. The former at least must be mainly a matter of luck, but Friday, she reminded herself, had always been her lucky day.

Not at first, however. She drew a blank in the Fellows' Garden and spent an unrewarding hour hovering round the back gate of the college. The easiest way, of course, would have been to march straight into the Fellows' Garden Hostel and ask for Mr Balliston's room; but she had an idea that such a direct proceeding would be not only indiscreet but also presumptuous, for if God meant her to meet Hugh, He would arrange it at His Own pleasure. She was bound, she thought, to wait; and she now decided on King's Parade as the next place to wait in. The quickest route thither lay straight through Lancaster and, as she reflected, right under the windows of Tom's rooms; so she mopped her brow and heaved a heavy sigh and walked all the way round by the Mill Bridge.

In King's Parade she had a cup of nasty coffee, spent half an hour reading the University Notice Board in front of the Senate, another half hour looking at college scarves in the window of Ryder and Amies, and then, heart sinking and hope fading, turned up past Great St Mary's to patrol the Market Square. Three times round and no joy. Into Heffers'. Out of Heffers'. Up Petty Cury and down again, across to Bowes & Bowes, back to Heffers', thence to the Ladies in the square to patch herself up (and did she need it). Up the steps, through the parked cars, along to the entrance of the Arts Theatre, look at the playbill (some modern rubbish about a Bolivian bandit), off down Bene't Street—are you mad, woman, cavorting round like this?—past the front gate of Lancaster (quickly, before that officious porter sees you) and straight on to the University Notice Board—for after all, someone might have put up a new notice since you were last there.

And so someone had. It announced that the Rylands Prize for Shakespearian Studies was awarded to HUGH EDWARD BALLISTON for his Essay on Shakespeare's Theories of Kingship. And here—merciful Jesus—was Hugh Balliston himself, pale, worried and nervous but unmistakably Hugh Balliston, coming down King's Parade in order to read about his triumph...

... There's that ferocious tourist woman again, thought Hugh as he walked down King's Parade. Reading the University Notice Board. What the devil has it got to do with her?...

... Very much to Patricia's surprise, Hugh did not turn aside to look at the Notice Board but kept straight on. He's seen it already, she thought. He's seen it, or he knows about it, and he's walking straight on and out of my life. And then she thought, perhaps he doesn't know, perhaps it just hasn't occurred to him, anyway I must try it, now or never——

'—Young man,' she positively bellowed, 'come here and read this...'

... Patently mad. Keep going. No. Don't just leave the poor thing there, you can't. Humour her. Wild, gleaming face, dress rumpled between quaking thighs, hair one crazy mess of decomposing curls—I should have kept going but it's too late now...

'Read this,' Patricia said.

Hugh read it, then read it again.

'Hugh Edward Balliston,' she said. 'That's you.'

He nodded.

'Aren't you pleased?'

'It's all so unreal,' he said. 'I wrote that essay and sent it in—why, months ago now. I'd almost forgotten. I thought they'd decided not to award the prize,' he burbled; 'they often don't, you know, if none of the entries is good enough. So when I didn't hear, I thought——'

'—Never mind what you thought. Darling, darling Hugh, you've won the bloody prize.'

This peculiar statement brought him to his senses again.

'How did you know my name?' he said.

'Never mind that. Is it a big prize?'

'Not in money. But it's a good one to win, because anyone can go in for it. Graduates, dons, anyone.'

'You beat them all,' she said, her voice ringing with pride: 'you beat the bloody lot.'

'Do you always say "bloody" so often?' Hugh asked. 'Who are you, anyway?'

Now or never.

'I'm Tom Llewyllyn's wife, Patricia'—he'd have to know sooner or later—'and I want to talk to you. We've never met but we were once at the same party. The Provost's party last Michaelmas. So we do know each other in a way.'

Her voice urged this with such a note of pleading that he could only nod assent.

'We will get a taxi in the Market Square,' said Patricia, remembering just in time that it was her role as laid down by Isobel to command and not to beg, 'and drive to my house for lunch.'

What am I doing in this taxi with this huge, ramping woman, who is shamelessly rubbing her knee against me and smelling of sweat? What ogress is this who has swept down from her lair to carry me off? Tom Llewyllyn's wife, she says. I thought someone told me that he'd married rather grandly—a Tory minister's daughter. *That's it:* the eldest daughter of Sir Edwin Turbot, grand vizier of the Conservative Party, now some years dead. Well, he'll be turning in his marble tomb if he knows about this lot—his daughter capering round Cambridge like a public whore . . .

. . . What shall I do with him now that I've got him? He's not responding to my knee. Never mind, there's the whole afternoon. Do as Isobel told me: just announce what's going to happen and take it from there. I'm Mummy, and Mummy knows best...

... A nice face really, under that upper-class arrogance. Vulnerable. Deprived. All very sad—and very clear. Tom Llewyllyn's died on her in bed, so she wants to be consoled. Badly, by the look of it. Well, she's not getting anything from me. Hugh's for Hetta ... Or is he? Hetta's not for Hugh. She hasn't been for over a week. Over a week, and not a peck on the forehead to show for it. And then again, this woman, this Patricia, it's not just sex she's after, it's me: she knew who I was, she was happy that I'd won that prize, she wasn't waiting just for anybody, she was waiting there for me. 'I want to talk to you,' she said. And all this clumsy business with her knee—it's quite plain she's never done this kind of thing before, she just doesn't know how to begin. Humour her. Why not? Hetta's dried up on me, and Sunday may well be the end of everything, and it's a long walk home from wherever we're going. So play up to her, Hugh Edward Balliston: cast your bread upon the waters, and see what the gods send back on the tide...

... He's pressing back against my knee. Bless his heart. But why does he look so white and ill? He ought to be so happy about that prize. Perhaps he hasn't been getting enough to eat, they're very poor, some of these boys, I must feed him up ... so what have I got in the house? *Christ.* Beans. Tinned sausages (skinless). Heinz Spaghetti—but no bread to make toast. Why didn't I think? I could have gone to Fortnum's yesterday before leaving London. Stop at a shop? Of course. But I haven't any money, I only brought two shillings and that went on the coffee in King's Parade, how to pay the taxi, there's no money at home either. Oh Jesus, Jesus Christ...

'Please let me.'

Seeing her distress, Hugh had at once taken out his purse and paid for the taxi.

'But I like Heinz Spaghetti and tinned sausages.'

... Well, he'd eaten it all, and there'd even been a cup of Camp Coffee—no milk, of course, but he said he didn't mind about that. And now she really must assert herself, get the upper hand, dominate like Isobel said. Mummy knows best.

'You look tired, Hugh,' she said. 'Come upstairs and lie down.'

... And really it wasn't too bad. She seemed to have got hold of some pretty way-out ideas from somewhere, and this one at least was a bit ambitious for a woman of her build, but it wasn't going badly at all ... even if she was a bit fierce with those huge teeth.

'Patricia, nice Patricia,' he said.

'Hugh, nice Hugh. Aren't bodies fun?'

'Yyyoowww. Try the other way again. Between your breasts.'

'All right, but don't look. My breasts are horrid. Like snakes.'

'Lovely long snakes, sliding and sliding. Go on ... go on ...'

'Mrs Llewyllyn,' called a female voice from downstairs, 'oh, Mrs Llew-yyyllll-yn. I saw you come home in your taxi, so I've brought Baby back a bit early.' And then lower but clearly audible through the open door, 'Go on, Baby darling. Run upstairs to Mummy.'

'Mummy, Mummy, Mummy ...'

'Into the wardrobe, Hugh.'

'Mummy, Mummy, Mummy ...'

'That's it. Mind your ... Hugh, I've *got* to shut the door. *Get it out of the way.*'

'Mummy, Mummy ...'

'Down between your legs—like *that.*'

Slam. And a rush of little feet on the landing.

'Oh Mummy, you do look funny. Why haven't you got any clothes on?'

'Because I took them off and put them in the wardrobe.'

'Why?'

'Because I've been resting.'

'But you *haven't* put them in the wardrobe. They're down here all over the floor. So what are you doing by the wardrobe?'

'I was just going to get some other ones out.'

'Can I help you choose them?'

'No. I've decided to put those ones on again after all.'

Patricia crossed the room, scooped her clothes off the floor and started to dress herself under the close and malicious inspection of Baby. She was very afraid lest Baby might notice Hugh's clothes, which were piled neatly on the chair by the dressing table, but she needn't have worried, as Baby was too fascinated by her mother's anatomy to have eyes for anything else.

'And now,' Patricia said, as she tugged her dress down over her sweaty rump, 'Mummy and Baby will go for a nice walk.'

'Where?'

'By the river, I suppose.' And then rather louder, so that Hugh could hear in the wardrobe, 'We'll go for a nice walk by the river and not get back till tea.'

'Shouldn't we make the bed first?'

'No. We can do that later. So we'll forget it, Baby. We'll forget it,' she called bleakly towards the wardrobe, 'just forget it. We just won't think about it any more.'

Mummy knows best.

As soon as all was quiet, Hugh extracted himself from the wardrobe (having not sustained any very serious personal injury), put on his clothes, and set out for Cambridge. Since Patricia and Baby were to be in the region of the river, and since it was clear that Patricia did not wish to set eyes on him again, he walked along the by-road to Trumpington, where he caught a bus.

As he was carried along the Trumpington Road and past

the Botanical Gardens, he attempted to cast an account of the day's events. First, the Rylands Prize: excellent. Second, this incident with Patricia Llewyllyn: that too would have been good in its way, if it hadn't had so ludicrous an ending. What a pity, he thought; we were both enjoying it so much; but as things turned out, it may have done positive harm. Not indeed to me, he thought, though it has left me jumpy and dissatisfied, but to poor Patricia, who may well think in terms of divine intervention (or something of the sort) and never attempt to rebel against her lot again. Certainly, her last few words before she left the bedroom with Baby had shown a grim determination to call the whole thing off for good.

But perhaps, he thought, that was only her first reaction to the shock of interruption. Perhaps she will think again. If so, do I want to go on with it? On the whole, he was disposed to think not. It had all been unusual, rather moving and very educative, and there was no doubt that Patricia's physical attributes were both ample and curious. But as against all this, it would be neither comfortable nor prudent to have an affair with the wife of a don. It was obvious that the obliging neighbour who had delivered Baby must already have smelt a sizeable rat, and though Tom Llewyllyn would doubtless take a fairly enlightened view of such quadrupeds, there was no denying that they carried dangerous fleas and were best left undisturbed behind the arras. And so, while Hugh was deeply regretful that the antics on Mrs Tom Llewyllyn's bed had not reached their proper culmination, he was, by and large, disinclined to make or even take any opportunity for their renewal.

In any case, he thought, as he walked from the bus stop to the main gate of Lancaster, God knows where I shall be after this business on Sunday. If the worst comes to the worst, I may not even have time to collect the Rylands Prize, let alone go a-wooing to Grantchester. I wish it were over, he thought: it is the right thing to do and nothing will stop me doing it, but I wish to God that Sunday was over and myself safely back with my books. And with Hetta, if she'll have me. The trouble is, he told himself as he walked into the Great Court, that this sort of thing never *is* over. Revolution is self-perpetuating. Once you start, you have to go on to the end—of the ever-receding end—or there's no point in starting. Mayerston will never set me free, unless he's defeated and got rid of; and if that happens, I may have to go too. I'm trapped, he told himself: I have no way out, ever . . . except by deserting Mayerston . . .

He was nearing Willow Bridge now, and among those who were standing on it and staring over Scholars' Meadow was Hetta. Or someone very like her. He quickened his step. Yes, surely it was. If he asked her, she would come to his room, listen to him, hear his troubles. She might even take pity on him, when she knew how unhappy he was, and give herself again despite her vow.

'Hetta,' he called, as he hurried towards the bridge, 'oh, Hetta.'

Hetta turned and waved.

'Oh, Hetta . . .'

'Never mind her,' said a voice by his side; 'I want a word with you. Now.'

Tom Llewyllyn.

'Here he is,' said Tom to Daniel Mond.

Tom had led Hugh fiercely across Willow Close and up into Daniel's rooms on staircase Omega. Daniel was lying full length on his sofa, looking pale and persecuted, fiddling uneasily with the silk scarf which he always wore round his throat. Tom shoved Hugh forward, like a police constable propelling a vagrant towards the station sergeant's desk, and then fell back to hover alertly by the door, as though he anticipated that Hugh was going to run for it at any moment.

'Oh,' said Daniel, and then, 'Ah . . . I've just heard about the Rylands Prize, Hugh. Well done. It must have been a wonderful essay.'

This was not what Hugh expected in the circumstances, and plainly not what Tom expected either. He now advanced and stood, almost threateningly, over Daniel's head.

'We are here to discuss a different piece of writing,' Tom said. 'Show him, Daniel.'

'Oh . . . er . . . yes,' said Daniel, and passed Hugh a sheet of folded quarto.

This was an anonymous letter, which said that Daniel was a reactionary Judas who had betrayed the prophet Beyfus. Daniel, it seemed, was also a high priest and a Pharisee, the false Jew who had spurned the oppressed and the humble among his people, whose voice was the voice of Beyfus. Daniel was a filthy Jewish Fascist and Daniel was Fascist Jewish filth.

'Your gang wrote that,' said Tom when Hugh had finished reading.

'No. Why should they? What good can it do them?'

'*Someone* wrote it.'

'Not me. Why show it to me?'

'Jacquiz Helmut warned me,' said Daniel in a placating voice, 'that this sort of thing was likely to happen. He warned me weeks ago.'

'It's the work of a psychotic,' said Hugh, 'or some one with a personal spite against Daniel.'

'Jacquiz said,' persisted Daniel, who was obviously finding it an effort to speak at all, 'that people would get angry. When they get angry, he said, they look for faces to punch, and they prefer Jewish ones.'

'Why?' asked Hugh, genuinely concerned to know.

'Because Jewish faces are clever and self-righteous.'

'Well, he was certainly right about that.'

'Thank you, Hugh . . . Your candour is appreciated.'

'Never mind all that,' said Tom. 'The real point is that people can easily get out of control. You know that, Balliston. You know, as well as anyone, that once you start stirring people up they may do anything. This,' he said, snatching the letter from Hugh, 'and far, far worse. So why,' he screamed into Hugh's face, 'have you helped your rotten, scummy friends to do this to Daniel?'

'How unfortunate,' said Daniel inconsequently (deprecating Tom's noise and fury but uncertain how to quench them), 'that this had to happen on the day Hugh has won the Rylands prize. Well done again, Hugh. I am pleased.'

'I wish I was. It's all been spoilt.'

'You've only got yourself to blame for that,' said Tom, who had sensed Daniel's distaste for his honking and was now speaking in a low voice that was parched and crackling with hate. 'I dare say you didn't write this thing, but you're to blame, because you've licked up the slime of envy from the gutters and gone round breathing it out in rant.'

Hugh ignored this.

'You don't look at all well,' he said to Daniel. 'Is there anything I can do?'

'Yes,' said Daniel. 'Stop making this horrible trouble for us all. Write your essays and give us pleasure. Don't let your good name get mixed up in all that,' he pointed a limp finger at the letter which Tom was still clutching. 'Stay away from that.'

'But can't you understand?' said Hugh wearily. 'That letter has nothing to do with the people I'm working for or the cause I serve. It's something different, separate, totally irrelevant.'

Tom grunted with anger.

'And *can't* you understand,' he said, 'that if only you and your kind had kept quiet in the first place, this letter would never have been written? You set the climate, for it, Balliston; you whipped up the hatred from which it sprang. What does Daniel care who actually wrote it? All he wants, all any of us wants, is to be left in peace.'

'But that's just it,' said Hugh. 'You're all so complacent that we have a duty to rouse you. You've let your consciences become so lethargic that if we don't make a row we'll never wake you up.'

'Look here, Hugh,' said Daniel, 'would you mind going away? I realise that your motives are pure and high-minded, and I'm quite sure that the young have a lot to teach us all, but will you kindly go away and leave us in peace and quiet?'

'*I* didn't ask myself up here,' said Hugh huffily, and flounced out of the room.

When Hetta saw Tom confront Hugh and lead him off to Daniel's staircase, she knew at once from Tom's face that something unpleasant had happened. At first she was minded to stay on Willow Bridge until Hugh came out again and then ask him what was up. But as the minutes went by, she realised that she was now late for her tea-time appointment with Balbo, and since it wasn't fair to keep the poor old darling waiting (and since she was in any case very hungry), she moved herself smartly off towards Sitwell's.

And so it came about that when Hugh left Tom and Daniel he did not, as he had hoped and expected, find Hetta waiting for him. Forgetting the friendly wave which she had given before he went off with Tom, he now assumed that she was deliberately avoiding him, and this, after his frustration at Grantchester and the disagreeable scene in Daniel's room, put him in a very bitter mood indeed. It was quite intolerable that the world should so misuse the winner of the Rylands Prize: who did they all think they were? Well, by the time he and Mayerston had finished with them, they were certainly going to find out: parasites, reactionaries, decadents, that's what they were, Tom, Hetta, Patricia, Daniel, the lot, and it was going to be made very plain to them that there was no longer any place for their sort in a well ordered modern society. Come 12.30 on Sunday, now only some forty-four hours away, he, Hugh Edward Balliston, was going to give them a very nasty shock.

'There's something very odd about that young man,' said Tom to Daniel as soon as Hugh had gone.

'He's sound at heart,' said Daniel: 'tiresome but genuine. Not at all odd as boys go nowadays.'

'I didn't mean that. I meant something particular—something I only noticed just as he was leaving. Daniel ... Balliston had a deep bite on the lobe of his right ear.'

'And so?'

'Biting ear-lobes is a trick of Patricia's.'

'For Christ's sake, Tom. Biting ear-lobes is a trick of any woman's.'

'It's a trick of Patricia's when she gets excited. She does it almost without knowing—and very painful it can be. Right across the top of the lobe, drawing blood. Balliston had blood there, Daniel.'

'Patricia doesn't even know him. She never comes in from Grantchester.'

'Yes, but that's just where she saw him. Weeks ago, Daniel, she saw him there and asked me about him ... in some detail. And she *does* come into Cambridge. The other day, so Wilfred the porter told me, she was waiting about outside the college for a good two hours. Wilfred went out and spoke to her: she was rather peculiar, he said.'

'Tom, Tom, Tom. What's that to do with Hugh Balliston?'

'And since she's been back from London, she's been acting totally out of character. She's encouraging me to stay here in college. She doesn't want me back in my own home.'

'*Tom* ...'

'It fits, Daniel. Anyway, there's something up with her, and I mean to find out what.'

Tom crossed the room to the telephone on Daniel's desk.

'Tom ... you're not jealous?'

'No,' said Tom between his teeth; 'just curious.'

He lifted the receiver.

'Tom dear,' said Daniel, 'put it down.'

'Why?'

'You're being unreasonable and unkind. You're getting worked up because of a coincidence which probably means absolutely nothing.'

'There's something going on, and I know it.'

'Whatever it is, let her tell you when she wants to herself.'

'Suppose she doesn't?'

'Then you'll have lost her confidence, in which case you'll have only yourself to thank.'

'That's the one thing I couldn't bear. I don't mind what she does, Daniel, as long as she tells me. Now, if I ring up and ask, she will tell me, because she's a very truthful woman, and then I can tell myself I'm still in her confidence. But if I don't ring . . . and she says nothing . . . what am I to tell myself then?'

'The truth. That you've failed her and she no longer trusts you,' Daniel paused and started breathing very heavily. 'Tom,' he said in a voice so small and thin that he sounded like a man calling for help from the depth of an immense chasm, 'please do as I ask. Please, Tom. Don't do anything unkind. I couldn't bear it now if you did something unkind. You're all—— Oh dear, oh dear, whatever am I saying?'

'Danny . . . what on earth's the matter?'

Tom put down the telephone receiver and came to stand over Daniel.

'I'm sorry, Tom. I'm not well. My throat. It gets infected again sometimes, it opens inside, you see, and it hurts me so much, Tom, and all this to make it worse.'

'*Opens inside?* What in God's name have you got?'

'I tried to kill myself once—oh, a long time ago, and I can't even tell you why—and . . . *this* is what I did.'

He clawed his silk scarf away to show the flushed, puffy lesion, six inches long.

'But it's worse inside, Tom, and it flares up at me. I've got anti-biotics, but I have to use the tablets more and more often, and every time they take longer to help. *Stay with me, Tom.'*

Tom looked down at Daniel and at last, briefly but gravely, he nodded his head.

'I'll stay, Daniel. But in a little while, I'm going to have you taken over to my rooms, because they're bigger and so we can both sleep there. And there I will be with you and take care of you, until you are quite better. And then you will come back to your own rooms here, and I will go back to Patricia. You understand what I am saying, Daniel?'

'Yes, Tom. You are saying that you are not a man who disappears when he is most wanted. The way Fielding Gray used to disappear.'

'Remember, Danny, I come from the people. Disappearing when you're wanted is very much an upper-class habit.'

Ivor Winstanley, calling on Jacquiz Helmut, was surprised to find two large packed suitcases standing at the ready by the door.

'Going away, Jacquiz?' Ivor said. 'In the middle of full term?'

'I have to consult a specialist about my health. Yours might benefit if you did the same.'

Ivor pondered this for some time. At length:

'There's nothing the matter with my health,' he said with some contempt.

'No? I should have thought your drinking was wearing you down a bit.'

'Nevertheless, Jacquiz, I'll stick it out here. I may be a decaying old sot, but I know whose salt I've been eating all these years.'

'Don't make heroic gestures, Ivor. Ageing and overfed scholars,' said Jacquiz Helmut, 'can seldom carry them off.'

'I am bound to admit,' wrote Robert Constable in his record, 'that matters are not turning out as I had hoped. Despite my lenient treatment of Hugh Balliston, the extremists have managed to twist the affair in such a way as to cause mounting indignation throughout the whole University and beyond it. If Balliston isn't exactly a martyr, he's not far off it, and something has occurred to increase his face value (so to speak).

'For he has just won the Rylands Prize with an essay so distinguished that the judges have recommended its publication at the expense of the Chest. As far as that goes I'm delighted, but there's no doubt that this achievement will turn Balliston into a more prominent figure than ever and make of him an even more powerful tool in the hands of his exploiters.

'These must surely be planning to make use of him as soon as possible; but *how*? If only I had the smallest clue, I might devise some workable tactic. As it is, however, they have learned their lesson from the failure of the Garden Hostel protest; they now realise that to advertise their intentions is to vitiate them, and they have kept very close indeed about their next move. Even that ass Tony Beck has given nothing away. One can only stand to, as it were, and be ready for anything from any direction, a nerve-racking predicament which I have not experienced since the war; and come to that, I could almost wish I still had my old company of Gurkhas at my back to see me through . . .

'One minor nuisance. Jacquiz Helmut has left for London this morning, on the plea that he must have a series of important consultations with his heart specialist. He says he must be away at least a week, and this will make trouble over the history supervisions at the worst possible time, just before the exams. A headache for the Tutor, who is not the most resourceful of men.

'And one routine bore. Tomorrow is Madrigal Sunday, and I must give the customary luncheon party in the Lodge after the madrigals. This kind of occasion brings Elvira out at her silliest. Although we have the five most competent college servants in to cook and serve, she somehow contrives to put even these off their stroke and turn the thing into a fiasco. Last year would have been catastrophe, if it hadn't been for some memorable jokes from Tom Llewyllyn, who just managed to save the situation. But this year we shan't have Tom to depend on, for he tells me that he is seeing after poor Daniel (who is ill and also badly upset by an anonymous letter he has received) and doesn't care to leave him. All in all, though, perhaps this is just as well, because it seems that Tom has invited that contemptible fellow Fielding Gray for the week-end, and if Tom were coming to the lunch I suppose Gray would have to come too, which would really be most disagreeable to me after all that has happened over the years ...'

Tom, Daniel and Tom's guest, Fielding Gray, were having dinner in Tom's rooms in Sitwell's. Because of Daniel's throat, Tom had ordered only the wettest dishes offered by the kitchen; but even so Daniel was making heavy going, this being due less to the state of his health than to the distaste which he felt at the appearance of Fielding Gray. When Daniel had last seen him fifteen years before, Gray had been a handsome if somewhat dissipated man of twenty-five; this evening he was not only middle-aged and obese but hideously disfigured in the face by the injuries which he had received while on active service in Cyprus in 1958. As Daniel had been warned of this, it should not have come as a shock, and indeed at first he was quite unworried by it; but as the evening went on, Gray's one red eye and pink plastic cheeks seemed to Daniel such an obscene travesty of the human countenance as to be proof positive of an evil which lay deep seated, not in Gray himself, but in God. This being so, Daniel tried to blame God and suffer Fielding Gray, which, given Gray's proximity and God's absence, was not an easy task.

'So you're never going back to London?' Tom was saying to his guest.

'Except for odd days, no. Tessie Buttock's been on at me about it—tired of London means tired of life, she says, it's the only quotation she knows—but I can do without London from now on. Anyhow it doesn't suit Harriet.'

'Harriet?'

'Harriet Ongley. My rehabilitator and companion. She thinks London is bad for my character.'

'And is it?' said Daniel.

'I wouldn't know, Daniel. You see, I haven't got a character any more. I've never really had one since I was rejected by this college.'

'So you told me,' said Daniel, 'the first time we met. It was false and self-pitying then, and it's much worse now. You were a perfectly adequate soldier—as far as I could understand it—and you're now a successful novelist. Which reminds me: I must tell you, Fielding, that I strongly resent the way you twisted the real facts in *Operation Apocalypse*.'

'*Apocalypse* was a novel, Danny. It was not intended to render events which actually happened but to tell a story which would entertain readers. Although it was *suggested* by what went on in Göttingen that summer, there is no further connection.'

'That's what I told him,' said Tom.

'Then why use my character?' said Daniel.

'To save myself the effort of inventing one.'

'But if you use my character, you should respect it.'

'The character in that novel,' said Fielding Gray, 'is simply a collection of words. It does not exist as a real entity, and there is therefore no question of respecting it as one respects a real human being. One merely disposes of it—i.e. of the words of which it consists—in such a manner as to hold the attention of the reader, thus encouraging him to pay out ready money for one's next book.'

'So that is your opinion of your art?'

'I never said I was an artist. I am an entertainer, Danny. I arrange words in pleasing patterns in order to make money. I try to give good value—to see that my patterns are well wrought—but I do not delude myself by inflating the nature of my function. I try to be neat, intelligent and lucid: let others be "creative" or "inspired".'

In Grantchester the conversation was less thoughtful but equally acrimonious.

'Bed time now, Baby.'

'No.'

'Nice bath first with Quacky Whacky, then into lovely warm bed.'

'No, *no*, NO.'

Christ, thought Patricia wearily, sometimes I wish she were dead. But better her for company than no one at all; at least there'll be some other human creature in the house during the long night to come.

'All right,' she said: 'one more game of Snakes and Ladders, and *then* bed.'

Snakes and Ladders; 'lovely long snakes, sliding and sliding'; Christ.

'You must understand,' Fielding Gray was saying over the brandy, 'that I do not want money out of greed. I want it only as a means to being independent.'

'Independent of Harriet Ongley?'

Gray tightened his grip on his brandy glass and pursed what passed for his lips. Clearly this topic, though he himself had introduced it earlier, was not a welcome one.

'That's another matter altogether,' he said thinly. 'What I'm talking about is making oneself independent of the system . . . being in a position to tell all the bloody bureaucrats and politicians to go to the devil. I want to be beyond any man's interference.'

'Independence as a denial of power,' said Tom slowly; 'a very respectable ambition. But doomed, Fielding. The bureaucrats and the politicians, the men who relish power, are determined to tie down every last one of us. At the moment, as you say, money can still procure a modest freedom; but this is an affront to the power boys and they're stopping it as fast as they can. First they tax your money; then they forbid you to use it except as and where they see fit; and finally they'll just sequester it—or render it worthless. Money as a means to independence is all but finished.'

'So you think there's no hope?'

'I think,' said Tom, 'that very soon the only way of achieving independence of movement or action will be through winning power for oneself first. You're trying to evade the power boys, Fielding; but under modern conditions the only way to do that is to beat them at their own game. You can't be independent of them any more, but you can rise above them.'

'Of course,' said Daniel, 'there is an easier way. If one is prepared to settle just for *intellectual* independence, there's not much they can do to stop you.'

'They can stop you publishing.'

'But they can't stop you thinking your own thoughts.'

'Can't they?' said Gray. 'A person who is thinking his own thoughts has a calm and satisfied look on his face which is very easy to recognise. As soon as *they* see that look, they can come and wipe it off.'

'Then one must live alone.'

'They can soon stop that. Rational use of available accommodation, they'll say: at least five people to every house—and one of them a government informer in case anyone presumes to think his own thoughts.'

'Do we have to depress ourselves like this?' said Tom. 'It's such a beautiful evening.'

They all stood by the window and looked down on the Great Court. Someone was playing the organ in the Chapel ('Where my sheep may safely graze') and Henry VI pondered piously over his fountain.

' "Sitis boni pueri," ' said Fielding, ' "mites et dociles, servientes Domino." '

'What's that?'

'I should have thought you'd have known. It's what Henry VI said to a group of scholars when he met them one day near Eton. "Be good boys," ' he translated, ' "gentle and biddable, serving the Lord." There is worse advice than that.'

'It hardly conduces to independence,' said Tom.

'But it could make for peace of mind . . . Who's that,' said Fielding, 'that young man walking down by the Chapel? *He* doesn't look very gentle or biddable.'

'That's Hugh Balliston. He's a good boy really,' said Daniel, 'but just lately he's had rather a confusing time.'

Early though it was, Hugh was going home to bed. He was unhappy and bored and lonely and also very afraid, so that temporary oblivion was really the only answer. And anyhow, tomorrow would be a long day.

I wish Hetta was with me, he thought. It's so lonely without her. Besides, that's just what I need to help me to get to sleep.

'Miss Hetta?'

'Mr Blakeney?'

'Were you asleep?'

'Yes . . . but I'm glad you woke me up.'

She tweaked him and giggled softly.

'Next week,' said Balbo, 'I thought we'd look at more churches. If you'd like to.'

'I'd love to. You explain them so beautifully.'

'We might start with Ely Cathedral. "Merrily sang the monks in Ely," ' quoted Balbo,

' "*When Cnut, King, rowed thereby;*
Row, my knights, near the land,
And hear we these monks' song . . ." '

'Oooh,' shivered Hetta, 'couldn't we go tomorrow?'

'No, Miss Hetta. We need a whole day for Ely, and tomorrow's the Madrigals. You wouldn't want to miss them, after all I've told you about them?'

'The Madrigals tomorrow,' said Daniel, as they turned away from the window.

'I thought that was in May Week,' said Fielding, 'at the end of term.'

'It is. The Cambridge Madrigal Society sings them from punts on the river. But tomorrow it's the Lancaster Madrigals—sung by our choir in front of the West Door of the Chapel. Immediately after Matins.'

'Very handy,' said Tom, 'Right under my back window.'

'But surely,' said Fielding, 'Matins and Madrigals don't mix.'

'This college,' said Tom, 'has always taken the Chaucerian view . . . that God should be heartily thanked for *all* his gifts. Although I am not a believer myself, I find a lot to be said for it.'

Although the spirit of Madrigal Sunday might be, as Tom Llewyllyn had observed, Chaucerian, the scene which was set for the singing of the Madrigals was more Edwardian than medieval. The Great West Door of the Chapel was open, giving a view of the interior as far as the screen, which thus formed a distant back-drop. Immediately outside the open door, on the two top steps, were ranked the adult members of the Choir, dressed in morning tails and grey top hats, the Reverend Andrew Ogden being on one wing and the Senior Choral Scholar on the other; while on the next step below them, in single line, were the Choristers, who were got up in Eton suits and straw boaters, the latter bound with ribands of the royal purple which divided, at the rear, into two strands and flowed down to the Choristers' bottoms. On the gravel path beneath the steps, arrayed in velvet cap and quartered tabard (red rose, lion rampant, lion couchant and white lily), stood the Master of the Musick. In his right hand he held a baton which resembled a Prussian Field Marshal's, and with this he would presently elicit song. At the moment, however, he was turned away from the Choir and watching the audience assemble on the north eastern corner of the rear lawn.

The grander or more far-sighted of this audience were

provided with comfortable chairs, of which there were three crescent-shaped rows cutting off the tip of the lawn. Behind the chairs, people strolled or sat about on the grass, some of them dressed, like those who were seated, in grey frock coats, and almost all of them conforming to the custom of the day, which was to wear, on the right hand lapel, a large spray of red and white flowers, white for the purity of the Blessed Henry's soul and red for Lancaster. A few of those seated, as well as a very few of those on the lawn behind them, wore pansies of the royal purple, a privilege reserved to such Lancaster men as could trace a true line of descent from knights or noblemen who had served King Henry VI in court or field or castle.

In the front row of the seats (all but two of which were now filled) was the Honourable Grantchester Pough, totally recovered, one would have said, from his recent mishap and concentrating his gaze on the choristers Dinkie and Dudu, whom he was to entertain to luncheon when the Madrigals were done.

'Gloozer's giving us that look,' said Dinkie.

'Shut up, will you. We're just meant to stand here and look pretty.'

'I shall start giggling if he goes on gloozing at me like that.'

'Well, look at someone else. Look at Lord Beyfus. He's with that lady you said you liked so much.'

For Lord Beyfus and Mona Corrington were also there in the front row.

'Ready?' said Mona.

'I'll do what you made me promise. But I do wish they wouldn't interrupt the Madrigals.'

'Madrigals,' snorted Mona: 'hey nonny nothing.'

This was not the view which Balbo Blakeney was expressing to Hetta Frith, with whom he was sitting in the second row.

'I wish,' said Balbo, 'that I could write a madrigal for you, Miss Hetta.'

'What would you say, Mr Blakeney?'

'I should say that your hair is golden and your lips are ruby. And that the smell of your flesh is like new-mown hay.'

'I don't think,' tittered Hetta, 'that it would be a very original sort of madrigal.'

'But I should mean every word of it. You in that pretty white dress ... the spirit of summer.'

'I'm glad you like my dress. I bought it specially. You did say white was the colour? White, with red and white flowers?'

'Yes, I did.'

'Then why are you wearing a purple pansy?'

Very modestly, Balbo started to explain, and was overheard by the most Honourable the Marquis Canteloupe, the shadow minister of Commerce, who had been taking part in a debate in the Union the previous evening and was now sitting in the third row with Somerset Lloyd-James (MP), his friend and jackal.

'I never heard such snobbishness,' said Canteloupe. 'Fellow in front boasting that his family goes back to Agincourt.'

Somerset took a squint in the direction indicated by Canteloupe.

'I think that's Balbo Blakeney the biochemist,' Somerset said. 'If so, he's a second cousin to Blakeney of the Marsh—you know, the Norfolk lot. They were made knights after Agincourt and barons at Henry VI's succession.'

'Nothing to boast about. Every Tom, Dick and Harry who could still stand up was knighted after Agincourt.'

'Not a bad occasion for it, all the same. There weren't many Canteloupes at Agincourt.'

'Nonsense. My ancestor, Gilbert Tyrrel, was in charge of the other-rank brothel for the whole campaign. He came back to England with 40,000 marks, a thundering great dose and a grant of arms as an esquire. So much,' said Canteloupe, 'for the sort of rubbish which went on at Agincourt.'

This conversation had been heard but not heeded by Mrs Harriet Ongley, who was looking for Fielding Gray. Early that morning, as soon as she woke up, she had a sudden intuition that Fielding was either drinking too much or otherwise getting up to mischief, and so she had decided to come to Cambridge and fetch him home to Broughton. She had looked for him all over the lawn and was now carefully scanning the seats. What she didn't know was that Fielding was with Tom and Daniel in Tom's set at the north end of Sitwell's, from the rear bedrooms of which they would have good sight and sound of the Madrigals. They also had sight of Mrs Ongley, whom Fielding now pointed out to his friends.

'Bloody bitch has come sniffing after me,' Fielding said. 'I suppose I should be flattered.'

'Does she often do this.'

'Only when I go somewhere associated with my past. She's afraid I may get sucked back into it.'

'What do you want to do?' said Tom. 'Shall I ask her up?'

'No. She hasn't seen me, thank God.'

'She'll enquire at the Porters' Lodge,' said Daniel, 'and they'll send her here.'

'Then I'll go quietly,' said Fielding; 'but until then we'll forget her. I see bloody old Somerset Lloyd-James has got himself here.'

'There's worse news than Somerset,' remarked Tom.

'What can you mean?'

'You see that tubby little man with the huge hat? About forty-five degrees and ten yards from your Mrs Ongley.'

'Yes.'

'Well, that,' said Tom, 'is Alfie Schroeder of the Billingsgate Press. He used to be a reporter but he's been a columnist for some years now.'

'I met him once,' said Daniel. 'A very decent little man.'

'Decent or not,' replied Tom, 'Alfie means trouble. He's devoted to his wife and family, and nothing would bring him all the way here from Willesden on a Sunday morning except for a very hot tip.'

'Perhaps he wants the cultural experience? To embellish his column.'

'In that case he'd bring his wife. If Alfie's here alone, wearing that hat, Alfie's smelt trouble.'

Which was exactly what Alfie had smelt. Although he enjoyed this kind of occasion (since he knew a good thing when he saw it), he would never have sacrificed a domestic Sunday to the Madrigals had he not expected a sensation in Three-D and Technicolor. Meanwhile, however, he was looking forward to hearing such of the Madrigals as would be sung before the sensation, and noted with pleasure that the Master of the Musick was now looking at his watch and tensing himself as for action. Which followed speedily. The ranks of Choral Scholars and Choristers parted at the centre; down the steps, from within the Chapel, came Provost and Mrs Constable; the Master of the Musick saluted them by raising his baton to his forehead; and the Provost, having bowed first to the Master, then to the Choir and then to the audience, handed his wife to one of the vacant chairs in the front row. He's wearing one of those purple pansies, thought Alfie (who did not know why they were worn, or that the Constables had held Reculver Castle for Henry VI and for many kings before him): he's wearing a purple pansy, Alfie thought, and he looks as proud as the very devil, and I wonder how he'll come out of this lot, when it starts.

And now the Master of the Musick held his baton high and all were silent. Even Mona Corrington was awed, and Harriet Ongley was frozen where she stood. Hetta clasped Balbo's hand; the Marquis Canteloupe, who badly wanted a drink, did not dare bring out his hipflask for very shame; and Somerset Lloyd-James forbore to sneer. Tom blinked back tears and Daniel closed his eyes to hide them; Fielding Gray forgot his wounded face; while Dinkie and Dudu, taut with anticipation, slightly parted their lovely lips and——

'—Spring, the sweet spring, is the year's pleasant king;
Then blooms each thing, then maids dance in a ring,
Cold doth not sting, the pretty birds do sing:
Cuckoo, jug-jug, pu-we, to-witta-woo.'

'... My sweetest Lesbia, let us live and love
And though the sager sort our deeds reprove,
Let us not weigh them: Heav'n's great lamps do dive
Into their west and straight again revive
But soon as once set is our little light,
Then must we sleep an everlasting night ...'

'What's that they're singing?' said Daniel to Tom, whose attention, after half an hour of madrigals, was beginning to wander.

'Campion,' volunteered Fielding Gray: 'a translation of Catullus. I once translated that poem myself. Very difficult because it's so simple. Luminous in Latin but trite in English, probably because——'

But this particular essay in comparative semantics, though holding its own in competition with Campion, was now to be silenced for ever by a new sound: that of a massive brass band, which struck into 'Jerusalem' like a battery of heavy howitzers. The noise, which totally swamped the singing of the Choir, came from the region of the Willow Bridge; all eyes which had hitherto been aimed at the West Door, now turned through an arc of 180°; and what they saw was this.

Marching off the bridge and on to the south west corner of the rear lawn was the band which had just begun 'Jerusalem', scarlet, gorgeous, trimly moving, and led by two white-booted drum majorettes whose thighs were exposed right up to their lacy knickers. Clearly, thought Alfie Schroeder, this ensemble had mustered in the avenue on the other side of the bridge, under cover of the trees; but even so, it was a tribute to the singers that no one, apparently, had noticed what was going on. For to judge from what now came into view there must have been a great deal going on. Swaying off the bridge behind the band was a large platform, borne aloft by some twenty men, on which a lone youthful figure was posed in an attitude of aspiration and defiance; and behind this again came a forest of placards (like the insignia carried behind the Roman Emperor in some extravaganza of the screen) bearing bold and lapidary legends which denounced Lancaster, its Chapel and its dons, while praising Beyfus, Balliston and various aspects of progress. Behind the placards marched a small but deadly-looking platoon of leather-jacketed boys; following them was a second platform and a second tableau, this one consisting of a huge and evidently vinous papier mâché cleric who was trampling sadistically on the belly of a real, live and absolutely naked girl; and after this there came a column, a very long column indeed (so Alfie could now discern as he peered into the distant trees) of young men and women.

First reactions were various. Harriet Ongley, who had lived for a long time in America, assumed that all this was a planned part of the festivities and was utterly entranced, forgetting for the moment her anxiety about Fielding Gray and her irritation at failing to find him. A surprisingly large number of the inferior spectators seemed to share her view of the matter and made way for the band with respectful admiration. Among those seated, however, there was no doubt that something was amiss: even the Marquis Canteloupe, who was not well up in the forms of Cambridge life, detected something untoward and remarked to Somerset Lloyd-James that 'this show' might well 'fuck up' the Provost's luncheon, to which they had both been bidden, so hadn't they better think of finding some bloody pub to eat in? Others were bound to take a less detached attitude, not least among them the Provost himself, who signalled to the Master of the Musick to get the gaping Choir into song again, and then walked round to the rear of the seats to confront the now rapidly approaching procession. In the Provost's wake went Ivor Winstanley, who had no clear idea of what he meant to do but imagined (wrongly) that Constable would be glad of his assistance.

'And I will stand at thy right hand,' shouted Ivor (who was not strictly sober, having celebrated Madrigal Sunday with elevenses of sweet and thick Marsala), 'and guard the bridge with thee.'

Constable answered with a glacial nod, then held up his right hand to halt the scarlet bandsmen. Just for a moment, such was the authority in his manner, the bandsmen seemed to waver in their march; but when Ivor Winstanley unintentionally parodied the Provost's gesture with a pompous imitation, all hope was gone. The band came on apace, while the two drum majorettes, having planted their long batons in the lawn, tackled Ivor and the Provost respectively, tossing both well clear of the axis of advance with two simultaneously executed movements of elementary jiu-jitsu.

Meanwhile, the squad of leather jackets had come doubling up on the left flank of the column and were starting to clear a passage through the rows of seats. This they did quickly and competently, only pausing to brush aside anyone who attempted to prevent them and to punch him in the teeth if he persisted. One such was Grantchester Pough, who punched back—very hard and very low, since the circumstances, as he saw them, rendered the Queensbury Rules irrelevant. What deeds he might have done that day, or what black fate might have overcome him at the last, it is interesting to conjecture; but in actual fact, realising that he had responsibilities which precluded his brawling like a common sailor, he suddenly broke off from the mêlée, gathered up the Choristers (who were still gallantly celebrating the sexual obsessions of Catullus) with one sweep of his long arm, formed them into file with a crisp order, and led them away across the Great Court to the safety of his rooms.

It was at this stage in the proceedings that even Harriet Ongley realised that more than a mere carnival was afoot.

She longed for her true knight to ride up and save her (where *the dickens* was he?), but her true knight, who opined that Harriet deserved everything she got, continued to enjoy the scene from Tom Llewyllyn's window.

'That chap they're carrying,' he said. 'He's the one we saw skulking about last night.'

'Hugh Balliston,' said Tom crossly. 'And a perfect damn fool he looks.'

And felt. Despite the banner which was carried in front of him and announced that he was both the victim of a dead age and the embodiment of a new, Hugh felt like a twit. Although he had fiercely declined to take the pills he was offered before the march began, he now wished he'd accepted them. The grinding and self-conscious effort to look like a cross between Rodin's 'Thinker' and Joan of Arc was making him sweat through his shirt and grind his teeth in mental rage. Too late now. He hadn't taken the pills and must find some other analgesic. Watch the antics, then; no better distraction from one's own ills than the observation of human antics.

These were manifold, but the two most entertaining at the moment were, first, those of Somerset Lloyd-James, who was running away towards the side gate beyond the Chapel as fast as his spindly legs would carry him, pursued by howls of laughter from Lord Canteloupe; and second, those of Lord Beyfus, who had placed himself at the head of the procession, in front of the majorettes, and was leading the way up the Chapel steps towards the West Door. On and up he went, his bottom sagging and wagging like that of a worn out catamite, his head held high, his arms outstretched in front of him, on and up he went, like a fat little Moses ascending Sinai, towards the cowering ranks of Choral Scholars—only to plant his right foot in a boater abandoned by the fleeing Dudu and fall flat on his face, his left ankle at the same time becoming gaily cross-gartered by the long purple ribands which Dudu had sported from his hat.

Some were later to allege that Beyfus bounced when he fell. What is quite beyond dispute is that the charitable Andrew Ogden came down from the top step to Beyfus's aid, reaching him at the same time as frantic Mona Corrington, who had rushed up from the gravel. Together they got Beyfus on his feet; but since his right foot was stuck through the straw hat and his left was much impeded by the riband which joined the hat to his left ankle, he promptly fell down again, this time on his back. Both Mona and Andrew blamed the other for this; the difference being that Mona was now resentfully determined to manage Beyfus all by herself, whereas Andrew Ogden, forgiving her with all his Christian heart, was still eager to co-operate. What ensued was a tug-of-war, each of them heaving away at one arm of the supine Beyfus, to no effect whatever except repeatedly to jerk up the poor old Hebrew's napper and bring it cracking down again on the edge of the stone step beneath it.

And now most assuredly would this farcical scene have dissolved everyone present into unquenchable laughter and thus broken up the entire demonstration (ah, would that it had indeed been so), had not Mayerston emerged from nowhere in particular and given a quick, quiet order to a mature-looking leather boy. The latter gathered five more; the six of them moved up the Chapel steps like panthers; and within ten seconds they had made a kind of bundle of Mona, Beyfus, Ogden, boater, riband and all, and carted the whole lot off like one large parcel.

Whereupon Mayerston mounted the steps and things became serious again.

Mayerston's first action was to gesture politely but dismissively at the two rows of Choral Scholars, who, doubtless feeling that they had stood their ground for as long as could be expected, obediently dribbled off the steps. Mayerston then turned towards the band (which for some minutes now had been marking time while continuing to play), pointed his right forefinger at one drum majorette and his left at the other, turned about to face the West Door, and marched lightly and smartly through it. The majorettes pranced up behind him and the bandsmen followed, neatly forming their four ranks into file as they went in order to negotiate the door which, though wide, could not accommodate four men in line with bulky instruments.

After the band rode Hugh, rigidly triumphant on his platform, and after Hugh the papier mâché clergyman, who, being nearly as tall as the door itself, had to be eased inch by inch under the lintel, while the naked girl beneath his foot diverted public attention from the awkwardness of this manoeuvre by screaming and squirming in realistic agony. Meantime, the leather boys had been sorting out the column of student marchers in the rear. This now stretched diagonally across the lawn, over the Willow Bridge and along the avenue (so Alfie made out) right down to the Queen's Road. Clearly there was not room for this entire mob in the Chapel, and equally clearly the organisers were determined, from whatever motive, to avoid overcrowding; for the leather boys were now both marshalling and thinning out the column, despatching at least two persons in three to join a rapidly growing group round the statue of Henry VI in the Great Court and only admitting to the Chapel a carefully selected minority. Quite what the principle behind the selection was, Alfie could not determine: it had nothing to do with physique or gender, though it was possible, he thought, that those allowed into the Chapel were chosen as the dirtiest and most ill dressed. The reason for this preference was obscure to Alfie, but the basic strategy behind it all was as plain as the nose on his face. Those left outside the Chapel in the Great Court, quite apart from perpetrating casual outrages, would be amply able to deal with any resistance which the authorities might now attempt to rally and with any external threat to those gathered inside the Chapel, who could set about their business (whatever *that* might be) without fear of interruption. Inside or outside, Alfie asked himself; and decided that the big news lay within.

But how to get in? The column was now being very smoothly processed. The chosen were being waved swiftly up the steps and through the West Door, the others efficiently diverted into the Great Court. If the leather boys wanted you out, you stayed out. 'Press,' shouted Alfie, wagging a card and waddling up the steps—and was ushered in with deep bows of gratitude and respect.

'But they won't let me in so easily,' said Balbo Blakeney, who had observed this little incident.

'Why do you want to get in?' asked Hetta.

'To keep an eye on the old place.'

'There's nothing you can do. It's a blessing you can't get in.'

'But I think I can, Miss Hetta. There's a little door into one of the side-chapels. Unlocked, as a rule.'

'Don't go, Mr Blakeney.'

'Must, Miss Hetta. Got to keep an eye on the old place.'

'Then I'll come too.'

'No place for you, Missy. You cut off home.'

'I'll come too.'

'And so will I,' boomed the Marquis Canteloupe, who had been listening to this exchange and now found himself (despite his earlier aversion) liking both Balbo and Hetta very much indeed.

'Right,' said Balbo, 'but don't make so much din about it. Noise gets on my nerves.'

And he led the way round the north west tower of the Chapel and then eastwards along the north wall. This was an area seldom visited by anyone, as it consisted of a strip of rank grass (lying between the north wall of the Chapel and the southernmost building of the neighbour college) which had once been the Lancaster coal dump and was now used for dustbins. Although the smell was abominable, the arrangement always pleased Balbo who was amused by the medieval juxtaposition of grandeur and squalor. Canteloupe and Hetta were not so amused and started to retch, but Balbo led on stoutly, and when they were about forty yards from the east end of the Chapel, he suddenly darted behind a buttress, pushed through a cluster of waist-high nettles, and seized a rusty ring which hung from a low studded door.

Alfie Schroeder, meanwhile, had been wafted down the Chapel on a wave of precedence and prominently ensconced in the Provost's stall against the east side of the screen, with a full view of the chancel. This was somewhat disconcerting, even to a man of Alfie's agnostic temperament, as the altar had been cleared to make room for Hugh Balliston, who was now enthroned on top of it and was gazing in the rough direction of Alfie with a fierce look of misery that might just have been taken for revolutionary zeal. Alfie wasn't fooled for a moment: that boy, he told himself, is rueing the day. Of even more scandalous interest, however, was the deployment of the papier mâché cleric, who had been set up so that his buttocks were supported by the lectern (which was some thirty yards to the west of the altar and slap in the middle of the aisle) and his two feet were straddling his female victim, the latter being prone on the floor with her bottom aimed in a suggestive manner as for a long range shot at the West Window. The band, which had at last dispensed with 'Jerusalem' and gone on to a samba instead, was drawn up in two long lines, which stretched down, one on each side of the aisle, from either wing of the sanctuary to the eastern end of the choir; and for the rest, all seats whatever, from the Doctors' and Masters' stalls down to the meanest Chorister's bench, were crammed with the scruffiest, hairiest and most hangdog assemblage which it had ever been Alfie's luck to contemplate. I was right, he thought: it *was* the dirtiest they were letting in here—the dirtiest because the most resentful. So what does that point to?

But this question was not to be answered for a while. Even the practised leather boys must have time to arrange the rest of the congregation in the west end of the Chapel, and to judge from the racket that arose from the far side of the screen this would take some minutes yet. Alfie did not know whether to be glad or sorry about the delay. The more delay, the more chance of intervention and anti-climax (notwithstanding the massed guard in the Great Court) and the less chance of a scoop for Alfie's column; but the less chance, also, of some really sinister outcome, such as Alfie (knowing a good thing when he saw it) would deprecate in surroundings like these. In any event, there was nothing to do but wait.

This, at first, had been what Tom and Daniel felt as they watched the events below, from various of Tom's windows.

'Best stay put and keep quiet,' Daniel had said.

But as more and more filthy boys and girls piled into the Chapel, and as the crowd grew larger and larger round Henry VI's statue in the Great Court, Tom became restless.

'I can't bear it,' he said.

'What can we do?'

'We can go up into Jerusalem,' said Tom allusively, 'and perish with him.'

'With whom?'

'Can't you see what they're going to do? They're going to pull down that statue.'

And indeed a small group of leather boys was already surveying King Henry's statue and the fountain at its base, while another such group was coming through the crowd with pick-axes and coils of rope.

'Stay here, Tom,' Daniel said.

'No,' said Fielding Gray. 'Tom's right.'

'It's nothing to do with you. You were never even in the college.'

'I was elected a Scholar. They turned me away before I got here, but I was elected a Scholar.' Fielding turned to Tom. 'I'll come with you,' he said.

So Fielding and Tom (having persuaded Daniel, though he pressed to come too, that in his state of health he could only be an embarrassment) went up into Jerusalem, which in this instance lay down in the Great Court. Fielding, however, never quite reached his destination. The moment he emerged with Tom from Sitwell's, he was boarded, so to speak, by Harriet Ongley, who came running up on her strong, shapely legs, while her globular face (usually placid and benign) exploded into reproach like a flying sea-mine.

'Just where do you think you've been?' she screeched, seizing Fielding's left arm with both hands. 'I'm taking you home right now.'

If Tom expected any resistance from Fielding, he was disappointed. Hanging his head in shame and resignation, Fielding suffered himself to be towed away, lurching and stumbling, round the edge of the crowd and off to the front gate.

So here I am, thought Tom, and what do I do now? He eased his way through the crowd in order to see what was doing near the statue. Round Henry's neck were tied two ropes, two teams to pull on which were now being recruited by the leather boys. Tom supposed that if this failed to shift the statue they would then start work with the pick-axes, which for the present lay discarded on the ground, just by the rim of the basin into which the fountain was playing from under King Henry's piously pointed feet. Tom eyed the pick-axes and pondered within his heart: it could work; they might call his bluff, and God knew what would happen then, but it could just work. Anyway, he thought, there was no time for delay. The two teams to pull on the ropes were already made up; the two ropes, forming an angle of 40°, were already stretched taut from the poor king's neck. At any moment the order would come to heave. Now or never.

Tom bent down and seized a pickaxe. He struck a nearby leather boy hard on the head with the flat centre of the pick, gave him, as he reeled, a shove in the mid-riff with the helve, and sent him tumbling into the shallow water in the basin. He then climbed in after him, stood astride the unconscious body, and raised the pickaxe on high. All this he did in about five seconds, so that scarcely anyone even began to take in what was happening until he gave a demoniac squeal for silence.

'Listen to me,' he called, in the high-pitched, fanatical chant which he remembered from the Welsh chapels of his childhood. 'If any man pulls those ropes; or if any man seeks to harm that statue; or if any man comes near me: then I shall strike down with this pickaxe into this man's throat beneath me.'

From the outer crowd rose a hum of curiosity, but in the region of the statue everyone was quite silent. Tom, lifting his weapon even higher, wildly contorted his face, in the hope that he would look mad enough to mean what he said; and for the time at least the mob seemed to believe him. In any event, no one moved. But for how long? And for how long, Tom thought, can I go on dilating my eyes like a dervish and holding up this pick, which is already weighing a ton? No, he thought, if I'm to stay here I must devise distraction, not so much for the crowd as for myself from my own discomfort; a distraction which will leave me still alert, will indeed help me to remain so, but will also help me to forget the dull ache in my face and my arms.

So he opened his mouth and started to harangue. In the crazy manner of the Welsh preachers he had heard so often before he escaped from his own people, he lilted and babbled and chanted of sin and damnation and death. Yet his burden was secular: the hell of which he spoke was of this world, the hell of envy and sloth, and the salvation which he offered was also of this world, by grace of intelligence, truth and hard work.

A sermon of a not wholly dissimilar kind was going forward in the Chapel. This was delivered by Mayerston, and took the form of a series of violent denunciations of the church, the clergy and the entire academic establishment, which was still associated with them. Each denunciation was framed like the verse of a psalm; and after every verse Mayerston would pause while Tony Beck and two assistant leather boys inflicted brief and vicious assault on the papier mâché cleric by the lectern, who was thus being slowly and symbolically dismembered.

'Let them consume away like a snail,' howled Mayerston, 'and be like the untimely fruit of a woman: and let them not see the sun.'

Bash, wallop, and away went a papier mâché arm.

'They grin like a dog, and run through the city: and the foam of their jaws doth stink like the bowels of dead men.'

RRRiiippp, and off came half the surplice.

'Behold, they were conceived in beds of dung; and their sons and their daughters coupled together in the filth of sewers . . .'

How very jolly it would be, thought Lord Canteloupe, if one could use language like that in the Upper House. And I must say, he thought (wrinkling his battered but still fruity face into a sumptuous leer), I rather like the cut of that girl. Like Maisie doing that trick with her bum when I'm slow getting off the mark. I wish I could get a better look . . .

For although the little chantry in which Canteloupe and his companions were secreted was almost opposite the lectern, the view which it afforded was poor, since there was a great deal of elaborate stone tracery screening side-chapel from upper chancel, to say nothing of a high box tomb, which blocked the line of sight where the tracery divided, and the row of bandsmen who flanked the aisle. Canteloupe now decided that he would try to peer round the tomb, and was edging cautiously past the Maltese Cross which was carved on one end of it, when Balbo plucked him back.

'Mustn't be seen,' Balbo whispered.

'Quite right. Sorry. What are you going to do?'

'Nothing as long as they just go on like this. They're not doing the place any harm.'

But in fact the proceedings were now changing dramatically in nature, though whether or not they threatened what Balbo would consider harm was still uncertain. The papier mâché cleric, having suffered a final indignity in the groin, had now tottered to the floor, and the girl had arisen from among the remnants, freed at last, as one was intended to assume, from ancient oppression. This release she celebrated by giving a few rather clumsy hops and skips mimetic of her new autonomy, in which, however, she was not long allowed to indulge herself.

'You are free of your old tyrant,' boomed Mayerston from his place; 'now go to your new comrade.'

Whereupon Tony Beck took her by the wrist and led her briskly up to the altar, on to which (not without vigorous upward pressure applied by Beck to her posteriors) she at length managed to clamber. Hugh Balliston bent down from his throne in welcome; the girl looked up and spread her arms in adoration; and after fifteen seconds of preparatory endearment, it became only too plain what was now about to happen.

'By God,' said Canteloupe: 'they're going to do it on the altar.'

'Desecration,' said Hetta.

'But no damage,' said Balbo; 'that's the important thing.'

But someone else thought otherwise. Out of a small door (which led into a vestry at the east of the choir and the south side of the Chapel) there now hurtled a furious and gibbering priest: Oliver Clewes, who disapproved of the Madrigals and had been sulking in the vestry ever since Matins. Surprised and cut off in his lair by the advent of the demonstrators, Clewes had doubtless deemed it prudent to lie low; but no clergyman, however revolutionary his opinions, could tolerate fornification on his own altar. Straight for this he now went; he grabbed up off the floor a pair of heavy candlesticks (which had been removed from the altar when Hugh was installed on it), and had time to administer two or three punishing strokes on Miss Liberty's succulent fesses before a tide of blue jeans and greasy hair surged up the chancel, burst on the steps of the sanctuary, and swept the wretched girl away from him.

Clewes now disappeared from sight, and Canteloupe, who had taken advantage of the interruption to move himself to a better peep-hole in the tracery, began to hope that the programme would be resumed. But there must be considerable doubt whether Miss Liberty was still in the mood, and in any case that of the mob had now altered drastically. It had been defied and it was out for vengeance, or so at least it was now told by Mayerston, who yelled from his stall the one word:

'SMASH.'

'For Christ's sake, man,' protested Alfie beside him.

'SMASH,' yelled Mayerston again.

'Smash, smash, smash,' the cry was taken up.

But no one seemed too sure what to smash (the miserable Clewes having been pulped already), except for Tony Beck, who now saw his chance to put his name for ever on the record.

'Smash,' he cried, and seized a candlestick.

'Smash,' he screamed, and climbed on to the altar.

'Smash,' he howled, and scrambled on to the foot-wide ledge at the top of the reredos.

'Smash,' he roared, taking back the candlestick and poising himself to strike through the most beautiful East Window in England.

But Balbo was there beneath him, standing on the altar and tugging at his ankles, and Hetta was there beneath Balbo.

'—Oh, wicked, wicked, wicked,' Hetta shouted.

—And Canteloupe was there doing his best to protect Hetta from the mob that hated her for loving Balbo for loving the window, and Hugh Balliston was there, trying to redeem himself in his own eyes by fighting side by side with Canteloupe.

'How could you all be so wicked?' Hetta cried, just as her mother would have done, 'how could you all be so wicked in this lovely place,' while Beck fell from the reredos and Balbo was dragged from the altar (but the Window, the East Window was safe), and Canteloupe and Hugh thrashed out all about them with their fists and feet, and someone (no one would ever quite know who) seized the candlestick which had been dropped by Beck and smashed it down on poor brave Hetta's skull.

When the police arrived (summoned by Somerset Lloyd-James, who was not a poltroon and had run away only for this purpose), they found Tom on the verge of collapse but still just retaining his authority beneath the statue. They then penetrated the Chapel, to find Balbo, Hugh, Canteloupe, Miss Liberty and several students in various but not serious states of injury and shock. Clewes they found to be severely though not lethally broken up. Hetta they found dead before the altar in her white dress. Tony Beck and Mayerston they did not find at all.

'I'm so glad you came,' said Hugh to Patricia Llewyllyn.

Patricia had come to Hugh's room in the Fellows' Garden Hostel. Mummy to the rescue.

'I had to, after I heard. That poor girl ... And what's going to happen to you?'

'I've been forgiven. They've put it round that I was the victim of moral blackmail while suffering from mental strain due to overwork. And after all,' said Hugh with just a trace of bitterness, 'I was wounded fighting for the right side.'

'Wounded?'

'A cracked rib.'

'I hope that'll give you a good lesson ... not to go in for things which you don't understand.'

Mummy knows her boy.

'I understand quite a lot about them ... now. I rather wish I didn't.'

'Forget it,' said Patricia: 'it's all over and done.'

Briskly, she unzipped her skirt.

'Now then,' she said: 'where did we leave off?'

'Snakes,' said Hugh: 'lovely long snakes, sliding and sliding...'

'So remember, next time,' said Mona Corrington, 'to look where you're going.'

'Will there be a next time?' said Beyfus, who was propped up against the pillows wearing a bandage like a turban round his head. 'I should have thought most people have had enough.'

'I haven't, for one.'

'No,' said Beyfus, 'I don't suppose you have. So what's your next step?'

'The International Committee of Anthropologists. It's time that made a bold bid for the bank. In fact I'm starting on a round trip tomorrow to try and get things buzzing.'

'You're going away, Mona? When I'm ill.'

'Only for three days.'

'Mona ... This last time before you go?'

So Mona sat down on the bed beside him, put his head on her bosom, and heard him at his prayers.

'What I can't understand,' said Jacquiz Helmut, who was now back from his medical consultations, 'is why the police took so long to come. You say this chap Lloyd-James telephoned them almost at once.'

'Yes, from the Porters' Lodge in Caius. But the police couldn't get into the college,' explained Ivor Winstanley, 'until they had the Provost's permission; and the Provost, like me, was out stone cold on the grass. So naturally it took some time before they were put in touch.'

'A fine piece of clowning ... And what's been done about Tony Beck?'

'He's vanished. With Mayerston, they think.'

'There's certainly no future for him here.'

'Nor much with Mayerston. They say,' said Ivor, 'although nobody can prove it, that it was probably Mayerston who hit the girl.'

'What was *she* doing there, I'd like to know? She wasn't even a member of the University.'

'Nor were half the others, it seems. A lot of them—particularly those in the Chapel—had come by coach for the day from places like Essex and Sussex. I thought they looked too awful to be ours, even in the distance. You don't realise how lucky we still are.'

'Perhaps,' said Jacquiz; 'but this kind of thing has come to stay.'

'Well, next time it happens I hope you'll stop here and lend a hand, instead of going off to your specialist. How did he find you, by the way?'

'Ticking over,' said Jacquiz. 'He recommends plenty of royal tennis this winter but no disagreeable exertion. He certainly wouldn't want me to get mixed up in revolutions. I pay him far too well.'

'The extraordinary thing was,' said Tom to Daniel, 'that Fielding didn't say a single word of protest. He just hung his head and went with her.'

'Leaving you in the lurch. I told you he was never there when wanted.'

'But this time it was different. He was removed by someone else, you see. Obviously she must have a very strong hold over him.'

'Perhaps that's what he wants people to think,' said Daniel, 'so that he's always got an excuse for disappearing when it suits him. Tom . . .?'

'Yes, Danny?'

'When are you going to disappear?'

'How can I? These are my rooms.'

'But very soon now I shall be well enough to go back to my own. And you'll have to go back to Grantchester. Oh, it's quite all right, you warned me clearly enough, but I'd just like to know when.'

'Not for a long time, Danny. Even when you go back to your rooms in Willow Close, I shall go on living here in college. So it'll be almost the same as now.'

'But how can you? Patricia . . .'

'Patricia,' said Tom, 'is a very honest woman, and I'm happy to tell you that I have kept her confidence. This morning she told me something which leads me to suppose that she will have no need of me for some while yet. Sooner or later, Danny, I shall have to go back to her. But this summer at least we can both enjoy together.'

'A very instructive business all round,' wrote Constable for his record. 'It has left me with two intentions, One is to learn jiu-jitsu, and the other is to dismiss the Master of the Musick. He actually allowed the choir to stop. Not so long, but it was only because I ordered him to that he got them singing again, and as everyone knows, no Master of Musick is worth his salt unless he can keep things going right through the last trump.

'In many respects, quite a lot of good has come of it all. Balliston has at last learned his lesson, and by pardoning him we have been able to give a public exhibition of liberal tolerance which will stand us in good stead in many quarters. Beck has gone—good riddance, on the whole—and so has Mayerston. Clewes has shown that he has some spunk in him. And Tom Llewyllyn's courageous performance should guarantee him a permanent Fellowship when the matter comes to the vote.

'Even the death of poor Hetta Frith has its brighter side. There's nothing like a death to sober people up, and Hetta's should be worth a good two years' peace to Cambridge . . . particularly after the very gruelling account in that journalist Schroeder's column.

'Meanwhile, the tedious question of what to do with our quarter million surplus is still dragging on. The Council voted on it for the fourth time this morning. Result: still ten each way . . .'

After the Memorial Service for Hetta Frith in Lancaster

College Chapel, Balbo Blakeney stood awhile under the tablet which had been set up.

HETTA FRITH
1948–1967
One Great-heart.

'Ah, Miss Hetta,' Balbo whispered, 'there were so many churches I wanted to show you.'

'She'd like that,' said the Marquis Canteloupe, who had come up behind Balbo and was pointing at the tablet; 'Bunyan, isn't it?'

'How did *you* know?' said Balbo before he could stop himself.

'My old nanny used to read it to me,' said Canteloupe, quite unperturbed. 'I've never forgotten. "My sword, I give to him that shall succeed me in my pilgrimage." Splendid stuff.'

'That's from a different passage.'

'But saying the same sort of thing ... My word, old fellow, you do look low.'

'I miss her so much, Canteloupe.'

'I know what. I'll introduce you to a friend of mine. Name of Maisie. Maisie will take your mind off it.'

'Who's Maisie?'

'Maisie's a tart. Not all that to look at, but believe me, she'll take your mind off poor little Hetta.'

Balbo considered this.

'So soon?' he said at last.

'The sooner the better,' said Canteloupe. 'Hetta won't mind. Even if she knows, she won't mind. She'll want you to enjoy yourself.'

'You talk as if you knew her. Yet you only ever saw her that one time. You didn't even know her name until she was dead.'

'That one time was enough. A girl who could stand up to all those yobs like that would never grudge you a romp with Maisie.'

'I don't see that that quite follows,' said Balbo, 'but

you're certainly right about Miss Hetta. She never grudged anybody anything.'

'Then that's settled. Here's a card of Maisie's with her telephone number' . . . Canteloupe scribbled on the back . . . 'and my recommendation. If I was you, I'd run up to London this very afternoon. But give her a ring first. She gets very booked up.'

Balbo looked from the card to Hetta's tablet and back again to the card.

'She bought a white dress for Madrigal Sunday,' Balbo said. 'She hadn't a penny in the world, but she bought a white dress, because I'd told her white was the colour.'

'Good for Hetta.'

'But why do you think she bought it?'

'To please you, I expect, and because girls like to be seen in the right thing.'

'No,' said Balbo. 'Miss Hetta didn't give a curse what she was seen in, and she knew she'd please me well enough if she turned up in rags. She bought that dress,' said Balbo, 'because I'd told her that white was in memory of King Henry's innocence. She was doing honour, Canteloupe, HONOUR, to a dead king because she thought of him in some sort as her host.'

'Don't upset yourself, old fellow.'

'I'm just trying to explain what Miss Hetta was really like. A jolly, sexy girl with bags of guts, yes; but so much more besides. She was . . . so delicate, Canteloupe. So delicate.'

Balbo put Maisie's card in his pocket.

'Delicate but dead,' he said, 'so thanks for the tip. Come on, and I'll give you a drink.'